Budapest Noir

Budapest Noir

Vilmos Kondor

Translated from the Hungarian
by Paul Olchváry

HARPER

NEW YORK · LONDON · TORONTO · SYDNEY

HARPER

First published in Hungary as *Budapest Noir* in 2008 by Agave
Könyvek Kft, Budapest. Reprinted by permission of Agave Könyvek.

BUDAPEST NOIR. Copyright © 2012 by Vilmos Kondor. English-
language translation copyright © 2012 by HarperCollins Publishers.
All rights reserved. Printed in the United States of America. No part
of this book may be used or reproduced in any manner whatsoever
without written permission except in the case of brief quotations
embodied in critical articles and reviews. For information address
HarperCollins Publishers, 10 East 53rd Street, New York, NY 10022.

HarperCollins books may be purchased for educational, business, or
sales promotional use. For information please write: Special Markets
Department, HarperCollins Publishers, 10 East 53rd Street, New
York, NY 10022.

FIRST U.S. EDITION

Library of Congress Cataloging-in-Publication Data
Kondor, Vilmos
   [Budapest noir. English]
Budapest noir : a novel / Vilmos Kondor ; translated from the Hun-
garian by Paul Olchváry.—1st U.S. ed.
      p. cm.
ISBN 978-0-06-185939-7 (pbk.)
1. Budapest (Hungary)—Fiction. 2. Hungary—History—1918-1945—
Fiction. I. Title.
PH3382.21.O555B8313 2012
894'.51134—dc23

                    2011028809

12 13 14 15 16   OV/RRD   10 9 8 7 6 5 4 3 2 1

Budapest Noir

One

Ever since the Balaton Coffeehouse reopened after a lengthy renovation, they'd started adding sugar to the coffee as a matter of course—unless you asked them not to. Zsigmond Gordon invariably forgot to ask. One such evening, he gulped down his cup of surprisingly sweet black coffee and waved a hand in resignation. Folding his copy of the *Budapest Journal*, he stood to pay the waiter and turned up his collar before stepping out onto Rákóczi Street. He glanced toward Blaha Lujza Square and noticed the neon lights of the newspaper building in the distance. He pulled a cigarette from his pocket and lit it.

A few yards away, a newsboy was frantically hawking his wares. Passersby in the evening crowd tore papers from his hand, and his apron sank farther and farther down his waist, weighted from their change.

Gordon started off toward the Erzsébet Bridge. Along the way he cast only superficial glances at the store displays and paid little attention to the automobiles jostling out on the road.

Dubious characters took their turns sidling up to him, trying to palm off a pair of silk stockings or some broad's no doubt unforgettable services. Without stopping, Gordon chucked aside his cigarette butt and checked his watch. If he hurried, he might reach Franz Joseph Square on time. He could always catch a bus, but he enjoyed the hustle and bustle too much to consider public transportation.

At the head of Károly Boulevard yet another newsboy was shouting at the top of his lungs.

"Gömbös has died! The prime minister is dead! His body is being brought back from Germany by train! Gömbös has died! The government has called an emergency meeting!" The boy's cap had slipped to the side, exposing a beet-red face. "Read all about it in the *Evening*! Gömbös has died!" the boy kept shrieking as he waved a paper at Gordon. "The latest news, in the *Evening*! The prime minister is dead! Buy a paper, kind sir!"

Gordon only shook his head. "I don't need a paper, son. I know the prime minister is dead." *I write the news*, he thought, *if, that is, the news lets itself be written*.

After getting to Apponyi Square, Gordon took a sudden right onto City Hall Street, and the relative peace and quiet afforded by this narrower thoroughfare felt good. But he couldn't shake the thought of the Róna case. For days now his mind had been on nothing else; he found it impossible to believe that Erno Róna, a detective who had helped Gordon on his crime beat, was guilty. It was all he could talk about—or tried to talk about—with anyone connected with Róna, but he kept coming up against brick walls.

Gordon cut through deserted, rain-drenched Erzsébet Square, and as he turned out onto Tisza István Street, the icy wind coming off the Danube nearly tore his hat off. He shuddered in the unusually cold October air.

The officer standing in front of police headquarters tipped his hat to Gordon, who'd already gotten used to entering the building through this new entrance—4 Zrínyi Street—normally reserved for detectives. All the on-duty officers knew him, practically letting him come and go as he pleased. This particular evening the on-duty officer was a young guy who, for reasons beyond Gordon's comprehension, always greeted him with overflowing respect: "Good evening, Mr. Editor!"

Gordon nodded and was already heading for the stairs when the officer called after him, "If you're looking for Inspector Gellért, he asked me to tell you he's not in just now. He's been called to an urgent meeting."

"No problem, son," said Gordon, placing his hand on the railing, "I'll wait for him in his office."

But the boy wouldn't let him go just yet: "Prime Minister Gömbös died today, and the . . . " Here he caught himself. "But of course you know this, sir."

"I know," replied Gordon, hurrying up the stairs to the second floor. In the hallway he turned right, heading toward the last door on the left. He knocked, but there was no response from Vladimir Gellért, chief inspector and section head. He let himself into the empty office, lit by a single lamp atop the desk. Gordon pulled the door shut behind him and stepped to the window. Gellért was particularly blessed: his office was among the few to command a view of the Danube. Gordon lit a cigarette and stared out at the river and beyond—at the Chain Bridge, which was aglow; at Castle Hill; and at the ships, some passing by, some anchored, as well as the tugboats trudging along. He crushed the cigarette into a marble ashtray and sat down in one of the chairs opposite the inspector's desk.

Gordon took out his notebook to review precisely what he planned to find out from Gellért. He'd spoken to the detective by telephone on Monday to arrange this meeting about Róna. There wasn't much Gordon could do, since the first hearing in Róna's case had been that morning. And yet he felt it his duty to keep digging for the truth.

The city had lately seen an explosion of currency smugglers, who, exploiting the monetary crisis, were vying to get their hands on serious profits—often with serious success. István Szörtsey's gang had an easy method indeed: his men, posing as detectives, simply confiscated money from other currency smugglers. One fine day a stock exchange agent named Arnold Bondi paid Róna a visit at his office to complain that he'd been cheated out of five thousand pengős. The detective, who specialized in common swindlers and cardsharpers, took out a photograph of Gyula Grósz, a man he and his colleagues had been watching for a while, precisely on account of the fake-detective scam. But Bondi didn't recognize the face. Róna advised him to file a formal complaint. Bondi did so, then regularly pestered the detective for the status of his case. When, on one such occasion, Róna informed Bondi that they were still working on it, Bondi left fuming. A couple of days later, Bondi filed a complaint through his lawyer alleging that the detective had accepted one hundred fifty pengős from him in exchange for pressing the fake detectives to return Bondi's five thousand. An investigation was ordered, and the first hearing was that morning.

Was Róna such an idiot? Would he have put his career—his pension—at risk for a measly one hundred fifty pengős? The case was murky. Although Vladimir Gellért was one of the section heads at Unit V, which oversaw homicide, while Róna worked at Unit IV, tasked with confidence crimes such as theft and fraud, they knew each other well and could always count on each other even if they weren't necessarily friends. And so Gordon felt sure Gellért would help him out. If nothing else, he would point him in the right direction. And if he didn't, why, that, too, would mean something, and perhaps even more so.

Gordon rose from the armchair. The wall clock read 9 P.M. The desk was in pristine order, as always. Gordon knew file folders containing active cases were in a pile on the left; the detective's thoroughly marked-up calendar was in the middle; and on the right was his typewriter, pushed to the side. In front of the calendar was an Art Nouveau bronze inkwell, and in front of that was the barrel of a pen and a little box full of nibs. Gellért often remarked that he finally just about got the hang of the typewriter, but he simply couldn't befriend the fountain pen.

For his part, Gordon had no problem with it, even if he did regard the quill as a backward and antiquated tool. He pulled his notebook from his pocket and placed it on the corner of the desk, bending to jot down a couple of questions, but paused. He figured he'd might as well sit down at the desk to write, as he'd done more than once while waiting for Gellért. He stepped around the desk and tried to pull out Gellért's chair, but it wouldn't budge. Gordon looked to the right and saw that the chair was stuck against an open drawer. This was a first. Over the past five years, Gordon had cultivated a truly exceptional relationship with Gellért, but not once had the immaculate detective left his desk drawer open. Indeed, he always took care to lock it shut, hiding the key in his vest pocket. Having freed the chair, Gordon took a seat and examined the open drawer. A file folder lay at the bottom—a standard official file folder, with an empty space where the title would have been written on the front. The corner of a photograph stuck out from the bottom.

Gordon sat there for a while in silence, motionless. He stared at the folder and at the corner of that photograph. He lit another cigarette. He threw the match into the marble ashtray, exhaled, and locked his eyes again on the photo. He balanced his cigarette on the edge of the ashtray and reached for the drawer, pulling it open a bit more, just enough to lift the cover of the file.

He took up the cigarette. Inhaling deeply, he lifted the file from the drawer and placed it open on the desk. It contained nothing but two photographs. The first depicted a young woman standing beside a covered table, a thick drapery curtain in the background. Her expression was at once forlorn and flirtatious. *You like me, right?* the girl's look suggested. *I know you like me; everyone likes me.*

Except for her smile and a pair of slender shoes, the girl was naked. She stood there lasciviously, her bright eyes awash with salaciousness and sadness. Long thighs; unusually full, round breasts; and dark, slightly curly hair that flowed over her shoulders. Gordon scrutinized her eyes. He realized it wasn't dalliance but defiance that he saw in them. Her body was faultless, lithesome, young. Or maybe not so faultless, after all. He held the photograph under the lamp and looked more closely at her left arm. An inch or so under her elbow was a brownish birthmark about the size of a two-pengő coin, hardly any bigger.

Gordon put the picture aside and picked up the other one. It, too, had been taken in a studio, but under entirely different circumstances. It was the same girl staring into the lens, her hair pinned up, her expression stern. Not even a trace of the defiance or, perhaps, the sadness could be seen. Regular features, vigorous eyebrows, bright eyes.

Gordon placed the two photographs back in the folder, then returned it to the drawer. He stood, adjusted the chair, and stepped to the window. He looked out at the city and then at his watch.

He was about to leave when the door opened. Gellért stepped in vigorously, but with an expression even glummer than usual. His blazer was wrinkled, and his glasses just barely concealed the rings under his eyes. Every motion of his lanky frame now bespoke exhaustion. Gordon turned to greet him, but the detective raised his hand.

"Don't say a thing," said Gellért, faltering out his excuse, "I know we agreed to meet this evening, but the chief of police called us to a meeting."

"The train carrying the prime minister's body is arriving tomorrow morning in the East Station," said Gordon.

"I can't say we expected him to die, especially since Darányi took over day-to-day affairs. I would have bet he'd resign. But when it comes down to it, it doesn't really matter."

"It doesn't," Gordon concurred.

"Sure, we had a plan in place for the prime minister's burial," explained Gellért, "but even so, we've got a million things to do. The chief has called all detectives, police officers, and gendarmes to duty so as to adequately secure the funeral procession from the East Station to the Parliament building."

"Will the interior minister lift the ban on public gatherings?" asked Gordon.

"Why would he do that?"

"Aren't the funeral procession and the burial public gatherings?"

"You're not serious, are you?" asked Gellért, peering out from above his glasses.

"No," replied Gordon. "Then I won't bother you anymore. Did you hear that Turcsányi-Schreiber testified for Róna?"

"Sure I heard. Dániel is an intelligent and logical fellow. If you don't mind . . ."

"Naturally," said Gordon, stepping away from the window. "No point looking you up until the funeral, I suppose."

"No," said Gellért, sitting down in his chair and pushing the drawer back in its place.

"I'll give you a call. Good night."

"Under order of Valiant Knight Miklós Kozma, the interior minister, and his secret order of the Council of Ministers, not a single officer of the law will sleep tonight," replied Gellért. He pulled his typewriter over on top of his calendar and rolled a sheet of paper into it. Blinking behind his lenses, he began to type. Gordon couldn't decide whether he'd heard a bit of sarcasm in the detective's voice.

THERE WERE NOTICEABLY FEWER PEOPLE ABOUT ON Rákóczi Street. Some bars and nightclubs had already closed, and the coffeehouses, too, were slowly emptying out. But Gordon saw an unusually large number of policemen and gendarmes, standing rigidly along the street in preparation for the long night to come. Passing by the Balaton Coffeehouse, he glimpsed a sign hung on the door: WE WILL BE CLOSED ON OCTOBER 10 DUE TO THE PRIME MINISTER'S DEATH. Though he wasn't particularly interested in coffee, he realized the notice hung on the door of every shop, restaurant, office, and coffeehouse.

The city had fallen almost completely silent by the time Gordon reached the editorial offices of the *Evening*. The night-duty concierge gave him a cheerful wave from behind the window of his booth. If it wasn't the demijohn of wine in his little cabinet that explained his good mood, then perhaps it was the prime minister's death. "Good evening, Mr. Editor!" he exclaimed with a tip of his hat. Leaning out his tiny window, he watched as Gordon vanished at the top of the stairs.

The newsroom was empty but for the on-duty typist. Ever since Gordon had started working for the *Evening*, this role was filled by Valéria. Even now she sat there at her desk, a sheet of paper rolled into her machine, the lamplight shining on her snow-white hair, dark glasses—her most prized possession—covering her eyes. She proudly showed this rare treasure to everyone in the office: mountain climbers' glasses equipped with leather side-shields brought home from Bern, Switzerland, by one of her girlfriends. By lamplight she could read only while wearing them, and—she insisted—she hadn't seen the sun in ten years. "The fate of albinos," she had once explained to Gordon. "But I don't mind. Here, everything is calm and quiet, and in the wee hours I can always get in a few hours of reading." Tonight she raised the volume in her hand: the latest in a series of mystery novels published by Athenaeum Press.

"What's wrong, Zsigmond?" Valéria asked, having lowered her book. "Can't you sleep? Has Krisztina sent you packing?"

"I won't have time tomorrow morning to write the article about that barber from out in Szentlőrinckáta."

"The dismemberment?"

"Yes." With that, Gordon went to his desk while Valéria raised the thin little book before her black glasses and went on reading. Turning on the lamp, he pulled his notebook from his pocket. He rolled a sheet of paper into his typewriter and began to type:

Budapest received news today of a shocking crime, a terrible murder in the village of Szentlőrinckáta: Frigyes Novotny, a 46-year-old barber, strangled Erzsébet Barta, the 30-year-old divorcee he'd been living with. After the murder, he dismembered the body, which he then burned. Though the victim was killed in March, her remains were only discovered when new tenants had moved into the

barber's home: János Zombori, a tradesman, and his wife.
Mrs. Zombori lit the oven to bake bread. When the fire
didn't take, she attempted to clean out the oven, making
the alarming discovery: human bones in the ashes. She
immediately ran to the gendarme post, where . . .

The phone rang. Gordon raised his head, but continued
typing when he saw Valéria pick up the receiver:

. . . she reported her discovery to the head of the local
gendarmes.

"Zsigmond!"
Gordon turned around.
"It's for you."
"Who is it?"
"He says his name is Kalmár."
Gordon ran over to the phone.
"How did you know I was here?" he asked.
"I didn't know, but I thought it wouldn't hurt to try."
"So, what is it?"
"The usual. Your beat. We found a girl."
"What sort of girl?"
"What do you think? A dead one."
"Who have you told?"
"I always begin with you," replied the cop.
"That I believe. Were you on the scene, too?"
"No, I'm calling from headquarters. You've always paid
my five pengős, so why wouldn't you pay me now?"

"Give me the address."

"You can be especially grateful for this, Gordon. It's right in your neighborhood."

"Don't go telling me the tram ran down some maid out on the main boulevard."

"I won't. You'll see the cops out front at the start of Nagy Diófa Street. There they are, standing around a very lovely and very dead young woman's corpse."

"Did she swallow a bunch of match heads? Jump out the window?"

"How should I know? But I think you should get moving if you want to see her. The coroner left for the scene ten minutes ago."

Gordon pulled on his trench coat, slammed his hat on his head, and grumbled something to Valéria on his way out.

WITHIN A COUPLE OF MINUTES HE'D ARRIVED AT NAGY Diófa Street. As soon as he turned the corner from Rákóczi Street, he saw the black hearse and, beside it, a few uniformed officers and two plainclothes ones. Gordon looked at his watch: it was past ten. Usually he avoided murder scenes; he'd seen quite enough of them, and after five years with the *Evening* there wasn't much that could surprise him. And yet he hurried now, for Kalmár had called him first; the next day—regardless of the prime minister's death—this is what every paper would write about. But he was the only one on the scene so far, and that was worth more than five pengős.

As the crime reporter at the *Evening*, Gordon knew the

countless modes of death better than he would have wished. Maids drank ground-up match heads to poison themselves and flung themselves in front of trams. Barbers dismembered their lovers. Divorcees slashed their veins with razors. Tradesmen's apprentices leaped off the Franz Joseph Bridge. Jealous civil servants cut their wives to shreds with butcher knives. Businessmen shot their rivals with revolvers. The possibilities were endless, and yet they were oppressively the same, for the end was always identical.

Hastily he went toward the guarded building, but one of the plainclothes officers stepped in his way. Gordon called out to detective Andor Stolcz, who waved to his colleague to make way. Notebook in hand, Gordon stepped over to the body, which was lying facedown right in the doorway like some discarded rag doll. Her face was turned into her shoulder; her black hair was sprawled out over her back.

"When did she die?" asked Gordon.

"She's still warm," replied Stolcz. "The coroner hasn't seen her, but I figure she's been lying here for an hour. It's amazing the telephone call came in so quickly."

"Sooner or later a gendarme or a police officer would have passed down the street and seen her."

"Assuming no one else would have."

"What did she die of?"

The squat, veiny detective shook his head. "How should I know, Gordon? We've only been here a couple of minutes. I don't see blood."

"Nor do I. Who is the girl?"

"Now that's the thing," said Stolcz, sticking his hands in his pockets. "We didn't find a thing in her purse. Just a few shreds of paper and a Jewish book."

"A what?" Gordon fixed his eyes on Stolcz.

"A Jewish prayer book." The detective reached inside the open back door of the automobile waiting on the sidewalk. "This," he said, producing a thick little package wrapped in a piece of white fabric. He unwrapped the book and held it out toward Gordon.

"Is anything particular written inside it?"

"Nothing. A few pages with their corners turned in. That's it."

"Nothing to identify her."

"I'll look at the list of missing persons back at headquarters," said the detective with a shrug, "but I doubt she would have been reported. And anyway, we just found her. Maybe in a couple of days someone will report her missing. You know as well as I do that more than one or two girls arrive in Budapest every day who wind up in this neighborhood. This isn't the first streetwalker to end up in an unmarked grave in this city."

Gordon nodded. But this was exceptional all the same: a dead Jewish girl on a street with such a dubious reputation. He took another look at the corpse. One of her feet was wedged under her body, and on the other foot he saw an ungainly, cheap, high-heeled shoe. Her skirt had slipped to the side, and there was a run in her brown stocking. Her peach-colored blouse shone from underneath her threadbare but good quality jacket. "She wasn't overdressed," Gordon remarked.

"Let's just say that for the work she was up to," replied Stolcz, "she didn't need to be." The left sleeve of the jacket had slipped above the elbow. Gordon leaned closer in the scant light. Then he squatted down. He took the girl's wrist and turned it toward the light. Just below her elbow was a birthmark the size of a two-pengő coin. His stomach churned, as if suddenly in the grips of a long-forgotten childhood fear.

Gordon glanced up at Stolcz, who was talking with the other plainclothes detective as the three uniformed officers listened in. He reached inside his pocket and took out a fountain pen. Carefully he reached out toward the dead girl's hair, and brushed it away from her face with the pen. The girl's eyes were open, opaque, the irises dull. And green.

For a couple of seconds Gordon stared at those green eyes, the bloodless face, the slightly curly locks of black hair. It wasn't hard at all to conjure up that sad, defiant smile he'd seen in Gellért's photographs.

Two

Since every coffeehouse had closed, Gordon hurried back to the newsroom. Valéria had begun a new novel, and she raised her head just as Gordon picked up the telephone to dial. He had to wait eleven rings.

"About dinner . . . tonight," he began.

"That you were late for again? Or did you want to cancel, Zsigmond? At ten-thirty?"

"I had a long day, Krisztina. Don't be angry."

"The devil is angry with you, but I could wring your neck. Tell me, why do I cook for you?"

"Because you like to cook. And I like your cooking."

"It's not so simple. You know that full well. And if you think flattery will sweep me off my feet, you're knocking on the wrong door."

"You think I don't remember your fits? You'd be the last person I'd try to flatter."

"But if you're not out to flatter, then what?"

"To say sorry; I had a rotten day."

"You're always having rotten days."

"Except when I'm with you."

"Zsigmond, Zsigmond, it's way too late. The rooster paprikash is much too cold for me to be in the mood to listen to
you."

"Then don't listen."

"Don't you worry, I won't. And before I hang up on you,
I'll tell you that Mór stopped by this afternoon and brought
another jar of jam. I haven't tasted it yet, but this time it looks
edible, surprisingly enough." With that, she slammed down
the receiver. Gordon shrugged and put down the phone. He
couldn't know whether Valéria was looking his way from
behind her dark glasses, but he suspected she was. He nodded
her way and then headed home.

THE NEXT MORNING GORDON WOKE EARLY AND STARTED
his day at the Abbázia Coffeehouse on the Oktogon, the bustling eight-sided intersection where the Grand Boulevard met
Andrássy Street.

"Good morning, Mr. Editor," the waiter greeted him
before leading him over to his usual table, placing the
morning papers before him along with the freshly arrived
papers from London and New York. The fellow then hurried off to get Gordon his breakfast. Gordon sat and stared
out at the Oktogon for a while. He'd often been asked why
he liked the Abbázia, since it was so passé compared to
the Japán Coffeehouse barely a block away. Gordon would
always shrug and reply, "Their coffee is good." Not that

this was true; the coffee at the Abbázia was average, and for one pengő and sixty fillérs, the breakfast wasn't exactly filling. Gordon liked it because he was a regular. He could sit at the same table by the window, watching the busy Oktogon in the morning and Andrássy Street decked out in lights at night.

That morning, however, the Oktogon was far from busy. It could have been 6 A.M. on a Sunday. The noisiest thing in sight was the tram, and he saw far fewer cars and buses than usual. Most shops hadn't even opened, and two out of the three coffeehouses were closed. The usual surging crowd had vanished: there were no onlookers; no maids headed toward the market on Lövölde Square to shop; no shoe shiners; no kids making a racket. Those passing by were clearly going about their business resolutely.

Gordon shook his head. It wasn't possible that everyone was mourning Gömbös. Nor were they worried about the government—Hungarians didn't worry over the government even when they should. Kálmán Darányi had been overseeing day-to-day affairs for a good month already, and Gömbös was missed by few. There certainly was no crisis. Of course, the government ministers all submitted their resignations, and the nation's regent, Miklós Horthy, accepted them. But it would be days yet before Horthy would formally assign Darányi the task of forming a new government. At such times Gordon didn't mind being a crime reporter. He had little affinity for politics, and when he thought about the impassioned and hot-blooded politicians clashing over which political faction Darányi would invite into his gov-

ernment alongside his National Unity Party, Gordon found
the whole affair simply ludicrous. He had no patience for it,
and he also knew this: he wasn't alone in his silent apathy.
The question wasn't really who Darányi would share power
with, but in what direction he would go. And unfortunately
he knew full well—he could see—which way the new
head of government was moving. It wasn't by chance that
Gömbös had been receiving medical treatment near Munich
of all places.

At the same time, Gordon was also certain that a huge
crowd had gathered along the route of the funeral procession
and in front of the Parliament building. Even in this country,
it wasn't an everyday occurrence for a prime minister to be
brought home dead from abroad.

Gordon grabbed a newspaper, *8 O'Clock News*. He flipped
through, then picked up the next. He got through the *Budapest
News* every bit as fast. In the city's German-language daily,
Pester Loyd, he read the accounts of the German stock exchange, the most vivid reading possible of that country's situation. Gordon noticed his coffee sitting in front of him on the
table and, beside it, a brioche. He leaned back in his chair and
savored the unusually silent spectacle of the Oktogon along
with his breakfast; he wouldn't have another minute's rest
until evening, that much was certain.

Gordon grabbed his hat and caught the next tram, watching the eerily deserted boulevard in the half light of dawn
until he reached Berlin Square. Just as all the police officers
and gendarmes had been ordered to the streets on account of
the procession, so, too, were journalists assigned to cover only

the funeral that day. Sports reporters, Gordon's colleagues on the police blotter, stock exchange correspondents, editors, and apprentices—all were focused on Gömbös. Gordon couldn't complain about his assignment; he was to go into the Parliament building to speak directly to the funeral's organizers, those doing the real work, versus those merely giving their names to the event. On Berlin Square he fought his way toward Kaiser Wilhelm Road through the crowd of people making their way to the West Railway Station carrying suitcases, bags, and baskets. No matter the occasion, there was always a huge hubbub at the station.

On Kaiser Wilhelm Road, however, it was utterly quiet and calm. Although the procession carrying Gömbös's body had long since arrived at the Parliament building, the police officers and the stone-faced gendarmes still lined the road, standing there so erect it seemed they might snap.

Gordon picked up his pace a bit. He'd already had enough, and he wanted to get to Krisztina on time today. He still had half an hour. Anything that couldn't be found out in that much time wasn't even worth it, he figured.

In front of the Parliament building stood an honor guard and even more policemen, as if concerned that someone might want to cart Gömbös's body off to a taxidermist. A small group of detectives stood by the main entrance. Gordon didn't even have to take out his ID; one of the detectives recognized him at once and waved a hand to the policemen by the door to let him in. Gordon gave an appreciative nod and stepped inside. The bier was already there in the rotunda under the building's imposing dome, filling the cavernous space with all due somberness but a bit too much grandeur. Gordon was just about to look for the person in charge of the funeral when he noticed three men behind one of the columns. He took a step back and to the side, to get a better look without being seen. There was nothing unusual about two of the three men; they, of all people, certainly belonged here. Miklós Kozma, the interior minister—a tad plump, with a full mustache and slicked-back hair, wearing a dark, simple suit—stood opposite Tibor Ferenczy. Budapest's chief of police had to lean down a bit to catch the interior minister's glib yet soft voice. The chief also wore a dark suit and his graying hair was likewise combed back; his eyes were piercing. Although the third man stood with his back toward him, Gordon had no problem recognizing the lanky, slightly stooped figure with his hands, as always, clenched behind his back. Gellért had been up and about all night, and so his jacket was just as wrinkled as before.

Gordon drew back farther into the shadows. *What was Gellért doing here?* Of course, he had to know the details of the funeral procession, but why was he beside the bier of all places? What was one of the heads of the homicide unit talking about so intensely with the interior minister and the chief of police? Gömbös's funeral was not an occasion for investigating a murder. Gordon glanced about for József Schweinitzer. In the best-case scenario the state had to be on the lookout for a modest public disturbance—at worst, an assassination. And this was the job of the state security police, under Schweinitzer's command. But Schweinitzer was nowhere to be seen, and the body language of these three men told Gordon no one else around would be privy to their discussion.

Having finished speaking, Kozma looked at Ferenczy, who said something to Gellért, whereupon the two senior officials went off toward the building's north wing. Gellért turned, and Gordon stepped out of the shadows.

For a moment the detective's expression was one of surprise, but for a moment only. He waved Gordon over.

"I see you really didn't sleep last night," Gordon began.

"You see well."

"In the thick of things? The interior minister and the chief of police are giving you orders in person?"

Gellért didn't reply, but it seemed he hadn't even heard the question. Fumbling about in his pocket, he pulled out a pack of cigarettes but realized at once where he was, slipping it back into his pocket with evident annoyance. He looked at Gordon. "What is it you asked?"

"Where is Schweinitzer?"

"How should I know?"

"I thought this was a matter of public order," noted Gordon.

"Yes, but this is an exceptional situation, and—" He cut his sentence short. "Why am I explaining this to you?"

"I don't know," said Gordon with a shrug.

"Then give me a ring next week. I've got to be off now."

"Just one question."

"Next week you can ask me a million questions about Róna."

"But it's not Róna I'm interested in right now."

"So what is it?"

"Last night a dead girl was found on Nagy Diófa Street," said Gordon, scrutinizing Gellért's expression for any reaction. But no.

"Great. It's been a while since we found a dead hooker there."

"How do you know she was a hooker?"

"On Nagy Diófa Street? Not far from Klauzál Square? If it had been an upper-class girl, rest assured I'd know about it. But since I don't know, she could only have been a hooker. Why are you asking me?"

"The case belongs to Unit V. And you're a section head there, if memory serves me right."

"First of all, the case is not my section's. If it were, I'd know about it. Second, even if it were mine, I wouldn't be dealing with it now. In case you didn't notice, we're burying the prime minister on Saturday. Unless the Communists blow up the Chain Bridge, I won't be doing anything else until Saturday night."

"The Communists want to blow up the Chain Bridge?"

"I don't have time for this," said Gellért with a dismissive wave of the hand. He turned around and headed toward the door leading to the Hunter's Room. Gordon thought about asking Gellért why the dead girl's photograph was in his desk drawer, but didn't. Gellért went through the door, and complete silence descended on the hall. Gordon took his notebook and went off in search of one of the men in charge of the funeral.

FROM THE PARLIAMENT BUILDING GORDON HEADED straight toward Krisztina's. He checked his watch when he reached the Oktogon. He had time to spare and didn't have to take the underground. Gordon liked to walk along Andrássy Street after dark, and without a soul in sight, this night was no exception. Turning up his collar, he walked along the deserted road under the trees, which by now were shedding their leaves. He turned right onto Szív Street, his steps echoing against the sidewalk, between the gray buildings. Under one doorway a couple was locked in a passionate embrace, but they broke apart on Gordon's approach. On the corner, a building's super was shoveling coal. Gordon nodded at the man, who wiped his blackened forehead.

Lövölde Square looked positively destitute, as if the life had been sucked right out of its buildings. Here and there a light glimmered in a window, but the air didn't move between the trees. At the market, the counters were empty and the trash had been cleared away; stray dogs and cats had eaten every single scrap the stall keepers had left behind.

Krisztina lived in the building on the opposite side of the square, on the fourth floor. The massive wooden door was open. Gordon walked up to the fourth floor, turned right at the landing, and headed toward the flat farthest back. Here, above the building's inner courtyard, it was quiet. Instead of the usual, cheerful cries of children from down below, two sparrows were wearily chirping to each other in the dried-out sumac trees.

Krisztina was already dressed for the evening when she

opened the door. She always managed to look elegant without outdressing Gordon, for whom fashion meant only that in the summer he wore a gray suit thinner than his winter one. Krisztina was wearing a wine-red suit, her ankles flashing from beneath her skirt. Under her blazer, the top of her white blouse was unbuttoned. She never wore makeup, nor did she now. Her glasses were perched on the bridge of her nose, but she would never wear them in public. She said they made her look old, which Gordon invariably dismissed. "Kid," said Gordon not long after they first met, "I've seen a few thirty-something women in my time, and believe you me, you can take at least five years off when telling anyone your age." "I don't care how many women you've seen," Krisztina had retorted, "and spare me the details. You yourself said that from now on there's just one lady in your life." Gordon would gladly have eaten his words, but he knew that doing so would have been in vain.

Krisztina put a dainty little hat atop her medium-length, curly brown hair, and Gordon couldn't have been grateful enough—he couldn't stand the wide-brimmed, gaudy hats so many women were wearing.

"Well?" asked Krisztina when they got into the living room.

"Well, what?" came Gordon's reply.

"You've forgotten, right?"

"No doubt. Just what have I forgotten now?"

"You're the one who wanted to go to the Zanzibar tonight. To listen to that cabaret singer from London."

"New York," Gordon corrected her, and with that, he

flung his coat onto the bentwood chair beside the bed. As much as he liked being at Krisztina's place, he did miss normal armchairs. She'd arranged her little flat in keeping with the latest trends. A simple bed in the corner, a two-level coffee table in front of the bed, with a white ashtray on top. At the opposite end of the room stood a dresser with three drawers, topped off with a porcelain figurine, and, above that, a long mirror in an unadorned frame. One of the flat's two plants rested on a little shelf: a potted flower whose name Gordon couldn't manage to remember. On the wall, one abstract painting and nothing else. Krisztina had fallen in love with the latest designs in Berlin, and she took care that nothing should disrupt the delicate unity of the room. On more than one occasion Gordon had sworn up and down about the lack of an armchair, but Krisztina wasn't particularly concerned with his grumbling. "In your own flat, you can sit about in those old-fashioned armchairs as much as you want," she said, at which Gordon shrugged.

Leaning against the doorjamb, Krisztina now waited for Gordon to finish up in the bathroom. He quickly washed his face, slicked back his hair with his wet hands, and adjusted his necktie before joining Krisztina, who, having removed her glasses, asked: "All right, then, not London but New York. So who are we listening to tonight?"

"Lucy and Nora Morlen," replied Gordon. "The Morlen sisters."

"And they're still performing tonight?"

"You think the Zanzibar is about to cancel their performance after bringing them over here, just because a prime minister has died?"

On reaching the corner of Szív Street, Krisztina turned right toward the underground, but Gordon nudged her gently toward the Oktogon. "Kid, just take a look at Andrássy Street. When have you seen it so quiet? Besides, we've only got to go as far as Teréz Boulevard. Surely you'll make it there in those high-heeled shoes."

"And will you finally tell me what kept you out so late last night?"

Gordon nodded. "Something happened on Nagy Diófa Street."

"Something always happens there."

"But not like this," said Gordon, buttoning his coat and taking Krisztina's arm. He described the past twenty-four hours. Krisztina listened in silence and spoke only when they turned onto Teréz Boulevard.

"And what do you want to do?"

"Do? What do I want to do?"

"Yes. What do you want to do? That's what I asked."

"Why do I need to do anything at all?"

"Because it's suspicious, Zsigmond. Don't you think so?"

"I'm not saying a few details don't add up."

"Add up?" Krisztina stopped in her tracks. "A few details?"

"Krisztina, don't go making a fuss. A girl died on Nagy Diófa Street. That's it. It's not exactly a safe neighborhood."

"Let me put it another way. Even if that picture hadn't been in Gellért's desk drawer, doesn't it seem suspicious to you that a Jewish girl should be found dead not far from Klauzál Square? In a seedy neighborhood like that?"

"Why should it be suspicious? Dohány Street is close by, too."

"How many Jewish girls from Dohány Street have you heard of who work the streets?"

Gordon looked toward Blaha Lujza Square. He shuddered at the shrill ring of the tram behind him.

"Not a lot."

"And surely you haven't heard of one with a siddur in her purse, and nothing else."

"What are you talking to me about some siddur for? As if I'm supposed to know what that is."

"Zsigmond, it's been five years already since you moved home, but there are a few things you still need to remember."

"Don't say it."

"But I will. Here and now, in this country, it does indeed matter who is Jewish and who is not."

"Now you'll go telling me again about your Saxon roots, and that back in Transylvania you even had Jewish friends and Romanian friends."

Krisztina pulled her arm from Gordon's, turned about-face, and headed back toward the Oktogon with determined steps. Gordon hurried after her.

"Don't be angry."

"You're such a boor sometimes that I don't even understand why I let you into my bed."

"Into *your* bed? You got that modern monstrosity from me."

"But I'm the one who sleeps in it. And you, only when you happen to remember I exist."

Gordon took a deep breath. He didn't want to ratchet up the tension any more. "All right. Don't be angry. I beg your pardon. I was a boor. And you're right, this whole affair is suspicious to me, too."

Krisztina nodded. "What are you going to do?"

"I have no idea. Unless . . ." He thought for a moment. "Unless I go find Vogel. Maybe he knows who took the nude picture."

"You just said that as if I'm supposed to know who Vogel is."

"The police reporter for *Hungary*," replied Gordon. "I even showed you that terrific series he wrote about the city's sex industry."

"About Csuli and his gang?"

"See there, you can remember if you want."

The Zanzibar's flashing neon lights clashed with the deserted boulevard. Gordon went ahead, and they left their coats in the cloakroom. They sat down at a table far from the stage. The bronze lamps on the tables emitted a reddish light, and the orchestra played in muted tones in preparation for the evening's main performance. Waiters bustled about with trays stacked full, couples cuddled, and the smell of cigarette smoke mixed with that of bean goulash and Wiener schnitzel.

Gordon lit a cigarette, then waved for the waiter. He ordered Krisztina a glass of red wine and French cognac for himself. The musicians stopped playing, and the MC announced that the program would continue with the singing sisters from

New York after a ten-minute intermission. The patrons grew louder, and Gordon was too busy scanning the audience to hear Krisztina at first.

"What did you say?"

Krisztina sighed. "That something happened to me today, too."

"Tell me," said Gordon, leaning on his elbow.

"I got a letter from London."

"From London."

"Right. They say . . ." She paused, reached inside her purse, and took out an envelope. "Read it."

Gordon reached for the envelope and took out the letter: "To Miss Krisztina Eckhardt, Budapest . . ." So began the letter, the figure of a stupid little penguin sitting atop it. Gordon skimmed it, then gave it back.

"Aren't you happy?" asked Krisztina.

"Sure I am."

"Don't you want me to go?"

"I didn't say that."

"You want me to stay?"

"I didn't say that, either."

Krisztina shook her head, looked toward the stage, and then took a sip of her wine.

"An English publisher saw your work on the Berlin Olympics," said Gordon, lighting another cigarette, "and decided that it's you they want in their design department."

"Exactly."

"Good. Don't get me wrong, I don't want to sound sarcastic, nor do I want to seem like a boor. But would you explain to me why a publisher that does not publish illustrated books and that uses the same sort of cover design for each of its books—white in the middle, with only a different border—needs a graphic designer?"

"So you know Penguin?"

"I do."

"Then you should know that not every cover of theirs is quite the same. Besides, I'd design other things for them, too."

"Sounds good."

"And I'd go only for a year."

"How can you be so sure?"

"In case you don't recall, a couple of weeks ago I was asked to design the materials for the International Eucharistic Congress. Well, *some* of the materials."

"That's a year and a half from now."

"I know. That's why I'd come back after a year. And as long as we're on the subject, you could come join me."

"In London."

"Right."

"I can't go, Krisztina, and you know this full well. Because of Opa."

"I know. So what do you say? Should I go?"

"If it's important to you."

"Is it important to you that I stay?" asked Krisztina.

"It's important to you that you go," replied Gordon.

IT WAS ALREADY PAST NINE BY THE TIME THEY LEFT THE club. Krisztina hadn't enjoyed the main act in the least, whereas Gordon had listened to the two American girls with rapture, pleased with their performance and their white smiles and sizable wigs, as they jumped about in their fishnet stockings.

"So go ahead and show me where it happened," said Krisztina, pulling her coat tighter.

"Where what happened?"

"The dead girl. Where they found her."

"On Nagy Diófa Street."

"I know," said Krisztina. And she headed toward Blaha Lujza Square.

"Now where are you off to?" Gordon called after her.

"Nagy Diófa Street," she replied. "I'll ask someone which doorway the body was found in."

Gordon sighed deeply, flicked his half-smoked cigarette onto the road, and went after her.

"What was she wearing?" asked Krisztina when he caught up. Gordon conjured up the image and told her. "Her nails? Her hands?" Gordon said the girl's nails were manicured. "Her hair, was it greasy? I mean, unkempt? Colored?" No, Gordon shook his head. Krisztina pressed on with her questioning, and Gordon patiently answered when he could. "What is it you noticed, after all?" she asked, looking at the corner of Wesselényi Street and Erzsébet Boulevard. "You would have made one rotten detective."

Gordon didn't say another word until they reached Nagy Diófa Street. He turned and stopped in front of the second building on the right. "This is where they found her." A window was thrown open above them: "Manci! Get yourself up here this instant!" came a drunken shout.

"And aren't you curious even now about what a Jewish streetwalker would have been doing here?" Krisztina fixed her eyes on Gordon. "And as long as we're on the subject, have you ever seen a Jewish prostitute? If you want my opinion, the question is not how she died, but how a Jewish girl—probably from a respectable, bourgeois family—ended up becoming a prostitute in the first place."

Three

In the morning Gordon got out of bed quietly while Krisztina was still asleep. He shaved carefully, then went to the closet for a clean shirt, taking care not to step on the creakier part of the parquet floor. In the kitchen, he pulled out a chair from under the table and sat down. He took out the jar of jam Krisztina had cleverly hidden in her purse, removed the cellophane, and dipped in a teaspoon. He'd expected worse. Mór's jams were more often failures than successes, but this one was decidedly edible. Not that Gordon could have said what kind it was, but it was tasty. Perhaps apple and gooseberry. Or quince and rose hip. Maybe pear and rhubarb. Or else the old fellow had his very own way of conjuring peaches into jam. Gordon shrugged and spooned the contents of the jar into his mouth. In the living room he took his blazer off the chair and paused momentarily in front of the vestibule mirror, where he adjusted his hat before closing the door behind him.

The super was sweeping the sidewalk in front of the building's entrance. "Good morning, Mr. Editor!" he greeted Gordon, with a smile that stretched from ear to ear.

"You, too, Iváncsik," said Gordon, and turned in the direction of Nagymezo Street. He might as well board a tram on Kaiser Wilhelm Road, he figured. He bought an *8 O'Clock News* at the tobacconist's and got on the tram. He changed at Apponyi Square and by eight-thirty was at the newsroom, where work was under way full-steam. Nearly every typewriter was occupied by someone feverishly typing away. Gordon glanced about, then walked up a floor to *Hungary*'s newsroom. There he was greeted by the same spectacle. He turned to the clerk sitting by the entrance. The fiftyish man might have unevenly buttoned his blazer, but he always knew everyone's business.

"Is Mr. Vogel here?" Gordon asked.

"Even if the pope himself were to die, Mr. Vogel would still start his day in the New York Café with a brioche and a cup of black coffee. Only once did he not take his breakfast there: when the Romanians occupied Budapest. And not because the place wasn't open. He said he didn't have an appetite."

Jenő Vogel had already finished his brioche and was reading the previous day's French newspapers while sipping his coffee. Gordon sat down across from him.

"Say, Gordon, how much do the Spanish Civil War and the situation in Abyssinia worry you?" asked Vogel, lowering his copy of *Le Figaro*.

"Each on its own or the two combined?"

"Combined."

"Not one bit."

"And on their own?"

"Why should I fret over it?" asked Gordon. "For some odd reason Mussolini needs Abyssinia, and he'll get it, he will. And if the Spaniards want to slaughter each other, even in the best-case scenario all I can do is take exception to it in principle. Because there's nothing I can do about it, that's for sure."

Vogel knit his brows, nudged his glasses up to his forehead, and took to pulling at his fleshy ear. "You didn't come by to talk about the Abyssinian situation," he informed Gordon.

"No," Gordon confirmed. "You know the inner city's sex industry pretty well, Vogel."

"You might say," said Vogel, casting Gordon a suspicious eye.

"I'm looking for someone."

"Who isn't?"

"Not just one someone, in fact, but two."

Vogel crossed his thick hands over his imposing belly and listened, motionless, his face not so much as twitching, as Gordon described the dead girl.

"I haven't seen her," he finally said, shaking his head.

Gordon wasn't surprised, but he continued. "Who takes nude pictures?"

"Why do you want to know?"

"Because I saw a nude picture of the dead girl."

"Who is that hooker to you?"

"No one."

"Then why are you interested?"

"Because I don't have enough for an article. Have you read the story in *8 O'Clock News*?" Vogel slowly nodded. "It was in there, too. It wasn't enough that I was there on the scene. That's just half a column on page seven."

"And you want page two."

"Or page one."

"Or page one," repeated Vogel. "A front-page story is a front-page story."

"Well?"

"I'm all ears," replied the rotund journalist. The rims of his wire-frame glasses had splayed out completely over his head.

Gordon sighed. "Next week I'll be having a word with Gellért about the Róna case."

"Which you'll share with me."

Gordon was silent. "I will," he said finally.

Vogel summoned the waiter and ordered a coffee and a cognac. "Will you have a coffee, too?"

"Black," replied Gordon.

"There aren't too many folks who take such pictures," Vogel began. "Based on what you told me about the photograph, there's just one person who could have taken it."

"I'm all ears."

"An ugly old lech, a real pig."

"I really do need more than that," said Gordon.

"His name is Skublics. Izsó Skublics."

"And where does this Skublics roost?"

"On Aradi Street. Not far from Hitler Square."

"I should leave your name out of it, right?" asked Gordon.

"Feel free to say it, but that will just make things worse."

The waiter arrived with the two coffees and the cognac. Gordon was just about to remove his blazer, but Vogel took the coffee, poured it into the cognac, and downed it all in three even gulps. "Are you coming back to the office?" he asked, springing to his feet.

"No, later on. First I'll take a look at this Skublics."

"You won't like him, but go ahead and take a look if you've got the taste for it."

GORDON KNEW THE CIRCLE AND ENVIRONS WELL; MÓR lived there, too, after all. But he was incapable of calling it— the Circle—Hitler Square. If something is a circle, well then, that's just what it is, he told Krisztina more than once. Not a square. Especially not Adolf Hitler Square. He'd also heard that the Oktogon would soon be renamed Mussolini Square. He shook his head and started off toward Aradi Street. Before turning onto Szinyei Street, he glanced up at a second-floor balcony door of one of the buildings on the Circle. It was closed. He'd try on the way back; by then Mór would surely be home.

He didn't even have to go looking for Skublics's building; he knew exactly which one it was. It was one of the blemishes on Aradi Street: a six-story apartment building with plaster flaking off its façade, a stairwell that smelled of piss, with hungry, stinking dogs in the courtyard and on the inner balconies that circled above it. Every time he'd walked this way, he'd always crossed to the other side of the street.

He stepped over a puddle full of water from someone's wash, it seemed, and began climbing the stairs toward the sixth floor. On one floor he heard shouting; on another, dogs fighting over something; and on a third, he saw two kids beating up a smaller child. On the sixth floor he walked the length of the rectangular passageway overlooking the central courtyard, but on not one door did he see the name Skublics. Finally he knocked on a window, from behind which came the smell of thick brown soup made with lard-fried roux. A woman of indeterminate age, wearing a kerchief, pulled aside the curtain. "Whadayawant?" she asked with a tooth-less mouth.

"I'm looking for Skublics."

"You can keep looking, but I don't know who that is."

"Supposedly he lives here."

"No one told me," said the woman, shaking her head and pulling the curtain shut. Gordon reached inside his pocket, pulled out a two-pengő coin, and with that knocked on the window once again.

"Whadayawant?"

"I found this under your window," he said, showing her the coin in his palm. The woman reached out for it, but Gordon pulled his hand back.

"What is that name you said, sir?" asked the woman, her eyes on Gordon.

"Skublics."

"Aha! Now that's different. I don't know what goes on in his place, but I'm not even interested, I'm telling you."

"I didn't ask."

"And I don't know what sort of girls go to him, morning and night."

"Which flat is his?"

"See the attic door?" The woman pointed. Gordon nodded.

"Well, if you open that, you'll see another door first thing on the right. Knock on that." The woman reached her sinewy, crooked hand out the window. Gordon dropped the coin into her palm and went to the attic door.

In the dark he could barely make out the door, it blended in so much with the wall. At some point it had been painted terra-cotta red, like the building's bricks, but now both it and the wall were grimy. He knocked. No answer. Again. Still no answer. He pounded. Nothing.

Gordon was just about to leave when a skinny girl with alarmingly white skin stepped out from the darkness. Her thin strands of greasy hair were woven in a knot, and her big eyes shone of fear. Even her pleated skirt was not enough to hide her spindly legs and bony hips. Her white blouse with its worn embroidery hung loosely on her frame, but even so, Gordon could see her sunken chest, her flat breasts. With a long finger she anxiously fiddled with a stray lock of hair.

"Please don't make noise," she requested.

"And who are you?"

"I'm . . . Mr. Skublics's . . . cleaning woman," came the girl's faltering reply.

"Then what are you doing out here?"

"I came early," she explained. "Mr. Skublics is never home in the morning, sir. He's always at the thermal bath, and I got here early."

"When did your train get in?"

"Six," the girl blurted out without thinking, but then it hit her, and wringing her hands, she continued: "Oh, please don't tell anyone, sir! There's no work to be had in Debrecen, which is why I'm here. And I don't even have a servant's license."

"You don't need a servant's license for what you're preparing to do," said Gordon, looking her square in the eye.

"You sure do need one for cleaning!" the girl protested.

"All right, kid. For that you do. But take it from me, this sort of cleaning doesn't lead to any good."

"What are you talking about?"

"Forget it, kid. I'm not going to the police."

The girl dropped to her knees and clutched Gordon's left hand, which she proceeded to smother with kisses. "God bless you, sir! May the grace of the good Lord be with you! There are six of us siblings, I'm the oldest, and . . ."

"Don't go explaining it to me," said Gordon, pulling his hand away. "I'll be back later. After lunch. Will Skublics get home by then?"

"The others said he would."

GORDON REACHED THE CIRCLE IN A COUPLE OF MIN-
utes. He saw that his grandfather's balcony door was now open. Every morning the old man would roam about the neighborhood markets—come rain, sleet, or snow—looking for fruit he was ever determined to turn into jam.

The building entrance was open, and so Gordon walked up to the second floor and opened the apartment door. Mór couldn't get it through his head that he no longer lived in the provinces, that locking the door was a good idea. From the sounds coming from the kitchen, Gordon could tell he was pottering about in there even now. The clatter of pots and pans mingled with the sound of the old man's cheerful cursing.

"Wonderful, wonderful!" he said, his face lighting up on seeing Gordon. He wiped his hands on the blazer that was buttoned askew over his round belly. Gordon had bought him at least three aprons, but the old man wouldn't hear of using them. He was like those veterans of the Great War who proudly wore their injuries. He wanted everyone to know that he was cooking jam. Not that he could have denied this had he wanted to: bits of fruit skin were stuck to his gray beard, and the jam of the day had even found its way to his bushy eyebrows. Opa was willing to make one concession only: although he didn't remove his blazer, he did roll up the sleeves along with those of his shirt. Of course, even if his shirt cuffs came away clean—he wore a clean shirt every day—the sleeves of his blazer provided a fairly accurate picture of his recent culinary experimentations.

"Son, I bought some marvelous grapes on Lövölde Square, I did!" He smiled broadly. "Simply dazzling. And just thirty-eight fillérs for a kilo. For the rhubarb I had to go all the way to the City Market, but it was worth it, boy, was it ever worth it. Just look at these nice hard stems." Reaching into one of his baskets, he pulled out five plump rhubarbs. Gordon shuddered; he didn't even like them stewed.

"What are you working on now, Opa?" he asked.

"Ha!" The old man's face lit up again, and he continued triumphantly. "Not even the Gastronome has heard of this! I thought of it a couple of days ago: grape-rhubarb jam!" He stirred the mixture bubbling on the stove. "If it works, I'll send him the recipe immediately. Immediately, I say!"

Gordon nodded. Mór was obsessed with getting his name

into the Gastronome's column in the Sunday issue of the *Budapest Journal*. It was as if his decades of healing others had vanished from his memory banks without a trace. He knew a great many people in the capital, so when he decided after his wife's death to move up to Budapest from his hometown of Keszthely, hours to the south on Lake Balaton, he could easily have resumed his medical practice or even taught. But no. The old man seemed bent on devoting his final decades to creating a jam the Gastronome would find worthy of publication.

"You didn't eat what I sent with Krisztina, did you?" he asked sullenly.

"I did, Opa," said Gordon. "What sort of jam was it?"

"Chestnut," replied Mór with a dismissive wave of the hand, "but I've figured out how I ruined it. As soon as I find really nice chestnuts at the market, I'll try it again."

"I thought it was good. Not that I could have said it was chestnut, but it was tasty."

"Well, you'll like this a whole lot better," Mór claimed, reaching into the pantry and taking out a small pot, which he proudly set down on the table. He took a brioche from the bread basket, spread a slice with some butter he took from the refrigerator, and applied a thick layer of the stuff from the pot.

Gordon was in no position to resist. But he would have liked to. While he couldn't stand anything sour, the old man, who found classical jams—strawberry, apricot, peach—gauche, experimented with more hair-raising recipes. Gordon took a deep breath, and then a bite of the jam-covered brioche. He watched Mór's ruddied face. Slowly Gordon nodded, quickly forcing down the whole slice.

"Well? Well?" asked the old man.

"I'm just asking, Opa, but shouldn't you have removed the seeds from the grapes?"

Mór threw a hand to his forehead. "For the love of God! I forgot. That one thing."

"And the sugar, too," Gordon mumbled, but the old man didn't hear, for he was back by the stove, stirring the simmering jam. "Opa, I've got a question," he continued louder.

"Question?"

"Yes."

"And what would that be?" asked Mór, his back still to Gordon.

"Well, two nights ago they found a dead girl on Nagy Diófa Street. She had no superficial marks, only her face had turned a bit blue. I'll go by the coroner's office, but what do you figure she could have died of?"

"Son, you're not asking me seriously," said the old man, turning around. "So many things that it's not even worth listing them all. Was it suicide?"

"I don't know."

"And why do you want to know?"

"Because I was on the scene, and I want to write an article about it, only there's nothing to write. Besides, something's not quite right about this girl."

"I'm not surprised," said Mór. "In that neighborhood there aren't too many upright ladies."

"This was no run-of-the-mill prostitute, Opa, but a Jewish girl who was probably from a bourgeois family."

"Is Dr. Somkuthy still the chief coroner?" asked the old man.

"Yes."

Mór stepped over to the telephone and had the operator connect him to the Institute of Forensic Medicine. Within a few minutes he was talking to Dr. Somkuthy.

"They'll be doing an urgent autopsy on the girl," he told Gordon after putting down the receiver.

"You didn't have to do that, Opa," said Gordon. "Really. I only asked you what the cause of death might have been."

"Son, since you've been working for the *Evening*, this is the first time you've asked me a question concerning an article of yours. So it must be important to you. I'll add that your question is foolish, for if anyone should know, you certainly should, that unless someone has a knife sticking out of their heart or has just been pulled out of the Danube, it's practically impossible to say what did them in without an autopsy. You can go to the coroner's office this afternoon."

MEANWHILE IT HAD BEGUN TO RAIN IN BIG, SWOLLEN drops. Gordon hugged the buildings as he walked quickly along Aradi Street without an umbrella. Silence now reigned in Skublics's building; only the stink accompanied Gordon up to the sixth floor. He opened the attic door and glanced around but didn't see the girl anywhere. He knocked on the inner door. In a minute a hoarse, smoke-saturated voice called out: "Get lost."

Gordon began pounding on the door. Again came the voice: "What do you want?"

Gordon said he'd gotten his name from Vogel and that he wanted a word with him. Finally, Skublics let him in. All

Gordon could make out in the dark hall was a stunted old man with an idiotic goatee. Skublics went on ahead, opening up another door.

Gordon found himself in a living room furnished with exceptional taste: carved furniture, leather armchairs, Turkish carpets, a crystal chandelier, and paintings on the walls. Just one thing was missing: a window. Gordon was beginning to suspect they were in the heart of the building, and he was certain that this flat was entirely windowless; yet it might well have a separate exit to the attic. Suddenly he found it hard to imagine he could be in the right place. This was not how he'd imagined the apartment of a black-market photographer. Just what he'd expected, he couldn't have said, but not this. Moreover, he saw nothing that so much as suggested that Skublics even had a camera.

"What do you want?" Skublics shot out his question once again. Gordon was now able to get a good look at him. The short old man was wearing a good quality suit, complemented by a gold-chained pocket watch. His hands were bony and his fingers long, like the feet of a sparrow hawk. He'd let his nails grow, and this only strengthened Gordon's impression that he was talking with an aged bird of prey. His sunken eyes topped off a face of baggy and pale parchment-like skin. He spoke fast, as if spitting out his words. "What do you want? I don't want to ask again. I don't care whether Vogel or someone else sent you, out with it!"

Gordon momentarily dropped his head and took a deep breath. He was just about to reply when a door sunk deep in the wall opened up, and out stepped the scrawny girl. She was buttoning her blouse. When she saw Gordon, her eyes turned away and she quickly went back where she'd come from.

"What do I want?" Gordon now asked in a quiet, menacing voice.

"What you saw here is none of your business," the old man proclaimed. "You can get going, as far as I'm concerned."

"Not until you answer my question. You took a picture of a young girl barely over twenty with slightly curly black hair."

"I don't remember."

"Of course you do," said Gordon, stepping closer to him. The old man did not draw back. "A green-eyed Jewish girl. With a big birthmark on her left arm."

"I don't remember any yiddie gal."

"No?"

"No."

"And what is that girl doing here?"

"I took her portrait."

"Full figure, nude?"

"It's my business who I photograph and how. It's not me who decides but my clients."

"Your clients."

"Them."

"Does the vice squad know about your little business?"

Skublics turned beet-red. Gordon had gone too far. He shouldn't have threatened the old man, at least not now and not like this. He couldn't have proven a thing, and it wasn't at all out of the question that the vice squad already knew what

Skublics was up to. What good would it do to file a complaint at headquarters? Nothing for now. Not until he learned what he wanted could he do a thing. Gordon was certain that Skublics had taken the girl's picture, and he was also certain that he wouldn't get anything out of him.

"I advise you to leave," hissed Skublics.

"I'll be back again," said Gordon, turning around and slamming the door behind him.

THE GRAND BOULEVARD HAD COME ALIVE. TRUE, IT wasn't quite as noisy and full of people as on most Thursdays, but the city was indeed starting to rise from the dead. Temporarily, at any rate, for Gömbös's wake had begun at three o'clock in the rotunda of the Parliament building, and a good many people planned to pay their respects at the prime minister's bier before the funeral on Saturday. While riding the tram to the newsroom, Gordon read the *Budapest Journal*'s coverage of the wake. True, the general public would be able to pay its respects, but in actuality, the Parliament building was open only by invitation. He had to be there on duty, and he already shuddered at the thought. He liked neither open coffins nor seeing corpses. Gordon loathed the thought that he'd have to stand there in front of the Parliament building and follow the funeral procession through downtown all the way to Kerepesi Cemetery.

Gordon had barely stepped into the newsroom when the crime section's editor, Gyula Turcsányi, greeted him with a shout: "A fine good morning to you, Mr. Gordon! May I ask where the hell your feet have been taking you? The whole office is working nonstop, and you're sauntering about town?"

Gordon would gladly have turned right around and left without pause, but instead he returned Turcsányi's stare. "I was working," he calmly replied.

"Working?" Turcsányi shot back. "And on what? If I may ask."

"On the Róna case."

"Who in the name of loving God cares a flying shit about that?" snapped Turcsányi. By now, even those who'd been typing furiously turned to listen. Turcsányi was capable of swearing on the verge of blasphemy when riled up. "Your place is here, not anywhere else. Róna is yesterday's news. In case you hadn't noticed, we're a daily paper—a newspaper. It's in the name! *News*-paper. We need news, Gordon, and Róna hasn't been news for a week already."

"And a dead girl was found in Terézváros. A dead Jewish girl."

"A Jew? As far as I'm concerned, she could be Hindu." Waving a hand in resignation, Turcsányi continued: "And I won't even ask why you didn't check with me." His anger slowly petered out. "Now go sit yourself down at your desk and write me an article about what the international press has been saying about Gömbös. And if you're not at the bier tomorrow at noon, I'll personally kick you from here to Hamburg, so you can catch the first boat back to America."

Gordon sighed deeply and, without a word, held Turcsányi's stare. For close to half a minute they just stood there facing each other: Turcsányi, the forty-plus, slightly paunchy editor whose clean-shaven face always wore a harried expression, and Gordon, hands in his pockets, head slightly bowed, eyes fixed and uncompromising. Finally, Turcsányi looked away and stormed off into his office. No one saw the interaction; everyone had better things to do than to watch the two of them stare each other down. They knew full well that Turcsányi was all talk, that he wouldn't let things reach their breaking point. He would never find a better crime reporter than Gordon. Turcsányi knew it well, and so did Gordon.

On Gordon's desk was a heap of daily papers from all over the world. The latest issue of the *Evening* was on his typewriter. Gordon picked it up and read a bit of the obituary: "It is to his credit that it isn't the nation burying itself," wrote the newspaper's deputy editor-in-chief, who went on to praise Gömbös for not subverting his constitutional role as head of government with a dictatorship tailored in foreign lands. Gordon put the paper back and took a seat. He picked up the first paper from atop the pile. *Popolo di Roma* began by writing that Gömbös had been a sincere friend of Italy. And, of course, of Mussolini. And Hitler. The *Times* of London referred to Gömbös as "Hungary's strongman," observing, "Gyula Gömbös, although an advocate of a one-party state who would have preferred military rule for Hungary—ideally conscripting every respectable Hungarian into his party—had *yet* been kept by his patriotism from breaking with Hungary's ancient constitution." Gordon didn't quite understand this, but he underlined it all the same. According to the conservative *Morning Post*, the Germans would "exploit the funeral to reemphasize, in diplomatic and military terms, German-Hungarian solidarity." Then he picked up the French papers. According to *Le Figaro*'s commentator, "Gömbös had been driven by a passionate love of his country. He worked ceaselessly for his nation's rehabilitation, and his aim had been the restoration of Greater Hungary. Gömbös was not exactly enamored of France. We fear that his predilection for friendly ties with Germany will outlive him. What is certain is that no big changes can be expected in Hungarian foreign policy." Gordon pulled the German papers from the pile, read on, and finally slid the typewriter in front of him, typing:

> The German press mourns Gyula Gömbös as a fervent Hungarian patriot, a statesman of European stature, and a most sincere friend of the national socialist German empire; as a leader who was first among foreign statesmen, and who was able to forge both political and personal ties with the chancellor, Adolf Hitler, as well as the interior minister, Hermann Göring.

It was past seven by the time Gordon finished writing. His head was abuzz from all the clichés, and he was sorry he'd even read the obituary in the *Evening*. He gave his piece to Turcsányi, who grumbled something about making sure to be there the next day at the Parliament building. Gordon nodded, then put on his jacket and his hat.

He would have headed home, but it occurred to him that the girl's autopsy would have been finished by now. He turned along Rákóczi Street toward Apponyi Square. The rain again took hold, and fog had descended on the city, but not even this could keep the newsboys from shouting their lungs out to let anyone in range know: Kálmán Darányi had been declared the acting prime minister. As if it could have been anyone else, thought Gordon.

As he passed by Nagy Diófa Street, Gordon took a look down the block but saw only a few windows shrouded in fog. He couldn't shake the image of the girl lying there like a rag doll. Or the photograph he'd found in Detective Gellért's drawer. He'd been on the crime beat for too long now to believe in chance. Moreover, the girl reminded him of the first article he'd ever written, for Philadelphia's Hungarian newspaper in December 1922. On the twenty-third, to be precise. A girl named Mariska Ifjú had committed suicide, and not even her mother suspected the reason. The girl had taken pills, a lot of them, and Gordon's editor, Ferenc Pártos, had sent twenty-two-year-old Gordon to check things out. The paper's owner and editor-in-chief, Béla Green, insisted that the story be covered, and by a reporter on the scene. The young woman lived in West Philadelphia with her mother, and hers was the first corpse Gordon had seen in his life. Mariska was lying on her stomach in front of her bed, her head against the edge, and Gordon couldn't decide whether it was merely his imagination playing a stupid game on him or if this girl and the one on Nagy Diófa Street really had been found in a similar position. With trembling hands, he took notes, stepping aside to avoid having to look at the sobbing mother or that pompous priest, János Murányi. He wrote as much as he was able to, and the same day he delivered the article to the newsroom on North Sixth Street. Later it occurred to him more than once that he might have guessed why Mariska had done herself in.

Gordon still believed he wouldn't be devoting so much attention to the case of the dead Jewish girl now if Skublics hadn't riled him up. Of course, a front-page story wouldn't hurt, either; if for no other reason than that it would keep Turcsányi's mouth shut for a while. He'd been writing about crime long enough to form an almost inexplicable sixth sense. He couldn't even tell Krisztina, but when his stomach churned like this, it was as if his gut was warning him: *Things are not what they seem*. Gordon couldn't even remember when he'd last felt this. A long time ago. It wasn't a yearning to reveal the truth that drove him as he wrote, as he collected facts and sometimes investigated. Gordon had never studied philosophy, but he suspected there was no such thing as the truth. Even if he could reveal the facts, what good would that do? Admitting it to himself was hard, but what interested him most was each person's fate. And death was the last stop on the road of fate; it all somehow led to death. Gordon was interested in the road. Whether he cared about these people he could not have said for sure, but their fates interested him more than anything else.

At Apponyi Square he boarded a tram. The Budapest transport company had again raised fares; Gordon couldn't even keep track anymore. He gave the conductor a pengő, pocketed his change, and sat down on the cold, damp wooden bench at the end of the car. Traffic was brisk on Üllői Street. Wagons, horse-drawn carriages, buses, and cars were all heading out of the city. The day was over.

Luckily, a car beeping its horn snapped him to attention; when Gordon looked up, he saw that his stop, Orczy Park, was next. He got off, and in the misty light of the streetlamps, he headed toward number 83. He knew the terra-cotta brick building housing the Institute of Forensic Medicine quite well, and the guard let Gordon in right away. He went down the stairs to the cellar, where a cold light was glowing. Dr. Pazár was sitting at a table in front of the cadaver room and having his supper: bread, a slab of roast bacon, onions, and beer from a clasped bottle. The big, bald man waved to Gordon to sit down.

"Want some?"

"I've already had supper."

"Who did you come to see?" asked Dr. Pazár with a full mouth. The doctor, whom Gordon liked very much, had served for years in the West Indies on a passenger ship, but he'd had enough of the sun and the tourists and returned to his native land, gladly accepting the coroner's position. Working nights didn't even bother him. He'd spent quite enough time as it was under the burning hot sun, he told Gordon. He loved the quiet, the calm, the cold lighting, and the patients, who might have been crotchety once but were no longer complaining by the time he saw them.

"A young girl. They brought her in the day before yesterday."

"For an autopsy?"

"Yes."

"Young, pretty, black-haired?"

"Yes."

Dr. Pazár nodded, then took out his cigarette case and held it toward Gordon, who took a cigarette. Gordon liked the coroner's obscure, aromatic cigarettes. He had asked several times, but Pazár never revealed his source. The doctor took a deep drag, placed the cigarette on the ashtray, and took one calm, final bite of his supper. Gulping down the remaining beer, he leaned back with satisfaction. He raised the cigarette once again to his mouth, inhaled the smoke, then suddenly sprang to his feet.

"Come on, let's go look at the girl!" He opened the glass door, and Gordon followed. The doctor stopped in the middle of the room. The refrigerated cabinets were to the left, the autopsy table in the middle, and behind that, some stretchers draped with white shrouds. Pazár went over to one of the stretchers and rolled it over and beneath the ceiling light. He took the end of the shroud closest to the head and pulled it back to the girl's waist. On her chest was a Y-shaped incision, and her face was whiter than when Gordon had seen her last. Her eyes were closed, and her black hair was wet and combed back. Her hands were beside her torso, the birthmark clear as day. Her breasts were as taut in death as in the picture. Her belly was flat. The incision alone disfigured her. Gordon was grateful for the doctor's aromatic cigarette.

"I don't know who put a rush on this autopsy, and I don't even want to know," said Pazár, looking at Gordon. "Shall I tell you or show you?"

"Tell me."

"The cause of death was intensive inner bleeding caused by a strong blow to the epigastric region. The left lobe of the liver was ruptured, and the consequent bleeding—as well as the circulatory and respiratory trauma this precipitated—caused the subject's death, which in my estimation occurred five minutes after the blow."

"In plain English?"

"Someone hit her so hard in the pit of the stomach that she died."

"I see," said Gordon. "How big a blow did it take? I've been hit in the gut before, too, but I'm still around."

"How big? I can't say exactly, but big. Big indeed. Other signs indicate that the victim was unprepared, that she was taken by surprise."

"In other words, someone socked it to her good."

"That's another way of putting it."

"Thank you," said Gordon, extending his hand.

"It's nothing," replied Pazár.

As Gordon headed toward the door. Pazár folded the sheet back over the body and pushed it back in place, switching off the light before following Gordon.

"Too bad," said Pazár, "she must have been a pretty one."

Gordon slowly nodded. "Yes, indeed."

"Someone really didn't want her kid to be born," the doctor drily observed. "She was in her fourth month."

Four

When Gordon awoke in his flat around 6 A.M., Krisztina was not lying beside him. He got out of bed and went to the living room. There she was, curled up in an armchair by the window. Strewn about the floor were sheets of paper, and a cup of coffee was steaming on the little table beside her.

"You got up so early to work?" asked Gordon.

"I woke up, and I'd rather work on these designs than loll about in bed listening to you snore."

Gordon leaned over and gave her a kiss. "Did you make me a coffee, too?"

"I did, but they didn't have the kind you like at the Meinl shop, so I bought the coffee at Arabia."

"It doesn't really matter," said Gordon with a dismissive wave of the hand. He poured himself a cup of coffee in the kitchen and added some milk, then went to sit beside Krisztina. "Will you be here all day?"

"Yes," she said. "I have to finish these designs, and it's best if I put this day of mourning to good use."

"I have to leave soon," said Gordon. "The whole office will be out there reporting on the funeral."

"But the procession doesn't start until after eleven," noted Krisztina.

"Yes," said Gordon, "I've got just enough time to go find Csuli."

"That Csuli?"

"That one."

"Then take care of yourself."

THE NEWSROOM WAS EMPTY EXCEPT FOR THE ONE PERson on duty. Not another soul to be seen—typewriters sitting idle on the desks, notes all over the place, and ashtrays full. Never had Gordon seen the office so desolate by day. Not even Turcsányi was in, and he was always in. Gordon looked at his watch: it was just after seven-thirty. He still had time to carry out his morning plans and get to the Parliament building by nine-thirty.

Despite the early hour, Blaha Lujza Square was even more deserted than the day before. Black flags hung everywhere, and though police officers lined Rákóczi Street, there was not a trace of civilians sauntering curiously about. He turned onto Hársfa Street and headed toward the Tick Bite. The door was slightly ajar, but the place had not opened up yet. Nine tables stood in its longish room, six on the left and three on the right. In the back there was a piano and, beside that, a bar; and a door in the back corner led to the kitchen. The tables were adorned only with clean tablecloths to start the new day, and the bar was empty. But Gordon was in luck. On the left side of the room, at the table farthest back, sat Scratchy Samu, drunk to the core. The tiny little man with the scratchy voice was wearing a grimy blazer, a red scarf, and a tilted cap. He had spent some time in Paris once—on what business, it was hard to say—and ever since, he'd tried to dress the Parisian way. Samu was a member of Csuli's gang; more precisely, he was its signalman, its chief lookout. Not that Gordon had much to do with him, but for some odd reason Samu was afraid of him. The few times their paths crossed, he always greeted the reporter with much more deference than necessary. Gordon stepped over to the bar and knocked on it loudly. Samu raised his waterlogged eyes toward Gordon but didn't recognize him. Roused by the noise, the bartender appeared—a fat, fiftyish woman with a hairdo that was all over the place—wiping her hands on her apron.

"We're not open yet," she told Gordon.

"I know," he replied, pointing to Samu, "it's just that that fellow over there is ready to die of thirst."

"I don't serve drinks on credit."

"I'm not asking you to," said Gordon, throwing forty fillérs on the counter. "Let's have whatever this will buy," he continued, "and make it decent pear brandy, not that poison."

The woman wanted to reply but had second thoughts. She wiped her nose, took out a bottle from under the bar, and filled two shot glasses. "Keep the change," said Gordon as he sat down beside a snoring Samu, whose head drooped on his chest. Gordon held one of the shots under the signalman's nose.

Samu snorted and jerked up his head. Blinking, he locked his cloudy eyes first on the glass, then on Gordon, who put the pear brandy down before him.

Samu didn't reflect for long. He reached for the shot glass with a trembling hand and all at once downed its contents. He shuddered, and Gordon watched intently as the life returned to his eyes.

"What do you want from me, sir?" he asked in a deep voice similar to the creaking of a carriage wheel.

"Take me to Csuli, Samu."

"To Csuli?"

"To him."

"But Csuli won't be happy about that."

"He won't be happy, Samu, to hear that you didn't take me to him when it was important."

"How important?"

"Very," replied Gordon, standing up. "Come on, we can't waste time."

Samu fretted a bit, but decided he'd probably be worse off not taking Gordon along. Adjusting his scarf and buttoning up his blazer, he rose unsteadily to his feet and headed toward the door.

"Shall I send this one back?" asked Gordon, pointing to the other shot glass. With surprising nimbleness, Samu stepped back to the table, downed the pear brandy, and gave a nod. "Believe me, sir, a man doesn't need a heartier breakfast than this."

"If you say so."

From the restaurant they headed toward Rákóczi Square,

Samu in front. Along the way the signalman kept gesturing to associates of his who were mostly invisible to Gordon: *It's okay, no need to worry, I know him, he's with me.* Gordon had to keep an eye out to see who Samu was communicating with in this singular language of thieves. A woman in a window watched as Samu ran his left hand along his blazer; a man leaning up against a wall observed him scratch his left earlobe with his right hand; and a teenage kid flashed his eyes toward them from inside a building doorway as Samu adjusted the visor of his cap. Gordon had to admit that Vogel had done an exceptional job with his series of articles. Everything was just as he'd described. The gang really did keep the neighborhood under surveillance every minute of the day.

Tisza Kálmán Square was lined by sullen, tired-looking buildings. Even the trees looked haggard, and the lawn— if you could call it that—was sparse and gray, with solitary clumps of grass visible here and there. A carriage was rumbling over the cobblestone, its insistent creaking echoed from all directions by the silent buildings. Gordon turned to see the signalman gesticulating dramatically: all at once Samu squatted down, tied his shoes, slowly stood back up, ran a hand over his lapel, and blew a puff of air onto the nails of his left hand before finally wiping that hand on his pants. Gordon didn't understand a single wordless action, and he couldn't even see to whom Samu was "speaking" so vivaciously.

"There, he lives in that one," said Samu, pointing. "The first door on the right on the third floor." He turned around and took off with unusually quick steps in the direction of Baross Square. Gordon looked around but saw no one. He walked carefully toward the building Samu had pointed out, avoiding dog droppings on the grass of the square, horse manure on the cobblestone. As soon as he reached the building, the front door opened. Whoever opened it was hidden in the interior's darkness even as Gordon entered. Gordon went up to the third floor and rang Csuli's doorbell. After a minute or so, he heard someone rummaging about. Then the door opened. When Csuli saw who it was, he immediately slammed the door shut.

"Come now, Csuli, even you know there's no use. You heard me coming," said Gordon loudly, "so just let me in." Csuli didn't answer. "You live in a lovely building," Gordon continued. "Much nicer on the inside than the outside. But why am I telling you this, seeing how it's not by chance you moved here. No doubt the neighbors also know how you earn your bread. The fact is, Csuli, my boy, that I could use a girl." Gordon was beginning to enjoy the situation. "A top-notch village tramp. A fiery one, mind you, not some sluggish slut, but the sort who—"

The door now opened, and a brawny hand reached out and yanked Gordon inside. Csuli slammed the door shut behind them and with booming steps went into the living room. Gordon followed. He'd seen a lot of flats, but he hadn't expected one like this, here. It was as if he'd wound up in one of the elegant, bourgeois flats near Szervita Square. Izsó Skublics's home was furnished poorly by comparison. In the corner stood a three-door Neo-Baroque hutch; the wooden door in the middle was adorned by a carving of the three Graces, and expensive china filled the shelves behind the glass door on each side. The writing desk had a castle carved right into its façade—which Gordon thought he recognized as the legendary castle of Sümeg—and a thronelike chair was behind the desk. Armchairs sank here and there into the plush Persian carpet, as did a round table with carved lion legs. In jarring contrast, however, the walls were replete with paintings and illustrations by modern artists. A heavy brocade curtain hung in front of the window, and in front of that was a sofa where Csuli himself now sat, wearing a taut, unwrinkled suit and immaculately polished shoes. Gordon could not decide if the man had woken up early or not yet gone to sleep. He'd heard that Csuli resembled the great Hungarian comic actor Szőke Szakáll, and upon seeing him now in person for the first time, Gordon had to agree.

For a moment Gordon just stood there in the doorway, taken aback. Szőke Szakáll himself could have been sitting on the sofa. The same plump frame, the same blond hair, the same double chin, and the same voluptuous smile he'd seen in the movies—only the glasses were different. Instead of Szakáll's tortoiseshell glasses, Csuli's were wire-frame and oblong, somehow transfiguring his smile. Csuli's expression was cold, calculating, menacing.

"I know you've made a name for yourself, but I know lots of people, and I demand that—"

"Demand?" snapped Gordon, plopping down in one of the lion-legged chairs beside the round table. He lit a cigarette and took a leisurely drag. "Demand? Now that's something. What do you demand? In the best-case scenario, you can demand a lawyer. Because this is the end of your little business, Csuli.

We'll see how demanding you are when the cops take you in. Because this time you've overshot the mark."

"What are you talking about?" replied Csuli, rising to his feet with surprising speed, given his proportions and the early hour.

"The Jewish girl found dead Tuesday night on Nagy Diófa Street."

"I don't know about any girl."

"In your shoes," said Gordon, "I wouldn't, either. The only problem is that everyone else knows the girl was part of your racket." From behind the cigarette smoke, Gordon watched to see if his ruse would pay off.

"Who are you talking about, you wretch?"

"Oh, I see that you really don't know her then." Gordon stood up. "I beg your pardon. My mistake."

"You're damn right you got it wrong. You have the nerve to come by here at this hour, you practically break the door down, shout in the hallway, and spout all sorts of lies."

"I must again beg your pardon. I only figured that I'd check with you before writing my article. I knew you'd deny it, but I had to try. So I'll write that you deny it."

"Deny? Me? What are you planning to write?"

"I was thinking something like, 'Csuli, the gang leader based out of Hársfa Street, denies that the girl found dead was working for him.'"

"You can't write that, because it's not true."

"Look, I wasn't seriously hoping you'd admit it. The point is, I was here and you denied it, and that I can write. After all, it's your girl they killed." Gordon turned around and headed toward the door. Now or never. He turned back. "And what's the worst that can happen to you? The cops can cart you off to the lockup for a couple of weeks. But the business will go on in the meantime, right?"

Beads of sweat appeared on Csuli's forehead.

"Even you know that would be the end of me."

"I know, I know, but there's nothing I can do. If she'd been a village girl-turned-whore, I'd say this sort of thing happens. But this was a Jewish girl from a good family. Only the general public will be more upset than the police have been at the news that she was pregnant. To send an expecting mother to the streets? Hell, Csuli, are you human? A pregnant woman's death is scandalous—even if she was a hooker—but socked so hard in the belly that she died? According to the coroner, death wasn't immediate, and was all the more painful on account of that. For both the girl and her fetus."

From Csuli's face it was obvious what was going through his head. He did some quick calculations—the dividing and multiplying—that led him to conclude there was no winning. Gordon meanwhile started off toward the apartment door again, but he hadn't yet reached it when Csuli called out, "She wasn't working for me anymore."

Gordon turned back, stuck his hands in his pockets, and listened to Csuli without a word.

"The girl had been recruited by Józsi Laboráns. It must have been a good two months back. She never did say her name. But she was a viciously pretty one; I just don't get it how Józsi Laboráns could have picked her up. He's always got such ladies . . ." Csuli waved a hand in annoyance. "We had no idea what her name was or where she'd come from. Nothing. Just that she was pretty, young, and Jewish." By now, Csuli was seated once again on the sofa, wiping his face with a handkerchief. "The customers liked her so much that she got quite the reputation. And one day a gentleman showed up in a fur coat, a hat, and cane, and he said we should talk. So we talked. You can't say no to such a gentleman. Then, the next day, the girl disappeared."

"Just like that. Like smoke."

"Well," Csuli faltered, "not so easily, though."

"How much did he pay you?"

The fat man raised his eyes to Gordon.

"You can't write that."

"Do you see a notebook in my hand? A pen?"

"You won't write it?"

"That's up to you. If you tell me what I want to know, then no. But you'd be well advised to know a lot, because it's been a while since I've had a front-page story. I'm listening."

"Five hundred pengős," Csuli finally replied.

"Five hundred pengős?"

"Yes. Gordon, right? You know gentlemen, too. Not that I'm complaining, because he could have had me carted off to the lockup instead. You think I drove a hard bargain? On the one hand, five hundred pengős; on the other, the lockup."

"Talk, Csuli," said Gordon, sitting down, "and start at the beginning." He looked at his watch. It was just past eight. He had plenty of time.

"But you know exactly how this sort of thing happens."

"I know. But do be so kind as to remind me. Or you know what? I'll look up Józsi Laboráns, and he'll tell me."

"You can look for him if you want. But you won't find him. He died a month ago of TB."

"A great loss," said Gordon. "Then there's no one left to tell it but you."

Csuli reluctantly began. One of Józsi Laboráns's girls, Teca, was caught by the detectives and sent to the lockup for two weeks. Józsi Laboráns felt the need to go in search of fresh labor. He looked around the "market," which is to say, along the Grand Boulevard and on Rákóczi Street. He couldn't help but notice this ebony-haired girl in front of a store window display. He hit on her, invited her to supper, and found her suitable. But he encountered unexpected resistance—the girl didn't want to go along with him. It was time for his tried-and-true "breaking in" routine. Józsi stepped away from the girl and over to a cop. He asked the cop if he was going in the right direction if he wanted to get to Andrássy Street, pointing toward the thoroughfare, which was just beyond the girl. The cop naturally looked in that direction, nodded, then told Józsi to keep going the same way. Of course the girl saw the scene, and because she thought this was about her, she got scared. Then Józsi went back to her and said he'd shown her to the cop, who now knew who she was, and if he saw her again, he'd arrest her. But if she stayed with him, continued Józsi, he'd protect her; he knew cops well, and it would take only a word from him to smooth things out. The girl believed him, and so she had to join Józsi, who told her what she had to do and how to behave on the street. He entrusted her to a friend of his called Dezső, who was a full-time signalman along the Grand Boulevard and accepted other "discreet" jobs as well. The girl moved in to Józsi's flat, where she was registered as a servant. She made good money for her services, and soon word of her spread among Józsi's clients.

When Csuli finished, Gordon looked at him incredulously. "You're telling me there are women who fall for this?"

Csuli gave a snorting laugh. "They all do, Gordon. You've seen lockups on the inside, right? Well, what woman wants to wind up there for even a week? She'll leave the place with syphilis so bad she'll be a stiff in no time, and even if she does avoid that or gonorrhea, she'll no doubt pick up a few nice little chancre sores."

"But why didn't she just leave Józsi?" asked Gordon.

"You see there, that you'd have to ask her."

"She's dead."

"This is what happens to these girls, Gordon," said Csuli, leaning back. "Or, if not, and they can stand it for three or four years, they end up in the provinces for a couple of years, and then it's off to Belgrade. You've been there, too; you know what they do to Hungarian girls there."

Gordon nodded. "And not just Hungarians."

"But that's most of them there. Before the war they got their hands on almost ten thousand Hungarian girls. Back then, Dušan Ranko led the business, now it's his son. A couple hundred Hungarian girls wind up there every year even nowadays, and then they take them east, to Sofia, Constantinople, Baghdad."

"I know the story, Csuli. But that's not why I came here."

"But I already told you everything I know."

"I wasn't saying you're hiding anything. Let's start at the beginning. Who was that gentleman who bought her off you?"

Csuli shook his head. "Gordon, even you should know that I wouldn't tell you, even if I knew. As it happens, I don't know."

"All right. Then you'll kindly prevail upon Skublics to talk to me."

"What does Skublics have to do with this?" the fat man asked, staring in surprise at Gordon.

"He took a couple of nude pictures of the girl."

"That type?"

"What type?"

"For a catalog," replied Csuli.

Not that Gordon had any idea, but he nodded. "That type."

"I figured as much," said Csuli. "A fellow doesn't pay five hundred pengős for a girl just for the heck of it."

"You see there," said Gordon, lighting another cigarette. "How can I get Skublics to talk?"

"That old goat? There's not a dirtier bastard in the city. If you only knew the sort of pictures he takes—pictures that can't even be used in a catalog. Why, he's got private clients willing to shell out twenty or even fifty pengős for that sort of picture. And he gives the girls five pengős."

"I'm listening, Csuli," said Gordon, blowing smoke.

Csuli grappled with something for a little while, but not for long. "Only a few guys know this about him, but one of my lookouts once saw him go to a meeting."

"What kind of meeting?"

"Not a scout meeting, that's for sure."

"Then what?"

"Skublics is a Communist."

Nodding slowly, Gordon processed this information, which, as Csuli knew full well, was worth its weight in gold. Even the police must have known how Skublics made his living. That sort of stool pigeon was useful to the detectives. But if it turned out that he was a Communist, why then, nothing could save Skublics from the state security police, headed by József Schweinitzer. And no one had escaped an encounter with them without a scratch. If they escaped at all. Most wound up in a detention camp for undesirables; Gömbös, along with Miklós Kozma, the interior minister, had made sure of that. The fewer of these types that were out in the streets, the better for everyone else. Hungary's Communists organized themselves in tiny cells and met in the greatest secrecy—never in the same place—and it was impossible to imagine what they could be up to. Not that Gordon believed the rumors that Szilveszter Matuska, who derailed the Vienna Express on a bridge near Budapest back in 1931, killing twenty-two, was a Communist and not just insane. But he knew Skublics was now in the palm of his hand.

"I see," he said, looking at Csuli. "Where does he go for meetings?"

"What do I get in exchange?" The fat man's eyes lit up from behind his glasses.

"I won't write a word about you."

"And you'll let me know if someone else is going to write about me for any reason."

"I can't promise, but I can try."

"Good. Then I can try figuring out where Skublics goes for meetings."

"You have until eight tonight. Tomorrow I'm meeting with Vladimir Gellért."

"I'll do all I can."

"That I believe."

GORDON HEADED DOWN A DESERTED RÁKÓCZI STREET toward the Parliament building. He boarded a tram and transferred to another at Apponyi Square. On Károly Boulevard there were more people milling about, walking with their heads down among the sparse but well-ordered line of soldiers and police. Gordon got off at Constitution Street and headed toward Kossuth Square. All the gas and electric lights along the road were on, but every one was shrouded by a black veil. The crowd seemed to murmur in unison, as if simultaneously praying. It was a couple of minutes after nine-thirty. Gordon had arrived earlier than planned, but despite his aversion to funerals, he didn't mind: it was a rare occasion when everyone was gathered together—both those who counted and those who did not. The uniformed honor guard that was to accompany the coffin extended in a line all the way to the main steps of the Parliament building. On the flagpoles jutting out from buildings along the route hung not only the Hungarian red, white, and green tricolor but also the flag of Gömbös's National Unity Party. Gordon shook his head and continued toward the Parliament building. Waiting on the square were the army, infantry, artillery, and cavalry units that would march after the indoor ceremony. All at once Gordon caught the drone of airplanes. Turning his head skyward, he saw nine planes fly in formation over Kossuth Square. Despite having read the official funeral schedule earlier, this display still surprised him. The storm troopers that belonged to the police units led by Dr. Gyula Kálnay clicked their heels and saluted.

The same detectives who'd stood at the main entrance before were there once again. Gordon nodded, and they waved him on. Several hundred wreaths lined the portico, and the guests trod slowly upward over the red-carpeted stairs.

No sooner had Gordon ascended to the rotunda than one of his colleagues noticed him and called him over. On his way, Gordon caught a glimpse of Turcsányi standing behind a column. Having seen Gordon as well, the section editor said a few parting words to his company and approached Gordon. "Just in time" was his grumbled greeting. "Before the procession begins, I want you to interview the British and American ambassadors." Pointing toward a group of elegantly dressed men in derby hats who were seated to the right of the bier, he added, "Hurry, they're not going to wait for you." Gordon nodded and went around the open coffin. He cast a sideways glance at the dead prime minister. Gömbös was lying inside decked out in the finest Hungarian ceremonial attire, surrounded by a sea of flowers, bouquets, and wreaths. Gordon recoiled. This corpulent character, this mockery of a soldier, this oldster with failing kidneys had

led the country? This was a man who'd had a free pass from
several European governments? This was the man who'd
led the National Unity Party with an iron fist and the man
whose word had made even Kálmán Kánya jump? Gordon
shrugged and stepped toward the group of seated gentlemen.

A smartly dressed man now stepped in front of Gordon with
a determination that belied his servile expression. Gordon recognized him as a deputy department head in the foreign ministry, as he asked the reporter what he wanted. "To interview
the British and American ambassadors," Gordon replied. The
man shook his head: not here, not now. Gordon finally left
with the promise that he would be able to speak with the ambassadors during the procession. He was on his way out when
the crowd suddenly fell silent. It was as if a schoolteacher had
struck a classroom desk with a reed switch. Gordon slunk
behind two hussars and looked on from there. For a couple
of minutes nothing happened. Then came the clang of un-
sheathed swords, the clicking of heels, and the click-clack of
stiff, soldierly steps. Gordon peered out from over the hussars'
shoulders.

First the Bulgarian ambassador, Stoil Stoilov, stepped up
to the bier and silently lowered his head. He was followed by
Galeazzo Ciano, the Italian foreign minister, and Kurt Schnu-
schnigg, the Austrian chancellor. Finally, a fat man with an
oily complexion started toward the bier. He wore black boots
polished to a sparkle, a leather jacket pulled tight around his
belly by a belt, and a flat service cap that covered his eyes.
Gordon shuddered. This was Hermann Göring, supreme
commander of the Luftwaffe, Prussian interior minister, the

man in charge of the four-year plan of the empire's military economy, and Hitler's most loyal backer and devotee. Göring stopped in front of the coffin, the Iron Cross hanging from his neck. He clicked his heels, threw back his head, and then, swinging his arms forward to clasp his hands, he stood in silence for a few moments. The quiet was broken only by the snapping of cameras and the popping of their flashes. Göring now turned around and took his seat to the right of the bier. He had barely reached his seat when Archbishop Jusztinián Serédi appeared, stood mutely for some moments, and then sat down to the left of the bier. Gordon glanced over at the Prussian interior minister, whose face remained unreadable, and suddenly Gordon recalled what Gömbös had boasted to Göring in the spring: by applying the fascist principles learned from the Germans, Gömbös would reshape Hungary within two years and would preside over the new state as its dictator.

Kálmán Darányi stood up and went to the steps leading to the rotunda. Gordon winced the moment he heard the sound of clicking heels. He glanced at the red velvet chair set apart on its own beside the bier. Hungary's regent, Miklós Horthy, now appeared on the steps in his admiral's uniform, his head topped off by a calpac, and his chest bearing the Grand Cross of the royal Order of Saint Stephen of Hungary. It was practically with piety that Darányi—in the company of the two speakers of Parliament, Sándor Sztranyavszky and Bertalan Széchenyi—greeted the head of state, who took determined steps toward the velvet chair, adjusted his sword, and sat down. Gordon shook his head with silent glee at the sight of the admiral's uniform. The regent, his face somber, knit his brows and stared into the air. Silence had once again descended upon the hall when the clergy arrived, with Lutheran bishop Sándor Raffay in the lead. Gordon looked at his watch. A few minutes past ten. He sighed deeply, took a seat in the rows reserved for the media, and proceeded to listen to one speech after another as the funeral began. After Raffay came Darányi, who in turn was followed by Sztranyavszky, and then Széchenyi and, finally, Béla Ivády, president of the National Unity Party. Gordon's head was buzzing by the end. It seemed as if this was the funeral for someone like the American president, Franklin Delano Roosevelt, instead. A champion of freedom, said the orators. A man who struggled for the rise of the nation; someone whose efforts brought the country order, security, and economic prosperity. A creative genius hammering out his people's future. Sometimes Gordon glanced up at the given speaker in surprise. Was it only now that he would learn how great a loss this was? A champion of democracy—luckily that was left off the list. Only then would the laudation have been complete.

During the eulogies, he passed his eyes over the elite who were on hand. A couple of them seemed to have fallen asleep. General Schamburg-Bogulski, head of the Polish delegation, undoubtedly nodded off, jerking up his head at one point, giving a quick, confused look around before deftly suppressing a yawn. Horthy sat there with an unruffled expression; at most, he would sometimes fiddle with the handle of his sword. Gömbös's widow, sons, and two siblings cried quietly as his mother stared glassy-eyed at the coffin.

After the eulogies, there came Siegfried's Funeral March

from Wagner's *Ring of the Nibelung*, conducted by Erno Dohnányi. Gordon was practically counting the measures to determine when the music would end. Once the final notes fell silent, the procession got under way, with Raffay in the lead.

Gordon escaped from the Parliament building in time to see the next act. A soldier held a simple wooden cross up high, and behind him six black horses pulled the hearse, followed by thirteen more carriages. The last two were perhaps the most notable: one held the wreath sent by Il Duce—Mussolini—and the other, a wreath of a thousand roses from the Italian king, Victor Emmanuel III. The pallbearers now also appeared, carrying on their shoulders the coffin, which was draped with the national flag and topped off with Gömbös's combat helmet and sword. By now, Horthy had removed the calpac from his head and was waiting on the steps to take the lead in the procession, behind three peasants donning sheepskin waistcoats. Gordon found this especially appealing. The man in the center, an older fellow with a white mustache, was carrying a silver tray and on that a little box containing soil from the village of Murga, so the prime minister could rest in the earth of his hometown. Gordon looked at his watch. It was already past eleven-thirty. The funeral procession would take a while, but there was nothing to be done. Turcsányi wanted an article compiled from interviews with the ambassadors, and Gordon would not find a better occasion than this. He buttoned his jacket and turned up his collar, sighing as he adjusted his hat. He started off with the mourners toward Kerepesi Cemetery.

The man from the foreign ministry kept his promise—by the time the procession reached Blaha Lujza Square, Gordon had already completed both interviews. He stepped out of the crowd and headed toward the Oktogon. With the trams out of service, he had to walk, but this didn't bother him at all. Indeed, he went by foot all the way to the Circle, where, in keeping with his habit, he looked up at the balcony door. It was closed. The old man was once again bumming about. Gordon sat down on a bench and began writing in his notebook. He hadn't been able to take notes during the procession, so it was now that he set down on paper those hackneyed phrases the ambassadors had rattled off. He could have conjured up the article from his head without any interviews at all; he'd known exactly what they would say. The U.S. ambassador, John Flournoy Montgomery, clearly disapproved of all the fuss—this much, Gordon could see on his face—but naturally he, too, chose his words diplomatically: Gömbös had been a European leader, his death was a great loss, Hungary had to look to the future, and so on.

When Gordon finished, he screwed the cap back on his fountain pen and, looking at the trees, once again fell to thinking about the dead girl, who was distracting him more and more. A while back, he'd heard talk around town about women chosen out of catalogs. Whoever was behind the girl's death was out of Csuli's weight class. Five hundred pengős for a woman? No matter how gorgeous she was, this was a ton of money. Csuli and his gang, including the likes of Józsi Laboráns, were lucky to make ten to fifteen pengős a day with their women. These were low-class characters who spent their money on drinks, cards, or horseracing as soon as they made it. The girls quickly withered and were sold to some hovel off in the provinces, unless of course some venereal disease did them in first.

Five hundred pengős was a big and thoroughly considered investment. Anyone who spent that much for a girl served important clients. And no doubt he didn't send the gals to bed down customers in some shady servant's room in some shady neighborhood like Terézváros. Gordon would have been lying to himself had he denied that there was anything unusual about this particular girl. But one thing was certain: no matter what he might find out about her, if he found anything at all, it would not be pleasant. And in all probability, he couldn't write about it. Even if he were to find the other girls who served this high-class clientele, not a single paper would be willing to publish the article. And yet . . .

"It's as if I was just looking at your dad," said Mór, plopping down beside Gordon and placing a basket of apples in front of him.

"Apple jam again, Opa?"

"Indeed!" proclaimed the old man. "Just look at how lovely they are. Eighteen fillérs a kilo. I didn't waste any time in buying five kilos."

"So you're giving it another try."

"I certainly am."

"It can't turn out bad. True, everyone says you can't make jam out of apples, but applesauce is the best-case scenario."

"You see, son. This is the challenge here."

"Remember when you cooked up that jam from some wild berries you found on a hill across the river?"

Mór shuddered, then gave a dismissive wave of the hand. "Don't you worry, son. Not even then did anything bad happen to me."

"Opa, for three days you didn't even come out of the bathroom."

"Well now . . . but it was tasty."

"As long as we're on the subject, Opa, how hard of a punch to the belly does it take to kill someone?"

The old man turned to Gordon and scrutinized his face. "So you've been to the coroner's."

Gordon nodded.

"Harder than hard," said the old man. "It takes quite a blow to cause death that way."

"That's what Pazár said, too."

"But you've also got to know where to hit, and how hard," continued Mór.

"You're trying to say that if I take a swing at someone, say, a woman, then . . ."

"What I'm trying to say, son, is that whoever did it has probably done it before. The chances of doing so by accident are quite small."

Gordon closed his notebook and put away his fountain pen.

"Tell me, son," said Mór, leaning back on the bench. "You know today's world better than I do. What do you think of this fellow Darányi?"

"What do I think, Opa? He's a politician. Maybe he'll be able to rein in the National Unity Party, maybe not."

"And if not?" The old man looked Gordon in the eye.

"You know Krisztina was in Berlin this summer, right?" asked Gordon.

"She was making some sort of drawings for the Olympics."

"You could say that. Well, she met a man called Günther, a longtime cop. A detective. This Günther was looking for a missing person. Don't ask me how they met," added Gordon in reply to the question in Mór's eyes. "You can never tell with Krisztina. Anyway, this Günther took Krisztina for a walk in Berlin. He showed her how the Jew-bashing placards on Alexanderplatz had just been replaced by Olympic ones. Well, one of the top figures in this German leadership paid a visit to Gömbös in the sanatorium near Munich. His name is Rudolf Hess. Have you heard about him?"

Mór shook his head.

"He used to be Hitler's deputy, and he edited *Mein Kampf*. This man conveyed Hitler's personal best wishes to our prime minister. And as you may remember, at a National Unity Party meeting not too long ago, those on hand enthusiastically sang the Horst Wessel Song—the Nazi Party anthem, that is. And then there was the Földes surveillance affair."

"Which was what again, my boy?"

"László Földes-Fiedler was tasked by the National Unity Party to put politicians under surveillance and prepare reports about them. Do you remember who stopped off in Budapest a couple of weeks back for a friendly chitchat? The German minister of foreign affairs, Konstantin von Neurath, and Goebbels. The latter was even received by our own foreign minister. Of course, the visit was purely personal. And not quite two weeks ago our interior minister ordered a ban on public meetings." Gordon was ratcheting up his temper as he spoke, and he just kept listing examples. "And Hitler's speech at the end of September? That if Germany had colonies and raw materials, then it could allow itself the luxury of democracy? The luxury of democracy? Opa, democracy is not a luxury."

"For you, my boy, in America, it wasn't. But here . . ."

"What was Gömbös up to in Rome all the time? Hunting with Mussolini?"

Mór stretched out his arms. "What are you getting at, my boy?"

"What is the name of this square you live on?"

The old man quietly replied: "Adolf Hitler Square. But Darányi will . . ."

"Darányi will what, Opa? Do you think he can stand firm against the hawks in the National Unity Party? Opa, this country of ours would just as well stand by Stalin, too, if he promised we'd get Transylvania and the northern highlands back after losing them on account of the war. As for the British, why, they're all talk; it doesn't cost them a thing to support revisionism. But the Germans? People believe they'll actually do it."

"My boy, it doesn't matter who we side with," said the old man softly. "Anything is better than the Communist rabble. Anything."

"Yes?" Gordon looked him in the eye.

"Yes." He nodded. "You weren't here in 1919. You didn't see what happened. Not only in Budapest, but where we're from, in Keszthely."

Gordon didn't reply. Mór's last sentence floated between them. The old man sighed, stretched, and stood up. "I've got apple jam waiting for me," he said, taking his basket and going into the building.

GORDON HURRIED TO THE NEWSROOM, TYPED HIS TWO articles in no time, and put them on Turcsányi's desk. The wall clock read six-thirty. He didn't have to hurry. He'd agreed to meet Krisztina for dinner at seven in the Abbázia.

With the trams not running, the city seemed to have entered a state of suspended animation. At the New York Café, the curtains were drawn and noise barely filtered out. On the Grand Boulevard only a bicycle messenger appeared now and again while pedaling feverishly to get a film reel from one cinema to the next.

The waiter in the Abbázia had Gordon sit down at his usual table. Only a few odd people were dawdling about in the coffeehouse. At the occupied tables, the conversations were hushed, and the waiters, having nothing better to do, sat on chairs by the kitchen and read newspapers or did crossword puzzles. Krisztina arrived a couple of minutes past seven. As always, Gordon noted with satisfaction that the men on hand turned their heads to look at her. Neither her outfit nor her expression was provocative, but she had a way of coming through a door that few women could match. Gordon pulled out her chair, and Krisztina nodded at a waiter (who, by now, was standing by the kitchen ready to leap) as she took off her hat and gloves. The lithe young man appeared beside them at once, as if he'd glided over on a film of water.

"A good evening to you, Mr. Editor, and to the fine young lady," he said. "May I suggest something for tonight?" Gordon nodded. "Well, our veal cutlet is fresh and tender, and the roast beef with fried chopped onions is simply divine. I would recommend butter-braised peas with the veal, and as for the roast beef, a double serving of onions fried to a special crisp, as well as boiled or fried potatoes." Gordon and Krisztina did not frequent the Abbázia for culinary pleasures. When they really wanted something delicious, they went to the Guinea Fowl, on Bástya Street, whose menu included fish and game broiled over coal ash. The Abbázia was close, pleasant, and comfortable, and their waiter always recommended the most acceptable dish of the day. He brought the menu under his arm only for show. He now took their order, which included coffee and a bottle of red wine.

Gordon quickly told Krisztina the story about Göring's appearance in the Parliament building and described the steel-helmeted storm troopers; Horthy on his horse; and the black-dressed, murmuring masses.

"Did anything else interesting happen to you today?" she asked after taking a sip of her wine. "Did you talk with Csuli?"

"I did," said Gordon. "I certainly did." And he caught her up on what he'd learned from Csuli.

"So the old lech is a Communist," said Krisztina, staring at her wineglass. "Then you were dealt a good hand."

"Not just any hand."

"Don't tell me you want to track down what happened to that girl?"

"I do."

Krisztina raised her eyes at Gordon and scrutinized his face. Gordon took out a cigarette and lit it.

"Why?"

"Because no one else is interested in her death."

"Not even the police?"

"Them least of all."

"How do you know?"

"It's been almost six years that I've been working with the *Evening*, practically always with the police. I know when they're investigating a case and when they're not. This time they won't."

"Why not?"

"Well now, that's another question. Gellért used the funeral as his excuse for inaction, which might even be true."

"Might even be true?"

"I don't know what will happen, Krisztina. This whole thing is suspicious to you, too, not just me. And if what Csuli said is true, and I can find evidence of these elite hookers . . ."

"You want to make the front page?"

"Are you kidding? With this? It could never be published."

"Then what?"

Gordon crushed out his cigarette as the waiter appeared and quietly set down their dinner. "Do you have some problem with me investigating this?"

"Zsigmond, you're a crime reporter. Not a detective, not a private eye. What do you know about investigations?"

"Just enough to know where to begin."

"Where to begin? You've been running about for days now with no idea of where you're going with this. Gellért would get further with his men. Why, even some detective from the provinces would."

"Are you trying to say I don't know what I'm doing?"

"What I'm trying to say," said Krisztina, "is that while you're used to digging into all sorts of affairs, here you suspect a murder. This is not like figuring out why some bank official shot himself in the head or why some clerk embezzled money from the glazier on the corner. Ask a couple of questions, and you've closed the case."

Gordon took a deep breath, held it in, and exhaled slowly. In lieu of a reply, he pulled his plate in front of him and proceeded to cut his veal with such force that the metal of the knife grated against the porcelain. Krisztina calmly saw to her own veal cutlet and didn't say another word until they'd finished supper.

"As you see it, I'm not qualified," said Gordon, putting his fork and knife down on the table.

"That's not what I said," replied Krisztina, looking him in the eye. "I just want you to watch out for yourself. If I know you, you won't sit still until you turn up something, no matter what it is."

"What could happen to me?"

"That's just it. There's no telling what you might get yourself into. Could you just think it over? Do you really need this?"

Gordon raised his eyebrows and picked up his wineglass, but he didn't drink; he just stared at the swirling, oily liquid. Krisztina watched him in silence, waiting patiently. "I've got to do something," he finally said, so quietly that on a normal evening she wouldn't even have heard him.

"If not for the girl, then for yourself," said Krisztina.

"What did you say?" asked Gordon, leaning closer, for at that moment a large and noisy group walked in.

"Do what you must do," came Krisztina's strident reply.

"I will. And if you don't mind, I've got to get going now to Csuli."

"I'll go with you."

"No you won't. It's not your sort of neighborhood, and although I've got Csuli, I have no reason to trust him. Go on home, or drink another coffee, and get some work done. Develop a couple of pictures. Potter about in your darkroom."

"I was beginning to think you'd tell me what to do."

"I wouldn't even try. But I'll tell you what you won't do. You won't go with me."

CSULI WAS SITTING IN THE TICK BITE, PLAYING CARDS. The tavern was permeated by the smell of beer and food, with shrill laughter, and with someone playing a sped-up version of the latest hit, "Gloomy Sunday," on the piano. Cigarette butts covered the floor, couples leaned against each other, drunks strutted about. Gordon walked up to Csuli.

"Wait for me in the kitchen," said Csuli without even looking at him. Gordon shrugged and went into the kitchen. There, a woman cook was trying to keep the chaos in check, and the kitchen boy was in the corner applying a cold compress to his hand. Gordon had never been inspired to eat in the Tick Bite to begin with, but this sight kept his appetite completely at bay. A block of lard was melting on the table in the middle of the kitchen, and beside it was an enormous heap of withering onions and potatoes; unidentifiable meats floated in a tub of water; and in front of the stove a cat was chewing on a bone. From the cook's crazed expression, it seemed she hadn't even noticed Gordon, who, having nothing better to do and feeling overwhelmed by the odor of burned lard, lit a cigarette.

He had to wait almost five minutes for Csuli. The fat man moved about in the kitchen, evidently feeling quite at home. He lowered a spoon into one of the pots, took a taste, and shook his head. "Don't eat here, Gordon. Or anywhere else where you get a whole meal for one pengő."

"I won't," Gordon replied, looking for an ashtray. Finally, he dropped the butt on the floor along with the others.

"Listen here," said Csuli, leaning against the table and causing it to slide out of place. "Skublics attends meetings in Józsefváros. And with your luck, he'll be there tonight, too. I got the dirt that he'll be one of the folks leading the discussion, which means they'll be there till dawn."

"Where?" asked Gordon. The Józsefváros district was big, after all—stretching from the National Museum downtown out into the sweeping residential districts well beyond Blaha Lujza Square and the Grand Boulevard toward Kerepesi Cemetery.

For a while Csuli fixed his eyes on Gordon, and then rubbed

his swollen hands together. "They meet in a cellar on Mátyás Square. They make themselves out to be coal heavers."

"Thanks," said Gordon.

Csuli watched him through narrowed eyes from behind his wire-frame glasses. "Don't thank me. I don't know why I'm helping you out."

"You know full well," replied Gordon. "Just one more thing."

"What?

"Scratchy Samu for tonight."

"He's yours. But bring him back in one piece," said Csuli. He ran his fingers nervously through his wavy blond hair before rolling out of the kitchen. On his own way out of the club, Gordon stepped over to Samu and quickly informed him of his task. "Don't be late," he added, "and don't have too much to drink." Pointing toward the fat man, he added, "If you muck it up, not only will I be angry, but Csuli will be, too." Samu nodded while silently repeating to himself the address and time. Finally he downed the last of his wine. "It'll all work out, Mr. Editor. I'll signal you a clear path, I will. Don't you worry."

Stepping out of the Tick Bite, Gordon turned up his collar and lit a cigarette before hurrying toward the newsroom. He pondered his course of action. Knowing Skublics, the old man would laugh in his face if Gordon simply tried to tell him he saw him at a Communist meeting. No, he needed much more than this. He needed evidence. A photograph. Ideally, one in which Skublics could be seen in the company of other suspicious characters.

He could ask one of the staff photographers—maybe Flórián Sziráki—to help him. Gordon liked the man and often worked with him, but he knew that Sziráki wasn't exactly renowned for his discretion. But he did know someone else, someone who took exceptional pictures.

On arriving in the newsroom, Gordon went straight to the telephone. Valéria looked up at him from behind her dark glasses but thought better of asking questions after seeing Gordon's expression. Gordon checked his watch: it was nearly eleven. If he wanted to catch Skublics, he had to hurry. He looked up a phone number in his notebook and dialed. Half a minute later, he nodded in Valéria's direction, then left.

As promised, the cab was in front of the building in five minutes. An Opel Regent that had seen better days pulled up to the curb. Behind the wheel was a man in his mid-forties, wearing a cabbie cap. "A fine good evening to you, sir," he said with a partly toothless grin. "Where to?"

"Lövölde Square," said Gordon, taking his seat. "And fast."

"Yes, sir," said the man, looking back briefly to check traffic, shifting the car into gear, and stepping on the gas. At the end of Rákóczi Street he swerved onto Rottenbiller Street, where he sped right by the horse-drawn carriages worming their way forward. Gordon held on to keep his balance. Not even five minutes had passed, and already they were on Lövölde Square.

"Wait right here," said Gordon, getting out. The driver nodded enthusiastically and began rolling a cigarette. "You won't have time to smoke it," said Gordon. "We're moving on in five minutes."

"Yes, sir," replied the cabbie, but he kept on rolling.

Gordon rang the bell for the super, who opened the building door with a tired face. Gordon pressed a pengő into his palm and asked him not to lock up because they'd be right out.

Krisztina was already in bed, reading. Freshly developed prints hung from the clothesline in the bathroom.

"Lucky you haven't gone to sleep yet," said Gordon, stopping in the doorway.

"What happened?" asked Krisztina, sitting up.

"If you want, now you can come help me out."

"With what?"

"Taking some pictures."

"Now?"

"Anything better to do?"

Krisztina shut her book and got out of bed. "Three minutes and we can be off." She went into the bathroom, pulling the door behind her without quite shutting it. "Go ahead and fill me in. I'm listening."

"Skublics is at a Communist meeting tonight on Mátyás Square. We need pictures of him there."

"I don't have a flash," said Krisztina.

"You don't need one, because I've come up with an idea."

"What?"

"I'll tell you in the car."

"The car?"

Gordon sighed. "I called a taxi."

"Then there's really no time to waste," said Krisztina, appearing in the bathroom door dressed for the task: trousers, a

short knit coat, hair in a ponytail. "I'm getting the camera,"
she said, stepping past Gordon.

NOT ONLY HAD THE DRIVER LIT HIS SMOKE, BUT HE'D
also rolled two more, parking one behind each of his ears. Having opened the door for Krisztina, he got behind the wheel.
"Endre Czövek is the name," he said, turning his head, "I'm
at your service, and I kiss your hand. Do you mind, ma'am, if
I smoke?"

Krisztina gave a wave of the hand. "Go ahead, Czövek.
Don't be shy."

"Yes, ma'am." Flashing his toothless grin her way, he
added, "Where to?"

"To Mátyás Square," replied Gordon. When they turned
onto Rottenbiller Street, he leaned forward and informed both
Czövek and Krisztina of his plan. "We don't have time to try
it out," he finished. "We'll have only one chance; we've got to
act fast, and we've got to get out of there even faster." Czövek
nodded somberly as Krisztina prepared her camera. By now
the taxi was on Fiumei Street, with the cemetery to their
left, but—wheels screeching as he turned—the cabbie took
a right instead, not once easing up on the Opel, even on the
cobblestones of Nagyfuvaros Street. But with a block to go, he
slowed, rolling quietly onto Mátyás Square. Gordon showed
him the address, and Czövek parked across from the steps to
the cellar, between a ramshackle truck and a cart. He cut the
engine and pulled his cap down over his eyes. Krisztina meanwhile took a place up front and slid down in the seat. She rolled
the window down all the way, set the camera on the frame,

noting its position, then put the machine in her lap and waited. Gordon slipped into a building doorway and lit a cigarette.

But for the shouts of a couple of drunkards, the square was quiet and still. The weather was perfectly suited to their purpose: neither raining nor foggy on the square. Little by little, the lights behind the windows overlooking the square flickered off, the drunkards moved on, and the silent night was broken only by the cries of a cat in heat.

Around 1 A.M. the cellar door opened, then closed. Gordon hurried over to the taxi. "Like we discussed," he said in a muffled voice. "You pay close attention, too, Krisztina. We'll have only a couple of seconds. When I wave my hand, go for it."

He didn't have to wait long in the doorway. After a couple of minutes the cellar door opened once again, and out stepped a large, grubby-faced figure in a disheveled outfit. From under the brim of his hat, Gordon watched the people exiting the cellar one by one. Finally, there appeared Izsó Skublics, talking with a thin figure as he stepped out onto the sidewalk. Gordon gestured toward Czövek, at which the driver started the engine. Krisztina set the camera in the car's open window, and when the headlights came on, Krisztina began rapidly clicking one exposure after another.

Skublics froze. As did the man beside him. Gordon turned around, and with quick steps he headed toward Népszínház Street. Skublics moved toward the car, but Czövek had already shifted into gear, and with wheels screeching he drove away. Krisztina hardly had time to shut the door. She gripped the camera tight as Czövek, a cigarette hanging from his mouth, rumbled toward Népszínház Street. Gordon was waiting for them at the corner of Conti Street. The driver slowed down and Gordon jumped in. A few blocks later they turned onto the Grand Boulevard, where they continued at a slower pace in the direction of Lövölde Square.

IT WAS PAST TWO IN THE MORNING BY THE TIME KRISZ-tina emerged from the bathroom. Hanging on the clothesline were the freshly developed pictures. Her eyes were red from exhaustion, but Krisztina pointed with satisfaction behind herself. "Only two didn't turn out. He's clear as day on the rest. Buying that lens was worth it."

Gordon stepped over to look up at the pictures. Skublics's expression was one of terror, whereas that of the man beside him was rather one of fury: cold, cruel, overwhelming fury. "This character looks familiar," he said, pointing to the other man. "I've seen him somewhere, but I can't say where."

"You can figure that out in the morning," said Krisztina from bed. "Now come on, come to bed with me."

Five

Now where did you take this? And when?" asked Kornél Kosik, looking up at Gordon. The political reporter was sitting at his desk, though it was Saturday. He had no choice: so much had happened during the week that he couldn't allow himself the luxury of a rest. And so he'd been in the newsroom putting his notes in order when Gordon appeared. Kosik now shook his head in disbelief as he stared at the picture. "Do you know who that is?"

Gordon studied the picture once again. His wavy, greasy hair combed back, the man stared contemptuously into the lens with grayish burning eyes. This was a face that was hard to forget. And yet Gordon shook his head. "He somehow looks familiar. I've seen him before, but I don't know where."

Kosik ran his fingers through his tousled hair. He stuck a key into the one drawer on his desk that had a lock and pulled out a thin little book with a blue cover. Gordon tried reading the title, but it was covered by Kosik's tobacco-stained fingers.

Kosik flipped through the book, which was filled with photographs accompanied by a couple of lines of text here, entire paragraphs there. On finding what he was looking for, he took a sheet of paper, used it to cover the text, and showed Gordon the picture. "Is that him?"

"Yes," said Gordon.

"In 1919, after the collapse of the Communist revolution here in Hungary," Kosik began, "he was sought nationwide. Not only had he joined the Red Army, but he also edited the *Commune* newspaper. He managed to flee to Vienna and from there to Bratislava. He returned illegally in 1922 and was arrested in 1923, along with seventy of his comrades, and sentenced to fifteen years in jail. But then, in 1924, through a diplomatic agreement, he and forty-one others were extradited to the Soviet Union. Starting there, the whole affair is murky. All that's certain is that he kept himself busy organizing Communist Party activities throughout Europe, and at some point became a member of the NKVD. You know what that is, right?"

"The Soviets' internal security apparatus. Its secret police."

"That's about right," said Kosik. "And he's fought in the Spanish Civil War, too. On the nationalist side, it probably goes without saying. It's not certain, but I've heard from various sources that he's been seen in Catalonia. And now here, in Budapest. Why, we've got evidence, too." Kosik tapped Gordon's photograph with his pen.

"Will you tell me his name, at last?"

"Why do you want to know?" asked Kosik, leaning back in his chair.

Gordon sat on the corner of the desk and pondered his reply. "I've got a proposal," he finally said.

"I'm listening."

"I'll give you the picture along with the address where it was taken."

"What do I get out of that?"

"Let's just say I don't keep the picture for myself," said Gordon, "and let's say I figured out some other way to get that name."

"Understood. And agreed."

"I have one more condition."

"Condition?"

"Yes."

"What would that be?"

"Wait till Monday morning. Don't go looking for Schweinitzer until then."

"Why do you think I'd go to the state security police?"

"Come now, Kornél. Come now."

Kosik took a deep breath and slowly nodded. "Monday will do. Besides, I figure he's already on his way to Moscow, so it's not as if they could catch him. His name is Gerő. Ernő Gerő."

"That's it. Gerő. What's he doing here?" asked Gordon, looking Kosik in the eye.

"Don't ask me. But I suspect he didn't travel home for Gömbös's funeral."

"Then you'll wait till Monday."

"I'll wait."

"You don't want to catch him," said Gordon, rising from the desk, "you just want a gold star from Schweinitzer." Kosik put the book and the photograph in his desk drawer. He then locked the drawer and put the key in his vest pocket.

Kosik looked at Gordon. "You have a problem with that?"

"Me? None whatsoever. You can do whatever you want with that picture."

GORDON LEFT THE NEWSROOM FOR THE TICK BITE. SAMU was not there. Gordon asked the bartender about the signal-man, but he only shook his head. "He left last night, and I haven't seen him since, though he always starts his day in here."

Gordon stepped out of the Tick Bite and lit a cigarette before heading toward the Grand Boulevard. All at once a scruffy, beer-scented man stepped out from a doorway. "Your name Gordon?"

"Who wants to know?" Gordon took a step back.

"Scratchy Samu."

"I'm Gordon."

"Samu says he's waiting for you on the Buda side of the river, on Ponty Street. Hurry up—he said that, too. That you should hurry up."

Gordon telephoned the taxi company from the New York Café and asked for Czövek. The young lady at the other end of the line was as polite as could be. "He'll be there in ten minutes, sir."

Gordon went outside to wait for Czövek. Not even five minutes had passed when the worn Opel Regent appeared in the sparse traffic.

"Where to now?" asked the cabbie with a grin.

"Ponty Street," said Gordon.

"Shall we hurry?"

"Let's hurry."

At the Oktogon, Czövek turned left onto Andrássy Street, not sparing his car. The traffic here was no worse. He drove quickly by the Opera House, which was still draped in black, and then from Count István Tisza Street he turned onto the Chain Bridge. Gordon looked at the Danube. Tugboats and barges were advancing with difficulty in the low river. Fog was slowly descending upon Castle Hill. At the far end of the bridge, Czövek turned from Adam Clark Square onto Fő Street, a block in from and parallel to the river, and soon took a left onto Ponty Street.

"Where, exactly?" asked the driver, looking back.

"I don't know," said Gordon, shaking his head, "but wait a bit." With that, he got out and stared at the steep series of steps that led up the side of Castle Hill to Hunyadi Street. He'd just turned around to get back in the cab when a dubious figure in a sport coat stepped up to the street from a cellar entrance.

"Your name Gordon?" Having received an affirmative reply, the man chucked away his cigarette butt and continued: "Samu is waiting for you at the start of Várfok Street."

Gordon had no idea what to make of it all. He got back in the taxi and told Czövek where to go. Not even now did the cabbie dillydally as he raced to the far side of Castle Hill. At the start of Várfok Street they stopped, and Gordon had barely gotten out when yet another shady character stepped up to him. "Anna Street," he said. On they went toward the top of Castle Hill.

The Mass had already begun at Matthias Church, and only a few odd tourists were left dawdling about on Holy Trinity Square. Gordon leaned forward toward Czövek. "Slow down here so I can peek down Anna Street." Gordon knew that Anna Street was short, comprising but a few buildings. There, not even a veteran lookout like Scratchy Samu could hide. As they rolled by, Gordon saw that he was right. Having asked for the cab to stop, he added, "Czövek, you just go on back to Holy Trinity Square and wait for me there." The cabbie nodded and the taxi turned around, vanishing into the thickening fog.

Gordon hurried onto Anna Street. He didn't want to be conspicuous, nor did he have to be: Samu would not have had anyplace to lie low, had he wanted to. At the start of Úri Street he stopped and looked around. There was no one to be seen. He then heard a soft whistle, and Samu stepped from a doorway on the far side of the street. His eyes were red, his stubble grayish, his face sunken, and his voice even raspier than usual as he said, "One Anna Street. First flat on the left." He continued, "He was on the move all night. Lucky I took a couple of lookouts with me to Mátyás Square, or else he would have gotten away."

Gordon nodded. "You sure made me run around. So you're saying he first went to Ponty Street, from there to Várfok Street, and finally over here. You sure he's in?"

Samu gave a weary nod. Gordon reached into the inner

pocket of his jacket, pulled out his wallet, and extended a ten-pengő coin to Samu, who only shook his head. "I don't work for you. I work for Csuli." With that, he pulled his cap down over his eyes and, coughing, dissolved into the fog.

Gordon stopped in front of 1 Anna Street. He looked around, then opened the front door. The tiny inner courtyard was gray, neglected, run-down. To the right, a set of stairs went up, and to the left, there was a door. By the wall, a dried-up plant in a flowerpot, a threadbare doormat, and hastily swept leaves. He stepped into the courtyard. The shutters were drawn on the windows of the flat the door evidently led to. Gordon began pounding on the door. One of the shutters moved almost imperceptibly. Gordon pounded even harder. The door finally opened a crack, and Skublics's eyes appeared.

"What in the fucking hell do you want?" he hissed. Gordon didn't reply; instead, he shoved the door in, together with the old man, and shut it behind him. Skublics came at Gordon from the fireplace, hands high above his head. Gordon waited for Skublics to strike before grabbing the old man's wrist and twisting the poker from his grip, forcing him into a grimy armchair. Silently Gordon reached into his pocket and pulled out the photograph, which he threw in the old man's lap. Skublics didn't move. At this, Gordon took a candlestick from the fireplace mantel. Lighting the candle with his cigarette, he held it in Skublics's face. The old man stared right back at Gordon, who now said, softly, "I won't ask you again who it is in that picture."

"What picture?" asked Skublics, his eyes wide. "This one?"

"No. The one I spoke with you about in your studio. If you can call it a studio."

"I don't know what you're talking about. Get out of here or I'll call the cops."

Gordon made a fist and then slowly opened his hand. "Go ahead," he said, stepping away and placing the candle on the table. "Call the cops. At least then they won't have to go looking for you."

"You . . ." snapped Skublics. Animal loathing flashed in his button eyes.

"Let's have it. Who's in the picture?"

"Why should I tell you? They'll nab me, anyway. You've already given them this picture here, and the state security police have men everywhere. I bet you're one of them."

"Skublics, if I were from the security police, I'd have broken down your door with gendarmes and summoned every paper to the scene. And don't be so sure about them. They'll get the picture on Monday. So you've got time to disappear."

"Why should I trust you?" asked the old man in a shrill voice.

"Trust me?" Gordon shot him a stare in reply. "You don't need to trust me. You do understand, don't you, that several pictures were taken?"

Skublics nodded. With his withered hands, he stroked his beard, and hope now flickered in his eyes.

"A couple pictures show only you. A couple show you in the company of the Communist Ernő Gerő. And there are other shots of Gerő by himself. So then, it's one of those I gave my man. Either you believe me or you don't."

"Let's just say I do."

"Let's just say. And let's also say I'll have that picture of you and Gerő sent right to Schweinitzer in the taxi that's waiting outside. Where does that leave you?"

Skublics did not reply.

"Don't go hoping they'll hand you over to the Soviets like they did with Gerő. You can hope for anything, but not that. They've got a dowry-full of Hungarian Communists, and they don't need another one. Especially not this sort, not an informer. True, you're not a state security informant, but what does it matter?"

The old man calculated feverishly. Finally, he reached a decision. "I don't know his name," he began. "But I do know who brought her there."

"I'm listening." Gordon sat down in the other armchair and pulled the candle closer to himself as he took out his notebook.

"One of Zsámbéki's girls."

"Who is Zsámbéki?"

"He's got exclusive girls in the center of town—in the fifth district."

"More precisely?"

"On Báthory Street. There's an apartment there, full of girls. Ten or twelve of them. But they don't do anything there. They just sit and wait. Because there's this book, a catalog of sorts. That's how our distinguished representatives choose their girls from the back rooms of the Parliament building. I take the girls' pictures. The gentlemen point to one, word goes out to the apartment on Báthory Street, and then they meet up in a hotel room."

"You're saying the girl was a tart for members of Parliament?"

"For upper-house gentlemen, too. Yes, mainly for them. The lower house is packed to the heap with boors and country bumpkins. Anyway, Zsámbéki is the one who found this girl. He got word that there's a cultivated, especially beautiful creature in Csuli's gang." The old man licked his chapped lips. "True, a Jew, but some want that. And she spoke several languages. So then, Zsámbéki went to Csuli and bought the girl off him. He dressed her up really nice and sent her over to me with Red Margo."

"Who is Red Margo?"

"She's the madam."

"She lives on Báthory Street?"

"No," said Skublics, shaking his head. "A few blocks away, in Falk Miksa Street."

Gordon wrote down the address. "So you don't know the girl's name?"

"You think I pay attention?"

"And what sort of picture did you take of her?"

"The sort you saw."

"Nothing else?"

"I wanted to, but Margo didn't let me."

Gordon's hand again tightened into a fist. He stood and stepped in front of the old man. "Get the hell out of here."

"You're telling me to leave my own apartment?"

"Leave the country, you swine. You wretched swine. I've heard there's demand in Paris for pictures of naked girls. You can meet up with your comrades there, too. And if you listen to me, you'll pull up stakes right this instant, because maybe you were wrong to trust me. Besides, who knows? If you don't get a move on, I might just write an article about you. Which our Paris office could publish, too. This sort of juicy story goes over well there." Skublics just sat there, staring at the carpet and stroking his beard. Gordon slammed the door shut behind him, walked out to Holy Trinity Square, and got back in the Opel Regent.

"Where to?" asked Czövek.

"Lövölde Square," replied Gordon.

"Shall we hurry?"

Gordon looked at his watch. It was a couple of minutes past noon. "Take your time. Lunch can wait."

GORDON COULD SMELL KRISZTINA'S POTATO PASTA WITH onions and paprika from the stairwell. On stepping into the flat, he saw Mór's overcoat on the coat stand. His grandfather often stopped by Krisztina's place, only a couple of blocks from his own, always bringing a jar of jam as an excuse. Today he had complemented his concoction with some crêpes.

"My apple jam turned out so well that I had to cook up some crêpes to tuck it into," he said, beaming. Krisztina grabbed the pot of potato pasta from the stove and set it on the living room table. "Come on, you two!" she called.

The three chatted over lunch, but Gordon didn't want to tell Krisztina in front of his grandfather what he'd managed to find out. As for the old man's newest creation, the crêpes, Gordon's initial caution gradually gave way to enthusiasm. "Opa, these aren't so bad. They aren't bad at all. How much sugar did you put in to keep it from falling apart?" he inquired.

"No small amount," replied the old man with a furtive smile, "no small amount."

After dessert, Gordon lit a cigarette and turned toward Mór.

"What are you up to this afternoon, Opa?"

"Son, I've got loads of pears waiting for me at home, and I bought some more rhubarb, so I've got plenty to do."

Gordon went on: "I only ask because I want to check out a boxing match this afternoon. There's this butcher from the town of Csepel who, I've been told, can outbox Harangi."

"No one boxes better than Harangi!" the old man exclaimed.

"You mean Imre Harangi, who won a gold at the Berlin Olympics?" asked Krisztina.

"That's the one," said Gordon.

"Son, I've seen quite enough blood in my life," said Mór with a wave of the hand, "and I'm not interested in seeing any more."

"As you wish, Opa."

"Zsigmond," said Krisztina, "you haven't forgotten that we're going to the cinema tonight, have you?"

"Of course I haven't," said Gordon, and he asked his grandfather to fill him in on the jams that awaited him this afternoon.

NO SOONER HAD GORDON STEPPED INTO THE IRON-works Sport Club near the West Railway Station than the familiar smell hit his nose: the mix of sweat, stifling heat, and cigarette smoke. He stopped in the doorway of the boxing arena and looked around. He hadn't been back among the cheering crowd for two weeks. He was relieved to finally take a break from his busy schedule.

Two rings stood in the middle of the enormous arena. Training was under way in one, while in the other they were preparing for the match. The league manager and the head referee were busy putting the competitors and their corner guys in their proper places, and—although it was a friendly, amateur bout—all concerned appeared to be taking it seriously indeed. A teeming mass of spectators surrounded the ring, many of them chatting enthusiastically, with coats flung over their shoulders; others, still in their overcoats, watched events unfold while standing a bit farther back from the crowd.

Gordon moved closer. Several people greeted him, and as he shook their hands, they exchanged a few words about the celebrated match back in June between Joe Louis and Max Schmeling, and of course about Harangi's triumph in Berlin. Gordon regretted not having been able to make it to the Olympics, but his paper didn't let him go. True, that hadn't stopped him from listening on edge, like so many of his compatriots, to the radio broadcasts from Berlin by the incomparable Hungarian sports announcer István Pluhár. He'd even been on hand in the Ironworks Sport Club boxing arena for Harangi's triumphant match: the radio had been placed in the center of the ring, and the crowd listened to it with rapt attention, as if the Olympic championship had in fact been unfolding live before them. When the ref held up Harangi's hand, everyone shouted along with the announcer, including Gordon, of course. It was a wonderful evening, and he'd been there in the cheering crowd when Harangi arrived home from Berlin with the rest of Hungary's Olympic team. In those moments, Gordon didn't care about anything else. He, too, flung his hat in the air as he joined the crowd accompanying Harangi out of Budapest's East Railway Station. He couldn't remember ever having been so happy about a boxing victory. Gordon had been a devoted fan of Harangi for years, transfixed by the boxer's self-confidence, nimbleness, unbelievably quick right hand, and air of calm superiority.

Gordon took off his overcoat and pushed his hat back from his forehead, giving the room a thorough once-over. Finally he found the person he was looking for. Jenő Strausz was standing not far from the ring, regaling two young men in shorts with his stories, as they listened with wide-open eyes. Indeed, Strausz had a story worth telling: he'd defeated Ralf Geyling in the international championship held in Budapest in February 1912. Strausz looked hardly a day older, and almost twenty-five years had passed. He might have been nearing fifty now, but every ounce of his almost two-hundred-pound frame was pure muscle. He stood out in the crowd, with his short-cropped hair, slightly stooped back, and meticulously shaved mustache. For decades he'd been raising the next generation of boxers and had played a role in discovering several greats.

At that moment, Strausz, having caught a glimpse of Gordon, broke into a smile and opened his arms wide.

"Zsigmond! Welcome! I wouldn't have thought you could make it."

"No one can be better than Harangi," Gordon replied, "but I just had to see this butcher from Csepel for myself. Does he have a name?"

Strausz knit his brows. "You won't believe it. Bruno Butcher."

"Bruno the Butcher," said Gordon.

"No, Bruno Butcher," said Strausz. "Just like that. Look, it could be worse. He could be Béla Baker."

"And what is his real name?"

"We don't know. He rose through the ranks of the Csepel Workers Bodybuilding Club, and everyone called him Bruno Butcher even then. That can't be his real name, but it doesn't really matter."

"Have you seen him fight?"

"If I'd seen him," replied Strausz, "I probably wouldn't even be here. Either he's just the same as all the other coal heavers and butchers out there—and then there's no sense seeing him more than once—or else I'll give him my every spare moment to make sure that he can think a little, too, and not just punch a big one."

"Who is he up against?"

"Micsicsák," said Strausz with a dismissive wave.

"Then it'll be a quick, bloodless match," replied Gordon, glancing at the far side of the ring. He did a double-take. "Am I right that that man there is Antal Kocsis?"

"You certainly are. Where he came from, and when, I haven't a clue, but here he is."

Winner of the gold medal in the flyweight class in the 1928 Amsterdam Olympics, Kocsis had emigrated to America in early 1930 and hadn't been seen in Hungary since. Rumors concerning his fate had surfaced regularly: he'd drunk away his money; his brain had been pummeled into jelly; he'd signed a contract in South America; and so on. Gordon knew not a single one was true. Even in America, Kocsis had made a name for himself in boxing, but on account of his good heart, he was constantly mired in financial struggles. He never could say no if a fellow Hungarian American asked him for a loan. Of course, he never saw the money again.

Squeezing his way through the crowd, Gordon headed over to Kocsis. The thin little fellow had his hair combed back and set with Brilliantine, and he was wearing a well-tailored suit and his familiar kindly smile.

"Antal!" Gordon greeted him. "Antal, what on earth are you doing here?"

Kocsis turned around, and on seeing Gordon he gave him a hug. "Zsigmond! For crying out loud, it's so good to see you. When was it we last met?"

"April 27, 1930," replied Gordon at once. "You were up against a Polish guy, and in the sixth round you knocked him out. Wajda—that was his name, wasn't it?"

"I couldn't say," said Kocsis, patting Gordon on the side, "you remember better than I."

"I did write about it, after all."

"You wrote about every match of mine you could make it to."

"I tried being there as often as I possibly could. Say, Antal, you just got back home, right?"

"Right," said Kocsis.

"Were you there at the fight between Louis and Schmeling in New York?"

"You bet I was."

"I want to know everything. Every single jab, hook, stick and move, clinch, block, and knockdown. The whole thing."

Kocsis's eyes lit up as he began recounting the legendary bout. He was so caught up in the story that he practically played out each and every round. A crowd soon formed beside Gordon and Kocsis. Even Strausz edged closer, but there were so many people standing there that he had to step up on the edge of the ring.

"And then Schmeling did a stick and move, dancing about and jerking his head out of the way again and again, blocking with his right hand. And then Louis approached. Schmeling held him in, and when Louis wasn't paying attention, Schmeling gave him a right hook, *bang*, and then another, and then into his belly, *bang, bang, bang* . . ." Kocsis continued fervently, and Gordon was so into it himself that he began involuntarily mimicking Kocsis's movements, grunting at the heavier blows and counting right along with Kocsis over the downed Louis. They were so caught up in it all that they hadn't even noticed that Bruno Butcher was already into the second round with Micsicsák.

Surprisingly, Bruno Butcher looked only like a middleweight: he hardly had a belly, and his arms were long and muscular. Micsicsák didn't know how to handle him. In the fifth round, all at once the butcher threw a merciless straight right into the pit of his willowy opponent's stomach. Micsicsák dropped to the ground and didn't move. The head referee leaned over him and started counting, and when Micsicsák still didn't move, he called in the doctor. He raised the butcher's right hand into the air.

Gordon waited a bit, then turned to Kocsis. "Antal, so what's it all about, a jab in the pit of the stomach?"

"What do you mean?" asked the boxer.

"Did Micsicsák collapse because he wasn't prepared for the jab, or . . ."

"Zsigmond, you can't really prepare for this sort of thing—especially not from a beast like this butcher."

"Let me ask one more thing. What happens when someone levels a jab that strong into the pit of the stomach of, say, a woman?"

Kocsis sighed. "What are you getting at?"

"Just a question, nothing else."

"Well, that could have a bad ending."

"How bad?"

"In the worst-case scenario, the girl might even get killed. Why do you ask? Are you preparing for something?"

"Me? Nothing. I'm just working on a case in which something similar happened."

"It all comes down to chance. I've been hit like that in my gut so hard the air just stopped dead in its tracks inside me and I couldn't even stand up. The air just got stuck, simple as that. It's practically impossible to prepare for a jab like the one the butcher just threw. His hand just shot in, and Micsicsák couldn't block. That was that."

Gordon nodded. Soon the next match began, and Gordon

stood there between Strausz and Kocsis until six in the evening: they lambasted the boxers and analyzed the punches, and during intermissions they conjured up famous old bouts. But around six, Gordon sighed. "I've got to be off."

"Don't tell me you're going to work?" asked Strausz.

"Yes. In a certain sense, yes." Gordon shook hands with Kocsis and with Strausz, said his good-byes to the others on his way out, and then he hurried out onto Podmaniczky Street and headed toward Berlin Square.

FALK MIKSA STREET—WHICH RAN FROM THE GRAND Boulevard near the Margaret Bridge to the Parliament building—was almost completely deserted. Expensive chandeliers, curtains, and an occasional fleeting shadow shone clearly from behind the tall windows of the narrow thoroughfare's elegant apartments. Gordon found the address easily. Standing in front of the building , he even found himself admiring what a grand neighborhood Red Margo occupied. It was understandable, of course: since Margo supervised and otherwise managed the girls in the apartment on Báthory Street, she had to live nearby. At the same time, Gordon was certain that the flat was not her own, but that the rent was paid for by the secretive Mr. Zsámbéki who had bought the black-haired girl from Csuli.

He rang the doorbell. The super appeared a couple of moments later. Without a word, Gordon pressed a pengő into his hand, whereupon the man sized him up. He didn't even ask who he'd come to see. "Fourth floor on the left," he told Gordon, then shuffled back into his little flat beside the stairs.

The inner courtyard was clean and ordered, with a few leaf-less bushes, a robust linden tree, and meticulously manicured flower beds.

Gordon got into the elevator and went up to the fourth floor. On getting out he turned left and stopped in front of the first door. No light filtered through the apartment window overlooking the courtyard. He knocked. A few moments later, the door opened.

The woman was a couple of inches shorter than he was, about five-eight. She had broad shoulders, a full bosom, round hips, and long, sinewy legs. She must have been about twenty-five, but the signs of age were already evident on her face. Tiny wrinkles occupied the corners of her fleshy, sensual mouth. Even finer wrinkles were starting to weave a web around her big, blue, bloodshot eyes with their long eyelashes. Her thick strands of brown hair could have used a bit of combing, and not even her part was straight. The lipstick was wider on one side of her upper lip than on the other side. She wore a wine-red silk nightgown that was wide open on one side and looked awful on her. She had a little run in her stocking just above her left foot. They shook hands, and Gordon felt that hers was soft, warm, and strong. This, then, was Red Margo, who, according to Gordon's source, had corraled the cream of the nation's crop of politicians into her bedroom and went to all lengths to satisfy their desires.

"What do you want, pretty boy?" she asked, leaning up against the wall.

"I'm looking for you on account of the Jewish girl."

"That's not how things work," said Margo, looking Gordon in the eye.

"Well, then."

"If you've managed to find me, you should also know how things work. Besides, I don't know what you're talking about or who you're looking for. There's not a single Jewish gal around here." She paused and asked, invitingly, "Or do you suppose that would be me?"

Gordon shook his head slightly. "Izsó Skublics said I should look for you."

"Are you Skublics's friend?"

"Do you think I am?"

"You can never know with him."

"Will you let me in?"

"Please," said Margo, opening the door wide. Gordon shut it behind him and followed the woman into the living room, which at one time must have been elegantly furnished but, by now, was rife with furniture by and large worn and faded. Disarray reigned supreme.

"So you're here asking about Judit Jeges," she said while removing a pair of lizard-leather shoes and a cup and saucer from an armchair so Gordon could sit down. Her voice was soft and lazy.

"Yes. But I'm mainly interested in knowing who killed her and why."

Red Margo knit her brows.

"You're saying someone killed her?"

"It looks that way."

"And you, I bet you think . . ."

Gordon interrupted: "I'm the detective here, and I don't like it when someone else takes over my role and starts asking questions."

Margo sized him up from head to toe. "You? A detective?"

"Let's just say I'm investigating," replied Gordon, pulling a silk stocking out from under him. He didn't know exactly why he'd said he was a detective. Maybe it would simplify matters, he'd thought, but he already saw he'd made a mistake. Margo sank into the other armchair and watched Gordon in silence.

"I'm investigating," Gordon repeated. "Not that I'm a detective. I'm a crime reporter for the *Evening*."

"So you're working on an article?" asked Margo.

"You might say so."

Red Margo rose and crossed over to a little table in front of the window, full of glasses and bottles. She poured herself a glass of gin, threw in a wilted slice of lemon, and downed the drink in one gulp. Then she filled another cup and set it down in front of Gordon on the coffee table. Gordon looked at the glass, and Margo, still standing, looked down at Gordon, who was trying to select the most appropriate approach. Margo obviously knew the girl, whose name—or, obviously, alias—was Judit Jeges. Gordon took out a cigarette and lit it. Margo stood by the window and stared listlessly down at the street, allowing Gordon to look her over. Evidently she'd gotten on her nightgown in haste, which was why it had opened on the side, exposing her long, sinewy thigh. Although the wine-red didn't look good on her at all, the nightgown accentuated the fullness of her breasts and her slender waist. Gordon saw her face from the side: her nose had a lovely arch, and her full lips curled downward. There was something feline about her glance—a glance that simultaneously suggested boredom and provocation. Provocation. Gordon sighed. Margo now turned toward him and raised her eyes to his. Gordon stared right back. Gordon knew full well that he had to choose his next step carefully. Something was not right with this woman. The last time he'd seen a woman drinking gin was in America, and not even there had it been a common sight. Not that it mattered, really. What did matter was that Margo, so it seemed, knew everything about Judit. Gordon finally cast aside his every possible tactic, leaned forward in the armchair, and prepared to tell Red Margo everything he'd found out about the girl. Margo kept staring at the street throughout, turning toward Gordon not even once.

"On Tuesday night, a dead Jewish girl was found on Nagy Diófa Street. Her name, as you said it, was Judit Jeges. The police, at least for the time being, are not looking into her death. According to the coroner, someone punched her so hard in the pit of her stomach that it killed her. Izsó Skublics claims someone bought the girl off Csuli, and that he, Skublics, took a couple of pictures of her. You brought her over there." After a momentary pause, Gordon concluded by asking, "What was her real name?"

At this, Margo turned, scowled, and put her glass on the table—or so she thought. She was off by almost a foot.

"I don't think I can help you," said the woman in a calm voice while looking at the spilled drink on the carpet.

"I'm not even sure," said Gordon, switching tactics, "that I need your information, after all. I think I can make do without it."

"If you can make do, that's fine. Just don't forget that I'm the only one who actually could help you."

"Is it money you want?" asked Gordon.

"That's right," replied Red Margo. "But not from you." With that, she spit the remains of the lemon rind to the floor, ran her fingers through her hair, then wiped her mouth with the back of her hand before breaking into a smile.

"All right, then, Mr. Journalist. I'm willing to work with you. Trust me, it won't cost you a thing. No, I'll get what's due me, anyway, before we reach the end of this game. Do you believe me?" she asked provocatively, looking at Gordon as if he were a block away.

This was not the moment to argue about money. "And I do hope you get what's due you," Gordon quietly replied.

"Believe you me, I will. Now listen here. You are not drunk, but I am. And I'm so drunk that I'll tell you everything you want to know. That's the sort of girl I am. When I meet someone I like, I tell him everything. You only have to ask. So go for it, ask!"

Though Gordon didn't understand what caused Margo to reconsider, he began asking questions. And the woman answered. Meanwhile, she sat down in the armchair opposite Gordon and crossed her legs, which made her nightgown open even more, allowing Gordon a view of her round belly, the beginning of the curve of her breasts. "What's certain," said Margo, "is that she went to a good school. She spoke

German perfectly, she was polite, and she knew how to wear fine clothes. We didn't talk a lot. Judit was withdrawn, she smiled rarely, and she was cold when handling men, which made them completely crazy about her." Red Margo smiled. "I should know. She was the most popular girl. Zsámbéki asked a lot of money for her. Some customers paid him as much as fifty or even a hundred pengős. Judit lived in her own world. When we sat down for a drink, she sometimes joined us. But she didn't drink and didn't say a word. She just listened."

"That's it?" Gordon looked at her. "Anything else?"

Margo shook her head. She stood and walked over to the little table once again, pouring herself another gin in a clean glass. Leaving out the lemon this time, she gulped the gin down. "There's one more thing."

"What would that be?"

"Whenever we had coffee, she always asked where we bought the beans. One time Manci didn't buy the coffee at Meinl, like usual, but at Arabia instead. 'I don't want any of that,' said Judit. 'It's the same coffee,' we told her. She looked at me and declared, 'I don't drink that stuff.' She crumpled up the paper she'd been reading and stormed out of the kitchen."

"That's it?" asked Gordon.

"That's it," replied Red Margo.

"There's nothing else you know?"

"I told you everything I know. Too much at that."

Gordon stood. "No. Just enough."

"Are you trying to say you already know who killed the girl?"

"Not yet. I still need to clear up one or two things to figure it out."

"Who is it? Who?" Red Margo snapped, completely sober. She seized his coat by the lapels. "Tell me who killed her!"

"I don't know yet."

"Be a good boy!"

"Not yet."

The woman let go of his coat, crossed her arms behind her back, and laughed in his face.

"Fine then. Keep it to yourself. Just go ahead and try figuring out what's true of what I said."

"No matter what's true," said Gordon, looking at Red Margo, "thanks all the same. For the gin, too." He turned and went toward the door. The woman stood by the window and didn't even look his way. Gordon shut the door behind him and was already at the stairwell when Red Margo called after him. "Wait a second, Mr. Journalist."

Gordon stopped and turned around. "For what?"

"There's one more thing."

"What?"

"Do you want to know?"

"What?"

Through half-shut eyes, Red Margo looked at Gordon. "You're the one here playing detective, isn't that right?"

"Go ahead," said Gordon, returning to the door, "tell me."

"Wait here," replied the woman, and she slammed the door shut.

Gordon waited. Minutes passed. He lit a cigarette. Finally,

Margo appeared with a letter in her hand. "I just remembered this letter."

"A letter."

"That's right."

"And you just thought of it."

"Just now. If you don't believe me or if you aren't interested . . ."

"What is it you want?" asked Gordon, exhaling smoke.

"Nothing," said Margo, leaning up against the doorjamb. "Nothing from you."

Gordon crossed his arms over his chest and looked at the woman.

"This is a love letter," said Margo.

Gordon held out his hand. The woman dropped the letter in. "It slipped out of her purse one time."

"And you picked it up."

"I wanted to give it back to her, but I didn't have the chance."

Gordon didn't say a thing. He slipped the letter into the pocket of his blazer and started toward the stairs. The woman once again called after him. "You don't know what you've got yourself mixed up in."

Gordon turned around.

"You don't know," Margo repeated, "what you've got yourself mixed up in. These folks don't kid around. Keep an eye out behind you." With that, she slammed the door shut and disappeared.

Gordon shrugged. What could they do to him? And who

did he have to watch out for? Would they shoot him? This was Budapest, not Chicago.

LEAVING THE BUILDING, GORDON TURNED LEFT, TOWARD Crown Prince Rudolf Square. The moment he arrived on the Grand Boulevard, he was struck by an icy wind off the Danube. He shuddered. Looking toward the Margaret Bridge, he saw dark clouds gathering in the sky. Gordon pulled his overcoat tight around him and walked over to the tram stop. The Comedy Theater was lit up, off in the distance, with expensive cars parked out front. The wind died down for a moment, and he heard music filtering out of a nearby coffeehouse.

The tram rolled to a stop with bells clanging. Gordon hopped aboard and got off on Berlin Square. As always, there was quite a crowd at the West Railway Station. The massive edifice seemed to pour out those freshly arrived and suck in those preparing for their journeys. Gordon stopped in the middle of the square beside a large concrete kiosk topped off by a clock prominently bearing the name of its sponsor, the Italian firm Modiano. From there, he looked back at the tram stop. He felt as if he was being followed. But no one looked suspicious. Not that he knew, of course, who might have counted as suspicious at this hour. Young men were waiting in front of the Westend Hotel, brooding away as they wondered if they could afford sixty pengős a month for a room or if they should move a bit farther from downtown, where they might get by on a bit less. A big poster in front of the Jolly Bar carried an ad for "Berta Türke's *Schrammelmusik* Band Playing Tonight."

Gordon shook his head. Was there a night when they didn't play? Berlin Square had a charm of its own, what with its ever-present mass of humanity, its trams and their constant cling-ing and clanging, its shouting cabbies, whistling policemen, and sundry spectacle of civil servants making their way from month-to-month rooms to the nearest bar, poor young boys from the provinces, and men who'd just left their wives for good. Inside the kiosk, right below the Modiano clock, was a tobacconist's shop. Gordon often bought cigarettes there, and the wounded veteran behind the counter gave him a cheery welcome even now.

"Mr. Editor! The usual?"

"Let's have it," said Gordon, slipping the pack of Turk-ish cigarettes into his pocket at once. "How goes business, Krámer?"

"Don't remind me," said the scruffy fellow with a resigned wave of the hand. "I'm sure Finance Minister Fabinyi is doing what he thinks best, you know, but it's us who get the raw end of the deal again."

"You mean that new rule making it illegal to loan out newspapers?"

"That wasn't the problem, sir. A gentleman would come in, ask for some tobacco, and skim the paper. No, I had no problem with that. Why, I even let regulars look at a paper or magazine for just a couple of fillérs." He shook his head before continuing in a newly dignified tone: "But if I got it back all torn up, he had to pay! I'm not saying it added up to much every month, just a couple pengős—okay, let's say ten. Now we can't do it. Now folks can't just page through the papers, you know, because it's been banned from the top."

Gordon gave a commiserating nod, then left the shop. He walked along Teréz Boulevard to Podmaniczky Street, turned, and followed that to Jókai Street. Mouthwatering aromas streamed out of a hash house on the corner of Horn Street, and Gordon nearly went inside, but he'd had enough for one day. He was exhausted, and he wanted to get home as soon as possible. Lovag Street was quiet at first, but as he approached Nagymező Street, the cacophony of sounds of Budapest's Broadway grew ever more intense. He looked at his watch. It was just past seven. He had just enough time to wash up and change. *A Night at the Opera* started at eight at the West Motion-Picture Theater, which was at the start of the Erzsébet Boulevard stretch of the Grand Boulevard. Gordon was not ashamed that he liked the Marx Brothers; nor was it by chance that he made an effort to watch the Fox International newsreel at least once a week. True, the constant war reporting from Spain and Abyssinia was a bit boring already, but sometimes there was a story from America. The other day, for instance, President Roosevelt—

"Sir, do you have the time?" asked a man in a hat who suddenly approached him.

Gordon looked up and, though he sensed there was trouble, could not do a thing about it. He was just about to take a step forward when someone seized his arms from behind him and held them tight. He tried looking up, but his hat slipped over his eyes, and it was in vain that he sought to tear his hands free. He was held in an iron grip. His attacker pulled him into a doorway. The other man now stepped in front of him and tore off Gordon's hat. Gordon jerked up his head, but a streetlamp shining behind his assailant kept the man's features obscured. He thought of shouting for help, but he knew it would be pointless. They needed only a couple of seconds to take care of him. One blow, one gunshot, that would be it. The man behind him held tight. Gordon tried scrutinizing the eyes of the man before him, but he still couldn't get a good look. Lightning-fast, the man socked Gordon in the gut. He doubled over and began heaving. The man behind him still had him in a certain grip. Gordon knew he shouldn't, but he prepared for the next round by tightening his stomach muscles. The second blow filled him with excruciating pain. Tears came to his eyes. His legs gave way beneath him. He tried catching his breath but couldn't. It was as if a lead cube locked away in his stomach was now seeping metal toward his lungs. He did everything to keep from letting panic get the best of him. The man raised his arm to ready for another blow, and Gordon tried slackening his body. Although it didn't hurt as much this time, his stomach contracted and he began heaving once again. A foolish thought popped into his mind: Lucky he hadn't had supper in the hash house, or he'd have been throwing up as well. Gordon could hear the man's fingers cracking as he made a fist. He didn't even see the fourth blow coming—which for once didn't land in his gut but on his chin. Gordon felt his lips tear and heard his teeth grind as they slid over each other. The man behind him now let him go. Gordon collapsed like a marionette whose strings had been cut. His head knocked hard against the pavement. He felt blood start running from his forehead. And yet he hadn't bitten his tongue. Perhaps something had stayed with him from all the boxing matches he'd seen: "Put your tongue to the roof of your mouth, don't think a thing, and just leave it there." On the ground, he wanted to spit but couldn't. Saliva mixed with blood dripped from the corners of his mouth. The man in the hat now leaned over him.

"You should call it quits here and now," he hissed. Gordon looked in his face. He saw little, but what he saw was quite enough. He caught a glimpse of his mouth, if it could be called a mouth at all. The lower lip curled downward, he had hardly any bottom teeth, and Gordon could make out only his canines up top. Above the mouth was a nose so terribly crooked that Gordon couldn't even imagine how its owner could take in air. "You should call it quits here and now," he resumed. "If you don't, your pretty little girlfriend won't look so pretty with a sliced-up face." Gordon groaned. He shouldn't have. Again he started heaving, and blood gushed from his mouth. The man with the crooked nose stood upright, dusted off his trousers, and stepped back. He kicked Gordon in the belly so hard that Gordon's world turned black. He didn't even feel the man level the one solid goodbye punch to his kidneys. But when he stepped onto the palm of Gordon's right hand, as if stomping out a cigarette butt, Gordon came to. A car turned onto the street, and the two men vanished in an instant. It was all Gordon could do not to focus on the pain, but he was afraid of losing consciousness again if he didn't. He lay there like the drunk vagabonds in front of the bars on Ülloi Street. The nausea was unrelenting. Finally, he tried sitting up by leaning on his right hand, but a sharp pain shot through him. He rolled onto his back and out onto the sidewalk, then slowly managed to sit up, this time using his left hand for support. He threw his back against the wall and felt his right hand. The slightest touch was enough to make the hand contract. The pain was great, but he tested his fingers one by one. With the exception of his index finger, which alone rested at an unnatural angle, every finger moved. Now came his wrist. He managed to move it left and right, though he heard occasional cracking. There was pain, of course. Slowly his breathing took on a more normal rhythm. He shut his eyes and took ever deeper breaths. At first, he'd wanted to vomit every time he inhaled, but some five minutes later the queasiness passed. He wasn't in a hurry; he knew he could not count on help.

A couple was approaching on the sidewalk. The woman wore a cocktail dress and a mink coat, and the man had on a tuxedo, hat, and a camel-fur jacket. On noticing Gordon's filthy, bloody figure, they hastily crossed the street. Gordon waited another couple of minutes. When he felt he had enough strength, he tried staggering to his feet. It didn't work. His belly throbbed, as did his hand. Again throwing his back against the wall, he began pushing himself to his feet. His legs were nearly straight when all at once he felt the building's foundation come to an end, and the ornamental brickwork begin. He took a deep breath, placed his hands just above his knees, and pressed himself until he stood erect. Dizziness set in. He leaned against the wall to keep from falling. The blood ran from his forehead into his eyes. He wiped it with his coat sleeve.

He checked to see how far he was from his building door. His flat was at the head of Lovag Street, just two buildings down, close to Nagymező Street. He had four doors to go. Pulling himself together, he pushed himself away from the wall and tried staying on his feet. This is when Gordon really felt the blow leveled against his kidneys. Had he been unable to grab hold of a brick jutting out from the building wall, he might well have fallen again. And he wasn't sure he'd be able to stand up one more time. Gordon leaned against the wall with his left hand. He would be strong enough.

Slowly, step by step, he moved forward. With his left hand he grasped another brick, then moved his left foot, then his right. *Left hand, left foot, right foot. Left hand, left foot, right foot.*

On reaching the door, Gordon had to gather all his strength to be able to knock. Then he turned around, fell against the door, and slid slowly to the ground. The door opened and the super looked out. On glimpsing the slumped figure, he moved to close the door, but Gordon called to him: "It's me, Iváncsik."

The super leaned down and looked into Gordon's face. He exclaimed in astonishment: "Don't you move, Mr. Editor!" Gordon had no intention of moving. "I'll help you right away." With that, he carefully reached under Gordon's arm, did his best to help Gordon to his feet, and led him to his little flat underneath the stairwell. The super's wife stood in the kitchen as if looking at a ghost. "Don't just stare like that. Irénke!" Iváncsik yelled at her. "Run, go get the doctor!"

"There's no need," Gordon moaned.

"Who are you kidding, Mr. Editor? The last time I saw this sort of thing was on the Italian front. We need a doctor right now."

"Go up to my flat," said Gordon softly. "Krisztina is waiting for me there."

"Right away," replied the super. "Irénke, don't just stand there twiddling your thumbs, you heard the man. Get a move on."

His wife hurried off as Iváncsik now slipped Gordon from his shoulder onto a stool. Not even a minute had passed before Krisztina appeared in the kitchen. But for her cheekbones, which were flushed, her face was a deathly white. She knelt down beside Gordon.

"Zsigmond, Zsigmond. What have they done to you?" she asked, reaching for his right hand.

"They ran away in the end," Gordon moaned, pulling away his hand.

"You stay here," said Krisztina, running her fingers through Gordon's bloody hair, "I'll call Mór."

Gordon replied, "Don't you worry, for once I'll stay right where I am."

When Krisztina returned, she was carrying a wet towel that she now carefully wrapped around Gordon's hand. She also wiped the blood from his face. When Mór arrived hardly ten minutes later, Gordon looked much better, given the circumstances. The old man took just one glance at him before pronouncing, "Call an ambulance."

"Not that, Opa. Not that. You're here, and that's just fine for me."

"Son, you won't get far with me. I was just a wretched district doctor, not a surgeon."

"Please try all the same, Opa," said Gordon. The old man sighed. "I'll examine you in your flat. If you can get up there, that is. If you can't, you're off to the hospital."

Gordon slowly staggered to his feet. Mór and Iváncsik each reached for an arm, then helped him up to the second floor. Krisztina had already opened the door and in the bathroom had put out a few sheets along with the first-aid kit they'd gotten from Mór. Gordon sank into a chair, and Krisztina gradually undressed him. Although she had to cut the trousers off him, she managed to pull the rest off. Using the sheets, she then washed Gordon's upper body and thoroughly cleaned the wound on his forehead and his lips.

"Can you go into the room, son?" asked the old man, eyes sparkling with worry from behind his round glasses.

"Yes, Opa," replied Gordon. With Krisztina's help, he went into the bedroom and collapsed on the bed.

"Krisztina, can you give us a minute?" said Mór. He then opened his medical bag and proceeded to examine Gordon. Once finished, he said, "If you don't piss blood tomorrow, you can stay at home. But if you do, it's off to the hospital with you." Krisztina, who of course had not left the room but was leaning up against the doorjamb, sighed with relief. "And your hand didn't break, either," continued Mór, "just one of your fingers snapped out of joint, that's all. I'll set it back in place. It will hurt, but I'll do it fast." Gordon nodded, and the old man grabbed his wrist tight with his left hand and his index finger with his right. First he yanked the finger forward, then pressed it back in place. Tears formed in Gordon's eyes.

"You didn't say it would be like this, Opa."

"And I haven't even tended to your head wound," said Mór. "You're just lucky it's not long, otherwise it would have to be sewn up, and I don't like doing that. The blow tore a vein, which explains the blood. Krisztina, hand me the iodine." He wrapped a matchstick in cotton, dipped that in the little bottle, then thoroughly cleaned out the wounds on Gordon's forehead and lips.

"Drink this, Zsigmond," said Krisztina, handing him a cup.

The old man nodded by way of approval. "Go ahead and drink it, son."

Gordon gulped down the plum brandy. His eyes slowly closed and his head slumped to the side.

Six

When Gordon awoke in the wee hours of the next morning, he felt firsthand the typical boxer's refrain: "In the ring it only hurts a little. Afterward it hurts more. But that's nothing. The real pain comes the next day."

Everything hurt. His head and his kidneys throbbed with pain, as did the fingers and palm of his right hand. But he could stand. He staggered out to the living room. Krisztina was sitting in front of the window, drawing by the light of the reading lamp. Leaning against the door, Gordon watched her. He had watched her draw on several occasions, sometimes for as long as a half hour. He'd seen many illustrators—mainly police artists and court reporters—but their work had never absorbed him so. Sometimes he, too, tried his hand at drawing, but he was incapable of decently depicting even a street map. Krisztina's hand moved over the paper with complete, consummate confidence. Hardly ever did she stop to think, and rarely did she make a mistake. She'd already illustrated several storybooks, and as only Gordon knew, when it came to drawing children, Krisztina's models were her relatives. She hadn't seen them for years, but she had preserved their memory since childhood. Since she was of Saxon descent, it was clear from the outset that she would study in Germany. Her father had relatives in Weimar, and so Krisztina attended the Bauhaus school there. She did not hold firm to this approach to art but gladly went about planning posters and building façades, and, indeed, the pavilion of the light-bulb manufacturer Tungsram at the Budapest International Fair was built from her designs. Never did she have a normal job, no matter what that might have meant. She always worked alone, on request, and never went looking for work—work always found her. Gordon often asked her: "And when will there be a Krisztina Eckhardt exhibit?" Krisztina hated being called an artist; the only thing she hated more was being called a suffragette. Men were both suspicious of her and respected her; behind her back they gossiped about her. Not that she cared. While she didn't deny that she agreed with the movement for women's equal rights, she wasn't too vocal about it, either. "People should stick to asking about what I draw and design," she often told Gordon. The upshot was that she didn't have girlfriends, either, in the traditional sense. She didn't understand women who suffered in bad marriages, women who kept lovers, and what she deemed the meaningless self-sacrifice supposedly endured for the sanctity of marriage and family. Rarely did she go out with friends, and when she did, it was with similar women. And they played cards. Bridge, which Gordon just

didn't get. For him, the only mystery greater than Krisztina
herself was bridge.

And so Gordon stood there in the doorway, his limbs
hurting, burning, throbbing. Mór was sleeping on the divan.
Krisztina rose to put a blanket over him. That's when she
turned and saw Gordon. She cast him an angry look and was
about to say something when Gordon brought a finger to his
lips. He motioned for her to join him in the bedroom.

"You'll find a letter in the inside pocket of my blazer," he
said when Krisztina entered the room. He was sitting on the
edge of the bed and trying hard not to move. "Bring it over to
me."

Krisztina found the envelope, looked it over, and extended
it to Gordon. "Read it out loud, Krisztina," he said. "I don't
think I could even pick it up." Krisztina opened the envelope
and pulled out a sheet of paper folded in two. She cleared her
throat and began to read:

My dear, sweet Fanny, I miss you like the devil. I miss
you terribly. What will I do with myself without you? The
days drag along, and not even the Torah helps. I look to
it for answers, but find none. I seek answers everywhere.
What is the answer if I love you with all my heart, and
our being together is more important to me than everything
else? What is the answer to their wanting to tear us apart?
It's not by chance that my father became a rabbi. Maybe
he doesn't really know the answer to everything, but he
acts as if he does, and that's enough for people to believe

*him. They respect him, they love him, they fear him. I
share with them only the last of these sentiments. My love
is now for you alone. Remember what I told you in that
restaurant? Well, don't forget it. And don't forget me,
either. I'll work things out somehow—how, I don't yet
know, but I'm constantly racking my brains. To finally be
able to be with you, to be able to freely kiss your lips, to
freely hold your hand, to freely look upon your lovely eyes.
I want to make up for everything—for everything—and it
is my firm intention that you should be the happiest woman
in the world, even if no one else wants this to be so. Your
devoted Shlomo.*

Krisztina refolded the letter and returned it to the envelope. "Don't you want to tell me what this is all about? What you got yourself beaten up for? Do you feel better, by the way?"

Gordon tried to smile, but his torn mouth made it look more like a grimace. Then, slowly, faltering, he told Krisztina the story of his visit to Red Margo.

"And this is so important to you that you're willing to get your brain knocked out because of it?"

"Now that they've already half knocked my brains out, yes."

"Zsigmond, don't you go playing the hero," said Krisztina, standing up.

"Calm down. I'm not playing the hero. But what else can I do? How could I look in the mirror if I didn't try catching the person who did this? How would you look at me if I didn't try?" Gordon didn't see the point in sharing the threat made by the man with the crooked nose. But he had to act, and fast.

Krisztina gripped the back of the chair so tightly that her knuckles turned white. Clearly she wanted to say something, but instead she turned around and left the room. She nearly knocked down Mór, who, disheveled and sleepy, stood in the doorway holding a tray, on it a glass of milk, a slice of brioche, and a jar of jam. "It's a waste filling him with your jam, Mór," said Krisztina. "He's so hardheaded he should be eating cement."

"My grandson, oh, my boy," said the old man, shaking his head, "you just eat this up now, and then we'll talk." He put the tray down by the bed and then sat beside the window. He watched in silence as Gordon slowly ate it all. "Last year's peach jam," he said finally, "that turned out pretty well." Gordon nodded approvingly, then tried standing up.

"Where to, son?" asked Mór.

"I've got business to tend to, Opa."

"For the love of God, you've got no other business than to be lying down and moaning."

"I can moan even without lying down," said Gordon.

"It will work better if you're lying down," said Mór, shaking his head.

"I can't do that now, Opa. I've got to go."

"Go? Where in the name of sweet holy hell do you have to go? You can't even get up, much less go. But even if you managed, you'd terrify people out on the street, that's how hideous you look."

"I've got to go to Dohány Street," said Gordon. "There's a rabbi there whose son is called Shlomo."

"If you ask me, there's not just one such rabbi out there."

"Then I'll find this particular one and have a talk with him."

"I'll go talk with them all," proclaimed Mór.

"You?"

"Yes, me. Zsigmond, you really can't go anywhere. You've got to rest. What do you want to find out about that rabbi?"

"About the rabbi? Nothing. I want to find out about his son, and I want to know everything about his girlfriend."

"I shouldn't ask why, right?" asked Mór, fixing his eyes on Gordon. He patted down his hair, and with his other hand he buttoned his vest askew over his wrinkled shirt and necktie gone awry.

"Don't ask, Opa."

"I'll go on one condition," said Mór.

"Condition?"

"That's right. Now you be a good boy and go to the bathroom and piss into this glass." The old man extended a water glass to Gordon. "If your urine isn't bloody, I'll go. If it is, you'll go—to the hospital. And for once I won't open a debate."

Gordon sighed, and staggering to his feet, he grabbed the glass and his cigarette case. Gritting his teeth, he went out to the bathroom. He closed the door behind him and, standing before the mirror, lit a cigarette. Exhaling smoke, he examined his face. He looked like some wretched boxer who'd run face-first into the glove of one serious opponent. A bandage

covered the wound on his forehead, above his left eye. Mór
had tied it tightly, but the blood had seeped through the gauze.
Gordon's lower lip was cracked and swollen. As he ran his
tongue over it, he winced. His eyes were bloodshot, to be sure,
but at least he hadn't gotten a black eye. All in all, he didn't
look too bad. Gordon had to forgo shaving and the use of his
right hand, which, bandaged as it was, still throbbed mightily.
The old man had put some magic ointment on his nightstand
for Gordon to apply to the wound. A clean suit and shirt, and
he'd look presentable enough.

Gordon stood in front of the toilet and raised the celluloid
seat. He took the glass in one hand and, wincing all the while,
began to urinate. When he finished, he raised the glass. Not
even a trace of blood. He set down the glass beside the sink,
carefully washed his face with cold water, combed back his
hair, and left the bathroom.

"Here you are, Opa," said Gordon, putting down the glass
in front of the old man. Mór held it up to the light and gave a
sigh of relief.

"Son," he declared, "I've never been so glad to see piss."

"All right, then," said Gordon, sitting down on the edge
of the bed. "But now you've got to promise me a couple of
things."

"Go ahead."

"Keep an eye out on the street. Is anyone following you?
Don't just pay attention to the pedestrians but also to the cars.
When you leave the building, look around carefully to see if
you spot a parked car with someone behind the wheel. Stick
close to the buildings as you walk, but move to the edge of the

sidewalk every time you pass a doorway. Make some sudden stops along the way and look behind you, but not conspicuously. If you see anyone who looks suspicious, don't confront them; sit down in a café instead, order a drink, then come home."

"Understood," said the old man.

"You might not turn up anything, by the way. It's Sunday, after all—Dohány Street and the streets around it are like a ghost town today."

"Don't you worry, son. I'll work it all out."

"Just be very careful."

"I will. And you will stay home and stay in bed."

"That's what I'll do, Opa," said Gordon.

"Krisztina!" Mór called out. Once she appeared in the doorway, he added, "Don't you let him get up. He's got to stay in bed, or else who's to say what will become of him." He stood up and mindfully rebuttoned his vest. Krisztina adjusted his tie, whereupon he pressed his hat onto his head and went out the door.

Hardly had his grandfather left the flat when Gordon rose up out of bed. With unsteady steps he went to the telephone and, using his left hand, picked up the receiver. But then it hit him that dialing with his bandaged, throbbing right hand would be impossible. He set down the receiver and tried dialing with his left hand, but it didn't work. Krisztina watched from the doorway as Gordon hobbled over to the window, picked up a pencil, and used it to dial. But the pencil kept slipping out of his hand. After the fifth attempt, he angrily threw the pencil to the floor and turned to Krisztina. "Would you help me already, for the love of God? Or are you enjoying this?"

"Who do you want to call?" asked Krisztina in an icy voice.

"The Sztambul Coffeehouse."

"And why?"

"Because I have to talk to someone."

"Well, now. You're kidding."

"Are you going to help me or not?"

Krisztina stepped over to the telephone and Gordon dictated the number by heart. When it rang, Krisztina handed him the receiver.

"Is Jenő Strausz there?" asked Gordon. Having heard the reply, he put the receiver back on the phone, returned to the bedroom, and with difficulty began getting dressed. Arms crossed, Krisztina just stood there and watched.

"Where are you off to?"

"I've got business."

"Business. After getting beaten to a pulp, you just have some business to tend to. May I ask what?"

"You may ask. I've got to talk to Jenő Strausz."

"And it can't wait until tomorrow? Or until you're once again in shape to go out in public?"

"It can't wait," he said, staring right back at Krisztina.

"Then maybe I can't wait, either, Zsigmond," said Krisztina, throwing down the gauntlet. "I'll accept Penguin's offer. And go to London."

"First help me get dressed, will you?" Gordon had managed to slip on his trousers, but getting his shirt on by himself was impossible. After a moment's hesitation, Krisztina helped him put it on. She tied his necktie, buttoned his blazer, and even put his coat on him. Gordon went out to the vestibule, where, with his left hand, he put on his hat. But the motion made him stagger, and he fell against the wall. His face winced in pain. Krisztina couldn't take any more of this. She grabbed her own coat off the coat hanger and picked up her purse.

"And where are you off to?" asked Gordon.

"If you think I'm going to keep helping with this rubbish of yours, helping you destroy yourself, you're sadly mistaken." With that, she slammed the door behind her and stormed off.

IT WAS A CLAMMY, ROTTEN MORNING. THE SIDEWALK was slippery from the drizzling fog, forcing Gordon to give up his plan to walk to the Sztambul. It took him a good fifteen minutes to reach Berlin Square. There he boarded a tram, sat down, and stared out at the city in its autumn guise. Pretty young girls holding tennis rackets were strolling across the Margaret Bridge. But Gordon didn't even try to crane his neck for a better look. Pulling himself to his feet, he signaled to the driver that he wanted to get off.

The Sztambul was a few yards from the stop. Despite the early hour, there was quite a crowd inside. One of the waiters opened the door for him, and he stepped into the smoky room, which smelled of coffee and fresh-baked rolls. The cashier was loudly pounding away at the register, waiters were zigzagging with full trays, and well-off young people from Buda, men and women alike, sat at the tables. Gordon glanced around. In the back he saw Strausz, in the company of Antal "Toni"

Kocsis. He started toward them, but on the way a sharp pain shot through his side so intensely that, using his left hand, he had to lean against a table. The young dandy seated at the table cast a wide-eyed stare at the genteel young lady seated across from him, then gave an indignant snort followed by the words, "Can't see because your eyes are in the way, my man? Drunk at this hour?" Gordon would gladly have knocked the young fellow's cup of coffee right in his lap, but he had more important things to do. Strausz, too, looked up on hearing the dandy's voice, and on seeing Gordon, he ran over to help. But Gordon gave a wave of the hand to let him know he could hobble on over to the table on his own. He did, however, let Kocsis pull out a chair for him.

"What happened to you, Gordon?" asked Strausz. "If I didn't know any better, I'd say the main character of one of your articles knocked you upside the head. But I know most of those guys are either dead or in prison."

"It's not me they should be beating up if they have a problem with the verdict," said Gordon, "but the judge." Having caught the eye of one of the waiters, he pronounced his order, "Black, strong, large, and fast." Then he told Strausz what had happened to him the previous night.

"And you don't know why they attacked you?" asked the old fellow.

"No," said Gordon, shaking his head.

"Zsigmond, guys don't just come at you and knock you out for no good reason," said Kocsis, with a befuddled stare.

"Unfortunately, they do," said Strausz. "Toni, you left this country a good while ago. A few things have changed since then, and not just currency." He shook his head. "Tell me, what did the guy look like?"

"He looked a bit shorter than me, average build, but I'm not quite sure. I didn't get a look at his whole face, but I did see his mouth and his nose. On top he had only his canines, and nothing down below. His lip was curled downward, and his nose was brutally crooked."

Strausz looked at Kocsis, who knit his brows. "Strausz, you think it's him, too?" asked Kocsis.

"Without a doubt," said the old fellow with a nod.

"Who?" asked Gordon, looking from one to the other. The waiter appeared with a mug full to the brim with black, steaming hot coffee. Gordon produced his cigarette case, pulled out a cigarette, and was grateful to the waiter for extending a lit match his way. He took a drag and a big gulp of the coffee, then looked at Strausz.

"His name is Pojva," the old fellow began. "We know him. So does Toni." Kocsis nodded sullenly. "A long time ago he started boxing on the amateur level, and he wasn't bad. Not that he was too fast on his feet, but he didn't have to be. His body was poured of bronze: they could hit him all they wanted, but he didn't feel it. There was such power in those fists of his that when he managed to find his mark, the person at the receiving end was out cold. But he didn't get far, since boxers with better technique had no problem dealing with him. Then, around 1925 or 1926, he was thrown out of the youth boxing league. He'd been winning more and more matches by breaking the rules, you see. He'd whack his opponents on the nape of the neck, lean into them, and he'd even use his elbows to beat them silly. That's not to mention hitting below the belt, holding his opponents down, or locking them in his arms— he did whatever he wanted. He didn't deserve to be called a boxer. What's more, he was mean-spirited, petty, and money-hungry."

"Not long before I left, I heard that he was working as a hired thug," said Kocsis.

"And of course he's still boxing," added Strausz.

"Where?"

"Where? On the city outskirts, in all sorts of dives. Without gloves, until blood flows. That's how he earns his bread. And of course he gets jobs as a hired thug, too, like Toni said."

"The sharks hire him?"

"Anyone who can pay. But it's not like it costs that much."

"And where do they hold these illegal boxing matches?"

"I don't know, Zsigmond," said Strausz. "And I don't want to know."

"I can find out," said Kocsis, leaning forward.

"Much appreciated," replied Gordon.

Suddenly beset by dizziness, Gordon almost slipped off the chair. Strausz helped him sit up straight. After composing himself, Gordon asked the old fellow to call him a cab. Strausz signaled to the waiter.

While waiting for the cab to arrive, Kocsis filled him in on the city's illegal boxing. "Zsigmond, you've got to forget everything you've learned up until now about boxing. They don't use gloves, and there's not always a ring. The ropes are a lot higher so they can't fall out. There's a referee—if you can call him that—but you can't get disqualified, and usually there aren't even rounds. The organizers toll a bell, then the two fighters go at each other for all they're worth, hitting wherever they can. The only thing that's not allowed is hitting below the belt. Punching the neck? Sure. Elbowing? Of course. The point is that someone ends up on the floor. The later the better—bets can be made as long as both men are still on their feet. Needless to say, the bookies rake in the dough. Sometimes it's them who run the fighters. There's no credit; you can put down only as much as you have on you. Some nights one of the bookies got his hands on almost two thousand pengős."

"How is it you know so much about this, Toni?" asked Strausz, staring at him with a look of surprise.

"Well . . ." said Kocsis with a shrug. But then the waiter appeared with the news that the cab had arrived. Gordon stood, dug a pengő out of his pocket using his left hand, and threw the coin on the table.

"Thanks," he said softly, then headed off, his eyes fixed on the door. Another waiter opened the door for him. Without looking his way, Gordon only nodded, then hobbled out into the foggy October morning.

As he stepped out onto the sidewalk, the waiting cabbie hit the gas and drove right onto the Margaret Bridge. A black Citroën rolled into its spot in front of Gordon. He didn't even have time to be incensed before a tall, mustachioed man stepped out of the Citroën. Gordon recognized him as Csomor, one of the detectives with Unit V.

"Good day," came Csomor's cheerless greeting. "Please get in, sir," he said, opening the rear door for Gordon.

"Why should I get in?" asked Gordon angrily.

"Because I asked you to," replied the detective, moving over to Gordon, taking his arm, and shoving him into the car.

Sitting in the backseat was Vladimir Gellért, a cigarette hanging from his mouth as he read the contents of a file folder.

"What's this all about?" demanded Gordon.

The chief inspector didn't reply but kept reading without so much as looking up.

"I asked what this is all about!" Gordon repeated.

"What could it be about?" asked Gellért, looking up. "We're taking you home. I see you're tired. And it would have been foolish for you to spend money on a taxi."

"I spend money on what I want."

"Start it up, Csomor," Gellért called out. The detective turned on the engine, then drove up onto the bridge. But at Crown Prince Rudolf Square, rather than staying on the Grand Boulevard, he took a right onto Falk Miksa Street. "This isn't the way to my place," Gordon loudly observed, and he wasn't surprised not to receive a reply. Csomor slowed when passing by Red Margo's building, and Gellért glanced up at the window. Finally, they came to a stop in front of the Parliament building. Csomor cut the engine.

"And now?" asked Gordon. "What are you up to?"

"The question, Gordon," said Gellért, closing the file folder, "is what *you're* up to. Are you snooping around?"

Gordon was so surprised that he couldn't even reply.

"Snooping around? Asking questions? Maybe writing an article?" Gellért continued.

"And if I am, what business is it of yours? And anyway, how do you know what I'm working on?"

"Come, now, Gordon," said Gellért, shaking his head. His face was paler than usual, and not even his glasses could conceal the dark bags under his eyes. The blazer practically hung from his lanky frame. "Don't you remember? A girl died. You even asked what the deal was with her. Well, we're on the case now. There you have it."

"Yes?" asked Gordon scornfully. "And where have you gotten?"

In lieu of an answer, Gellért continued puffing on his cigarette.

"I asked where you've gotten."

"You're out of line, Gordon. You're talking with a chief inspector of the Hungarian Royal State Security Police. You're not the one asking questions. At least *I'm* not playing detective."

Gordon slumped back in the seat, exhausted. His kidneys were throbbing with pain, his right hand smarted at every motion, and blood trickled from the wound on his mouth.

Gellért looked at him through a cloud of smoke. "What are you asking questions about a dead prostitute for? What are you up to visiting the medical examiner?"

Gordon opened his mouth to speak, but the detective continued. "Why did you hasten the autopsy? Maybe it was you who got her pregnant? You were scared word would get out? And as long as we're on the subject, what are you up to scheming with Csuli?"

It took just a moment for Gordon to forget his pain. He sat up and listened attentively to Gellért.

"So you got a little beating," said Gellért. "Such things

have been known to happen. You could have come away worse. Pojva is usually much more determined."

Gordon wasn't even surprised to hear this. He'd practically been waiting for Gellért to bring it up.

"Everyone's scared to death of him out in that slum he lives in, those ramshackle wooden barracks out in eastern Pest that used to be a POW hospital—you know, the Mária Valéria Colony. Looking at you, I'm not surprised they're scared. No matter. But if you're thinking you can just slip him some cash and he'll spill the beans on who hired him, well, forget it." Gellért rolled the window down a bit, blew out the smoke, and looked at the Parliament building, the flag at half-mast, the guards. Without turning toward Gordon, he went on: "Leave your little investigation be, huh? If you listen to me, you won't go digging into the affairs of respectable Budapest businessmen. Don't go snooping around the villas up on Rose Hill. It's nothing but honest folks who live up there. If you're looking for trouble, you'll find it, too, except no one's going to help you." Gellért now gestured to Csomor, who started the engine. Through narrowed eyes Gordon watched Gellért, who kept staring out the window. Csomor drove along Báthory Street to Kaiser Wilhelm Road, and from there to Nagymező Street, finally stopping at the corner of Lovag. Csomor got out from behind the wheel and opened the rear door. Gellért now looked at Gordon but didn't say a thing. Csomor helped Gordon get out of the car before returning to the wheel and heading off.

Gordon pressed the doorbell and slumped against the building wall. In a matter of moments Iváncsik opened the door. "Good, you finally turned up, Mr. Editor," he said excitedly, helping Gordon into the foyer. On the way up the stairs, he added, "The doctor is very angry that you disappeared."

Mór did indeed look furious, but on looking twice at Gordon, the anger left his face. "Into the bedroom," he said to Iváncsik, and after closing the door he helped the super get Gordon inside. They sat Gordon on the bed. Mór removed Gordon's coat and handed it to the other man. "Put this on the coatrack, Iváncsik." The super nodded and left the room. "Wait a second," the old man called after him. "Take these two pengős and go get some sort of lunch from the Jolly Bar."

Iváncsik nodded again. "Yes, sir, I'll be back in no time."

As soon as the super had closed the door behind him, Mór looked at Gordon, who was busily trying to extract a cigarette from his case. The old man helped him out and gave him a light.

"Where were you, son?"

"Not now, Opa," he replied. "I'll tell you later. Why don't you tell me instead what you found out."

"It wasn't easy," Mór began. "You know how many people I found out on the street? Because, of course, I couldn't just go ringing any doorbells."

"How did you go about it, Opa?"

"It doesn't matter, son," he said. "What matters is, I did it."

"I was sure you would."

"Anyway, the father of this particular Shlomo—there are three Shlomos, you know—is Rav Shay'ale Reitelbaum, a rabbi. Have you heard of him?"

"No," said Gordon, shaking his head. "Should I have?"

"They say he's the smartest of rabbis. And maybe he is."

"Why?"

"Because he acted fast when he sensed trouble."

"What trouble?"

"They say that Shlomo was courting the daughter of the merchant Szőllősy."

"Fanny," said Gordon with a nod.

"If you know, why did you send me?"

"I didn't know, Opa. And did you talk to this particular Shlomo?"

The old man shook his head in disappointment.

"Then I will."

"You won't, either."

"Why not?"

"Because Rabbi Reitelbaum put his son on the train to Hamburg six weeks ago, and from there immediately on the ship to New York. That's where Shlomo will attend rabbinical school."

"And there, he's far enough away from Fanny," said Gordon, crushing out his cigarette.

The doorbell rang. Mór stood up and left the room and in a few seconds reappeared carrying a meal can.

"The good man brought rooster paprikash," he announced. "With spaetzle. And pickles. Not exactly diet food, but this is what you need right now." He went into the kitchen, and when he reappeared this time, he was carrying a tray with the food.

Gordon fell ravenously upon the food. He did not feel his

wounded mouth, nor did it bother him to be eating with his left hand. Once he finished, Mór took the tray back to the kitchen. When the old man returned, Gordon was sleeping on his side. His breathing was labored and vexed, and remained so even as Mór pulled the curtains shut and sat down in the living room, attentively reading the *Gastronome's Cookbook*.

Seven

It seemed to take about fifteen minutes for Gordon to come to from an unsettling dream, but in fact hardly a minute had gone by. With aching limbs he rose to his feet and headed slowly to the telephone. Mór was snoring away on the divan; an entire switchboard might have been ringing, but he still wouldn't have woken up. By the time Gordon reached the phone, it had fallen silent. But the ringing came again a couple of minutes later.

"Zsigmond," said Krisztina in a distant, panicked voice.

"Yes? What's wrong?"

"Wrong? I'm not sure. Something must be wrong."

"Tell me."

"I woke up about fifteen minutes ago. A bad feeling came over me, and my eyes suddenly popped wide open and my stomach knotted up. I got up to check if maybe someone was in the flat. But there was no one. That's when I went to see if

I'd locked the door. Which is when I saw the sheet of paper stuck to the glass."

Gordon sat down in the armchair.

"I opened the door," Krisztina continued. "It was one of your articles. Then I looked down at the doormat. Lying there was a dead hen, its neck broken."

"I'm listening."

"This is what they'd written on your article, in red ink: 'Stupid hen, if you don't tell him to call it quits, we'll wring your neck next.' You there, Zsigmond?"

"Of course," he replied. "Put down the phone, don't move, and don't let a soul in. I'll send Opa over. I can't go, I've got business. Opa will bring you over here. Don't let in anyone but him."

"But Zsigmond . . ."

"This once don't give me any *but*s, just do as I say," replied Gordon, and he put down the receiver. He went to the bathroom and slipped on his robe, then went back to the living room and sat down on the chair by the divan.

"Opa," he called to the old man. "Opa, wake up."

Mór kept snoring. Gordon gave him a gentle nudge. "Opa, rise and shine."

His grandfather's eyes popped open and Gordon helped him sit up, then waited for Mór to rub the sleep out of his eyes. "What is it, son?" asked Mór.

"Opa, you've got to get Krisztina right away and bring her over here. Someone left a dead hen on her doormat along with a note saying if she doesn't stop me, they'll wring her neck."

"I'll get going right away," said the old man with a look of alarm.

"Get yourself ready. I'll call a cab in the meantime."

The old man dragged himself to his feet and went to the bathroom. By the time he returned, Gordon had also begun to get dressed. "Opa, you can go down in front of the building already, the cab is on its way. Go get Krisztina, come back here, and don't let anyone in except me."

"Can you get dressed on your own?" asked Mór as Gordon, gritting his teeth, pulled on his trousers.

"Sure, Opa, don't you worry about me."

Since Gordon couldn't manage to button his shirt, he went to the closet and took out a sweater he'd gotten from Krisztina. Getting on his blazer was an easier task, as was his trench coat. Before heading off, he took a pack of Egyptian cigarettes from his desk drawer and shoved it into his pocket.

THE GRAND BOULEVARD AND RÁKÓCZI STREET WERE AL-ready in the throes of the usual Monday morning rush: pedestrians heading to work, cars and buses honking their horns, runaway horses sweeping carriages along at breakneck speed. Gordon gave the concierge a nod, went up to the newsroom, and put down his coat in the cavernous space that was slowly coming to life. He took a notebook and a pencil and headed to the cellar.

Only a single light bulb was on in the hall. His steps echoed as he went over to the heavy iron door that was always unlocked. He stepped in, reached to the left, and switched on

the light. The cold room was flooded with light. Long rows
of shelves spread out before him, shelves holding all the back
issues of the *Evening*, the *Budapest Journal*, and *Hungary* in
chronological order. In the case of the *Evening*, this meant
just twenty-six years; but the *Budapest Journal* had eighty-six.
Andor Miklós, owner of this conglomerate, had purchased
the entire archives back in 1920 along with the *Budapest Journal*, and spared neither time nor money to catalog it all. The
catalog cards practically took up more space than the bound
issues from each year. By the wall stood wooden cabinets of
the sort used in libraries, with a slip of paper on the front of
each drawer showing what was inside.

He wouldn't admit it to anyone, but Gordon didn't like this
system. During his years in America he'd learned the system
there, but try as he might, he just couldn't get the hang of this.
True, he didn't take too much trouble to learn it, either, since
the man in charge of the archives, Benő Strasser, knew everything there was to know about the newspapers. He and Valéria,
who worked only at night, were the odd ducks of the house.
Strasser claimed that ever since the founding of the *Evening*
back in 1910, he'd come to work every single day, summer and
winter, Christmas and Easter. He sat down behind his desk,
took out his pencil and notebook, and proceeded to read the
previous day's papers from front to back, taking notes on everything. Rumor had it that he even read the advertisements
and radio program schedules. Not for a moment had Gordon
doubted that this was so. There was Strasser behind his desk
from eight in the morning until five in the afternoon, filling up
one index card after another with his notes, smoking nonstop.

Andor Miklós, while he lived, regularly went down to the cellar to get his take on various issues, for no one had a better handle on the concern's publications than Benő Strasser.

Gordon paused while standing there in front of the shelves and let out a big sigh. He didn't even want to touch the index cards, and so he took the first issues of both the *Evening* and the *Budapest Journal* for each month from 1933 and sat down with this stack of papers at the desk opposite the entrance. No, not at Strasser's desk—not even Gordon would have dared do that—but at the desk reserved for visitors. He knew what he was looking for; he just didn't know where it was. He glanced at his watch. It was seven-fifteen. He had time to read until Strasser arrived.

Exactly at eight the door opened, and in walked the chief archivist.

Strasser was a tiny little man with a wiry face that, despite his decades spent under artificial light, bore no eyeglasses. Having removed his jacket and then his blazer, he slipped an elbow guard onto his arm and a green visor onto his head, and only then did he turn to Gordon.

"It's got to be important if you're here so early," he said.

"It's important, Strasser, very important. I've got some digging to do."

"Go ahead and dig."

"It's not just urgent, but important, too." Gordon leaned over Strasser's desk, reached inside the pocket of his blazer, and pulled out the pack of expensive Egyptian cigarettes. The archivist's eyes sparkled at the sight. He took the pack from Gordon's hand, gently opened it up, and took out a cigarette. He ran his fingers all along its length to feel the crackling, gave the cigarette a sniff, and produced a box of matches, whereupon he lit the cigarette with boundless pleasure.

"What is it you want, Gordon?"

"I want to know everything there is to know about Szőllősy, the coffee merchant."

"The owner of Arabia Coffee?"

"Him."

"Everything?"

"Everything possible."

"Let me guess," said Strasser, now giving Gordon a closer look. "You complained to him about his coffee, and in his rage he gave you a good whacking?"

"Something like that," replied Gordon with a shrug.

The archivist adjusted his elbow guard and visor, pulled out his desk drawer, and removed an enormous book. This was the catalog of catalogs—the heart of the archives, which Strasser alone understood. "Come back at four," he said, looking up at Gordon.

"Four?"

"You want me to put it in writing?"

"No need, Strasser. Your word is more than enough."

"If it's enough, then you can come back by noon. But no earlier."

"I'll be here at twelve," said Gordon, putting on his hat. He pulled the iron door shut behind him carefully lest he should disturb the archivist.

ALTHOUGH EVERYTHING STILL HURT, HE HAD AN EASIER time moving about than he'd had the day before. His hand was the worst. The wound on his forehead no longer throbbed with pain, and if he pulled the hat down over his eyes, it even covered the bandage. His mouth was still swollen, true, but it no longer hurt to speak. Since sudden movements sent a sharp pain shooting through his kidneys, well, he didn't move suddenly. But his hand. He stuck it into the pocket of his coat and tried not to think about it.

Gordon boarded the tram on Blaha Lujza Square. He sat down beside the window and looked out at the city. Pedestrians chilled to the bone trod the morning streets, wearing gloves and turning up their collars. Those who couldn't afford gloves stuck their hands in their pockets or else warmed them for a few moments by a chestnut vendor's stove. Ships were moored by Margaret Island, and resolute rowers were out training on the water. There wasn't a trace of the families that had come out in droves in the balmy days of summer: of children clumsily making their way about on tricycles, of women pushing baby carriages, of men strolling along with folded newspapers wedged under their arms. Occasionally a cab carrying passengers from one of the island's hotels turned onto the bridge, but Gordon saw no other signs of movement.

He got off at the last stop, Kálmán Szell Square. This was home to the tobacconist's shop that sold special, foreign cigarettes. And so many other things, too—of course, only to the initiated. Kovách, the tobacconist, was a vigorous, healthy-looking fellow with ruddy cheeks and a meticulously crafted beard and mustache.

"Two packs of the Egyptian, Kovách," said Gordon by way of greeting. The man reached under the counter and, after rummaging about for a bit, finally produced two packs. "Would you like anything else, Mr. Editor?"

"Not now," replied Gordon.

"Come now, sir, you don't even know how much I have here under the counter. Lots and lots of lovely things. Lots." He stood, came out from behind the counter, and hung the CLOSED sign on the door. Gordon watched him with curiosity, even though he was in a hurry. Kovách disappeared through the door behind the counter, and when he reappeared, he was holding two wooden trays and a willow basket. "Please do take a quick look over these, sir," he said, now producing his merchandise of uncertain origin. "Here is the new Parker Vacumatic fountain pen," he began. "Its novelty is that you can see how much ink is in it. Herman Klein, over on Próféta Street, sells another Parker pen, the Major, for eighty pengős, and I sell them for twenty-nine. I've got a couple nice Longines and Omega wristwatches, too, and you won't believe how little I'm selling them for." Gordon shook his head. "Then I beg you humbly, dear sir, do buy some of these splendid stockings. They go for a whole lot more in the Heilig Stocking Shop, you know. This pair of sheer silk Signorians are just two pengős, and you won't even guess how low the denier rating is on them. The same thing is three-fifty at Heilig. No? No. I understand. In the back I've got a completely new and never before used Orion 44 shortwave radio, and I'm not even asking a lot for it, actually . . ."

"I've got to go, Kovách. Besides, I've never bought anything from you except cigarettes."

"That's true, sir, but you never know when you might have a change of heart."

"Hope dies last, huh?" Gordon remarked.

"What was that, sir?"

"Never mind."

Kovách put away his merchandise in no time, then opened the door to let Gordon back out onto the square. In the time he'd been inside the tobacconist's shop, the square had awoken, too. Trams came and went, a few odd hikers were setting out for the hills even though it was Monday. Newsboys were vying to outshout each other. Women were on their way to the nearby market. Gordon hurried on. He didn't like being in Buda. For some reason Pest was closer to his heart; there, at least, he felt at home, insofar as this was possible at all.

Having jostled his way through the crowd on Széna Square, he walked into the Buda Castle Coffeehouse. There was quite a hubbub there, too, but this was the one place that Vécsey was willing to have his morning coffee. Gordon was not the only one who knew where to find Leo Vécsey—if not behind a desk in the newsroom of *Hungarian Police News*, then he sat here in the Buda Castle Coffeehouse writing and translating away. Ever since he was appointed editor of the newspaper two years earlier, he hadn't written crime news. He'd had enough of that and much preferred editing, which left him time to translate and even write poetry. Despite this, however, he knew more about the city's crime scene than anyone. He knew all there was to know about con artists, cardsharpers, swindlers, and the cops chasing them down.

Not that they were friends, but they knew each other well, and whenever they'd crossed paths while working on a story, they'd always felt obliged to help each other out. Vécsey re-

spected Gordon for the years he'd spent in America. Gordon
couldn't understand why, but he knew better than to ask.
Whenever the question occurred to him, he heard Vécsey's
common refrain: "Zsigmond, what goes on in this country
of ours isn't crime, it's comedy. You get burglars with names
like Duck-Billed Bill, hookers called Danube Doozy. These
folks aren't criminals, they're dilettantes. It's a waste of time,
really, even to give my opinion when you ask." He repeated
such words often to Gordon, but then invariably proceeded to
detail how many people had been shot to death that week in
Chicago and how many millions of dollars had been embezzled in New York. Vécsey was always putting down America,
which led Gordon to conclude that he would have much preferred to have been a crime reporter for a Chicago newspaper.

"Zsigmond, you sure did step on someone's toes," said
Vécsey, fixing his deep blue, almost embarrassingly penetrat-
ing gaze on Gordon.

"It's nothing," said Gordon with a wave of his hand—
his left hand. "But, hey, I heard that one of your books was
bought in Hollywood."

"*Life Is a Circus*," said Vécsey.

"Well, then you'll be rich and famous."

"Or not."

"Did you get a lot of money?"

"Not so much that I don't have to work."

"And what are you writing now?"

"A poetry collection."

"What's the title?"

"*The Exiled Heart.*"

"Does it say whose heart has been exiled, and why?"

"Now that you say so . . ." Vécsey smiled. "Do you want a coffee?"

Gordon nodded. Vécsey signaled to the waiter, then crossed his arms. "You didn't drop in by chance."

"No," Gordon acknowledged. "Something happened that outdoes the usual doings of the Downtown Association of Amateur Evildoers."

"I'm listening."

"A dead Jewish girl was found on . . ."

"Nagy Diófa Street," said Vécsey, finishing Gordon's sentence. "One of Csuli's men filled me in."

"Then you've heard of Skublics, too."

"Of course," said Vécsey, leaning back in his chair. He unbuttoned the coat of his superbly tailored suit and reached for his coffee with a sinewy hand. "He disappeared so fast that he left everything in his studio. As if he just went up in smoke."

"In a manner of speaking," said Gordon.

"I get you. But there's one question, Zsigmond. What do you want to do? You can't write an article about it."

"I know that perfectly well," said Gordon, raising the cup of coffee to his mouth and putting it back down at once. The hot liquid nearly burned his mouth. "But I do have a plan."

"That's helpful," said Vécsey approvingly. "A plan is always useful. Just don't go telling me this is where I come into the picture. Because I'm not interested in any sort of plan. Especially not this sort."

"I need information. Nothing else, Leo. Information."

"That, you can ask for. Maybe I can serve up a bit."

Gordon took out a cigarette. He'd quite gotten the hang of using his left hand. Vécsey gave him a light. "What sort of information?" he asked as his brow darkened.

"Politicians and prostitutes."

Leo raised a hand with dramatic flair and gave a soft whistle. "Both have a price."

"Leo, I'm asking seriously."

"I know you asked seriously, but I don't want to answer seriously. You won't write an article, anyway. There's just no way you can write this."

"We've already agreed on that. There's a flat on Báthory Street, which is where the girls are. And there's a book, or let's call it a catalog, from which the politicians can pick and choose. Skublics took the pictures of the girls. The whole thing is led by a woman called Red Margo, who works for a certain gentleman by the name of Zsámbéki."

Vécsey watched Gordon through narrowed eyes. Again he crossed his arms, leaned back, and for a little while he rocked back and forth on the two rear legs of the chair. When he came to, he said, softly, "Not just them. Not just our politicians— members of the lower house and the upper house. But foreign politicians have also seen that . . . as you put it, catalog."

"Are the police in on it, too?"

"Not actively," said Vécsey. "Those who need to know, know, and of course they don't do a thing."

"I get it."

"No, you don't get it. You don't get it at all. Not only can't you write about it, but you can't even talk about it with anyone. For example, we didn't even meet today."

"Let's not get carried away, Leo."

Vécsey leaned over the table.

"Have you heard about Schweinitzer's state security commando unit?" he asked in a muffled voice.

Gordon shook his head.

"You don't want to hear about them, either. And you certainly don't want to meet up with them."

"What is it they do?"

"You don't want to know. Believe me, Zsigmond, it's better if you don't know. If you don't keep that tongue of yours in check, Bárczy will give Schweinitzer the order."

"That Bárczy? István Bárcziházi Bárczy?"

"How many do you know?"

"The undersecretary in the prime minister's office?"

"That's right, and don't play dumb with me. What are you out for?"

Gordon pulled his bandaged hand from his pocket and placed it on the table. "At first the dead girl was a professional labor of love. Maybe it would make a nice little article, I figured. The story seemed interesting. But everywhere I turned, I ran up against brick walls. That just piqued my interest. On Saturday night I was all but beaten to death. Early this morning someone left a broken-necked chicken in front of Krisztina's flat—with a note saying that if I don't stop, they'll wring her neck next. I can't stop now."

"But you should."

"And where will I get doing that?"

Vécsey paused to reflect. "Nowhere," he finally replied, and leaned back. "They won't believe that you've quit. No matter who's behind it all. You were right—this isn't Budapest, it's Chicago. Not every gangster needs a weapon."

"So you see. Even if I could just get over them beating me up, threatening me, and setting their sights on Krisztina, and even if I could just wave a hand to get that dead girl off my mind, not even then could I just call it quits. But I haven't gotten over it, and I haven't waved that hand. I've got to do something, because if I don't, then . . ."

"Don't say any more," Vécsey interjected. "I understand."

"But there is one thing I still don't understand," said Gordon, crushing his cigarette. "The day before Gömbös's funeral, I was there at the wake. I saw Interior Minister Kozma, and you know who he was talking with?"

"No."

"Well, not with Schweinitzer. Not with the head of the state security police but with Vladimir Gellért."

"It's not that surprising," replied Vécsey.

"No?"

"Both Kozma and Gellért are military academy graduates. They were in the same class."

"Bárcziházi went there, too," observed Gordon.

"That's right, but he was several years ahead of them."

Gordon nodded, stood, and threw a pengő on the table. "All the best with Hollywood. And thanks."

"No thanks needed."

"Tell me just one more thing," said Gordon, leaning against the chair.

"What would that be?"

"What do you know about Szőllősy, the coffee merchant?"

"The owner of Arabia Coffee?"

"Him."

Vécsey scrutinized Gordon's eyes. "Aside from the fact that in 1933 he bought himself an official certificate giving him the title of Valiant Knight?"

"Does that sort of thing cost a lot?"

"Why, do you want to buy one, too?"

"No, I'm just curious."

"Well, if you ask me, the title of Valiant Knight is worth every cent to a Jew who converted to Christianity."

GORDON GOT BACK TO THE NEWSROOM WELL AFTER eleven. Gyula Turcsányi was sitting in his office, a red pencil in his hand, with which he was struggling to edit a small pile of articles.

"I'll say!" he shouted on casting a furious glance at Gordon. "Eleven o'clock, and you've seen fit to show up at work. Maybe back in America this was in vogue, but in case you haven't noticed, you're working in Budapest. We're fussy about work hours, you see. A reporter is at his desk by nine and writing an article, or else he's rolling the article out of his typewriter one moment and delivering it to my desk the next. Or haven't I told you this before? Well?"

Only now did Turcsányi finally look up and see Gordon's unshaven face, wounded lips, the bandage sticking out from under his hat, and his limp right hand just hanging there.

"What in blazing hell happened to you?"

"An accident."

"You were in a fight?"

"Not for fun."

"Was it at least with a reporter at a rival paper? Over which one of you should write about the latest girl to do herself in by swallowing match heads?"

"I've got to rest my right hand. The doctor told me not to use it until Friday."

From behind his desk Turcsányi took stock of him.

"I can't type, either. And I certainly can't write."

The section editor slammed his red pencil on the pile of articles before him and gave a deep sigh. "Then go on home, and by Friday learn how to write with your left hand. Or to type. Or both." He then took a typed sheet of paper from the pile and resumed reading.

Gordon went down to the archives. As usual, the door was shut. Once inside, Gordon saw that Strasser was busy putting one pack of bound newspapers after another on a pile on a desk by the wall. He was utterly immersed in the task. Sometimes he'd take the pencil from behind his ear, write a note, page through one of the packs, put the pack aside, resume searching, consult his catalog, and scratch his head. Gordon knew full well that the archivist must not be disturbed at such a time.

Naturally, even now, a cigarette hung from his mouth. Gordon sat down in the visitor's chair and he, too, lit a cigarette. It was a couple of minutes past noon. Strasser took the packs of newspapers and returned them one after another to the shelves. Once finished, he plopped down behind his desk, read over his notes, and stared at the ceiling for quite a while. Then, all at once, he sprang up, rushing headlong to a particular shelf. Grabbing a pack of papers, he paged through them, taking the pencil from behind his ear to write something down. "I thought so," he grumbled, then returned to his desk. Adjusting his elbow guard, he spoke.

"I'm done, Gordon."

"Wonderful."

The archivist set his notes down in front of himself and looked at the reporter. "You didn't ask for this in writing, so I didn't write down the sources. Maybe I'll remember if it's important, but don't bet your life."

"I don't need to know when and where the articles were published, Strasser, much less by whom. Your word is enough."

"So then," said Strasser, craning his neck. Gordon was on pins and needles and would gladly have given Strasser a good shake to get him to start talking. But he knew it was worth waiting. He knew full well that if he'd hired a private investigator, the man would have found out ten times less in twice as much time, and he would not have kept as tight-lipped about what he was up to. "So then," repeated the archivist, "Valiant Knight András Szőllőshegyi Szőllősy was born in Budapest in 1876. His father was already officially called Tamás Szőllősy, or more precisely, Tamás Rotenau Szőllősy. He arrived in Buda as an Ashkenazi Jew after the 1848–49 revolution and there opened a general store. Just when he converted to Christianity is hard to say exactly, but it was sometime in the late 1850s. And so he didn't have his son christened with the foreign-sounding name Andreas, but under the Hungarian name András. His wife also took the Roman Catholic faith. Szőllősy's father became really well-to-do when he moved his business across the river to Pest in 1867. András was the only child, so he was sent abroad for schooling. First he studied in Antwerp, then Berlin. In 1902 he returned to Budapest and immediately went to work for his father, who, however, died in 1905. A year later, in 1906, András got married; his wife's name is Irma Petneházy. They had a daughter in 1914 who was christened Fanny. During the first two years of the Great War he traveled a lot, mainly to Africa. He was among the first to make business ties in Abyssinia. By 1919 he already had five stores in Pest, but their proceeds paled in comparison with that of his coffee imports. For a while he was the main supplier for stores in Vienna and Belgrade. It was from there that, in 1920, he entered the German market. He was deft at maneuvering his way around the touchy political situation of the time, managing to avoid the storm clouds at every turn, and before long he'd opened several stores in Germany that also operated as wholesale outlets. One in Berlin, one in Munich, one in Bremen, and one in Nuremberg. In 1933, our country's leader, Miklós Horthy, made him a Valiant Knight and simultaneously named him his confidential advisor. Since the start of the year, the bulk of his coffee exports have gone to Germany, where he is one of the biggest suppliers. He lives in the Buda hills, more precisely, at 48 Pasaréti Street. His office is in Pest, on Kaiser Wilhelm Road. He drives a Maybach DS8 Zeppelin sedan, license plate MA 110. He's known to be reserved, and spends a lot of time in Germany seeing to business affairs. He doesn't go to the theater, and he has almost no social life to speak of. His wife, Irma, is much more active, belonging to various women's associations. The greatest disappointment in Szőllősy's life is that he didn't have more children, and so he doesn't have an heir for his business."

Gordon didn't even try to take notes on Strasser's hollow, colorless speech. The archivist would not have made a good radio announcer, but then again, he didn't aspire to be one, either.

"Say, Strasser," Gordon asked, "may I have your notes?"

Strasser took thorough stock of Gordon. "I've never done that before."

"Nor have you ever seen a journalist who wanted to work but couldn't, because someone almost broke his hand."

"Well, I've already seen more than one journalist in my time who couldn't work, and then there are exceptional cases."

"This is precisely such a case," said Gordon, standing up and setting down yet another pack of Egyptian cigarettes in front of Strasser.

"That's also how I see it," he said, slipping the pack away in no time, then pushing his notes toward Gordon. "I don't know what use you can make of them. Don't tell me you want to write an article about him? Because that would be interesting."

"Why?"

"Szőllősy has never spoken to the press. Definitely not to us or anyone else. He's been written about, but he's never commented on himself."

"Why so secretive?"

"You see there, that's your job to figure out if you want to. It's not like I can do that from down here in the archives. Not as if I'd want to, I should add."

GORDON WENT UP TO THE NEWSROOM, STEPPED OVER TO the telephone, and dialed. Mór answered.

"Are you two all right, Opa?"

"We're all right, son. How long do we need to sit here for?"

"Not long. Have the super get you lunch, but don't go anywhere until I get home. Can you give the phone to Krisztina?"

"Hold on there, son. What is this all about? What have you gotten yourself mixed up in?"

"I'll tell you, Opa, but I can't talk about it now. Tell Krisztina I'm on the line."

While waiting, Gordon pulled up a copy of the *8 O'Clock News* and began paging through it. He paused at the announcements column, which comprised five short texts, each a couple of sentences long. He read the first, though he knew full well what these announcements were all about: "I hereby notify my most esteemed present and future clients that as of October 10, I have Hungarianized my family name from Klein to Kutas. Sincerely, Dr. Endre Kutas, attorney." The other announcements were the same. Doctors, merchants, lawyers— all people whose surnames suggested dubious ancestry who were obliged to announce that they'd adopted Hungarian names. The only surprising thing was that—

"Zsigmond."

"Are you all right, Krisztina?"

"Yes," she replied. "Better. I wouldn't have thought this would have made me so upset."

"Don't be angry."

"It's not your fault."

"But it is."

Krisztina pondered the matter for a couple of moments. "Okay, it is. Were they the same people who beat you up?"

"Yes."

"Do you know who they are?"

"I have a hunch."

"A hunch."

"Yes."

"But you're not telling me just now."

"Exactly," said Gordon, casting his eyes around the newsroom. No one was looking his way. Gömbös belonged to the past, and Gordon's colleagues were now all busy at work on other stories.

"And?"

"And what?"

"How long are we sentenced to confinement in the flat?"

"When I get home, we'll talk over everything. Now I've got to go. Watch yourselves." He put down the phone.

For one reason alone, Gordon wasn't sorry that he was unable to work. In recent days speculation had been rife about whom Kálmán Darányi would invite into the government alongside the National Unity Party. Why was this such a big mystery? He'd invite the same people who'd been there up to now. Horthy had appointed Darányi as prime minister on the day of the funeral, so Darányi had functioned as the acting head of government only for a couple of days, a position that had been a mere formality in any case.

So the newsroom was now abuzz with journalists churning out reports on the formation of the new government. The *Budapest Journal* was on the desk beside Gordon. He paged through it. Nothing showed Horthy's confidence in Darányi more than his having appointed him so quickly; and Darányi promptly moved to consolidate the trade and industry ministries, giving István Winchkler the boot, and naming Géza Bornemissza the head of the newly unified ministry. He also replaced the defense minister, Valiant Knight Jozsef Somkuthy, with Vilmos Roder, the general in command of the nation's infantry. But the government's key figures would stay right where they were, Gordon surmised. Bálint Hóman would remain culture minister; Tihamér Fabinyi, finance minister; Kálmán Kánya, foreign minister; and, of course, Miklós Kozma, interior minister. Gordon understood the newsworthiness of this; and at the same time, he didn't. Ultimately, it didn't matter who was at the helm of the government and who belonged to the cabinet. Nothing would change, anyway. The papers had to appear, and they had to run the news, even if, in fact, it was the same old news.

ON BLAHA LUJZA SQUARE, GORDON BOARDED TRAM NO. 4 and once again read thoroughly through Strasser's notes. He transferred at Kálmán Szell Square to Tram No. 14, got off at the head of Italian Row, and walked from there onto Pasaréti Street. Although his kidneys still throbbed with pain, moving felt good. And it gave him time to ponder what to do next.

There was hardly any traffic on Pasaréti Street. In this neighborhood of villas, a nanny walking a child or pushing a baby carriage occasionally turned up on the sidewalk, but for the most part the apartment buildings stood sullen, un-approachable, and vain behind thick hedges and tall fences. The fallen leaves had been raked up in preparation for winter. Gordon glimpsed gardeners busily at work as he passed by a couple of villas. Smoke poured from the chimneys, but there were few other signs of life.

Forty-eight Pasaréti Street was likewise guarded by a tall fence, but not quite tall enough to block the view of the opulent building behind it. It couldn't have been built more than ten years ago. Stairs climbed up on both sides to the ter-race. The boxed shutters over the second-floor windows were closed, the balcony was empty, and nothing stirred beside its lace curtains. Rows of birch trees populated the yard along with a few other trees, and a magnificent larch at least fifty feet tall was sagging from its many clusters of cones.

Gordon approached the gate and rang the bell. A maid soon appeared, wrapped in a shawl.

"Who are you looking for?" she asked with suspicion.

"I'm from the *Evening* newspaper, and I'm looking for the master of the house," replied Gordon in a tone of voice meant to persuade this girl that her only duty was to let him in.

"He is not home. His lordship is in his office." Chilled by

the brisk autumn air, she pulled the shawl tighter around herself. Gordon nodded. This was exactly what he'd expected.

"And her ladyship?"

"She is home."

"Then what are you waiting for?" Gordon cast her a piercing look. "Let her know I'm here."

"Yes, sir," said the girl, opening the door. Gordon followed her into the building. A pleasant warmth enveloped him in the vestibule. He looked around. This home had obviously been arranged with exceptional taste, yet it wasn't homey in the least. Everything sparkled, everything was lovely, everything was elegant. Gordon handed his jacket and hat to the girl and followed her into the living room. Expensive, massive pieces of furniture greeted him. Persian rugs. Biedermeier armchairs, chairs, and a divan—original, figured Gordon. A crystal chandelier, a Zsolnay vase, and a brocade curtain. As if he were in a museum or in an elegant furniture store, nowhere a personal object, a wrinkle on a tablecloth, nowhere a book left behind. Gordon sat down in the armchair beside the coffee table, which was lovely but uncomfortable. He saw no ashtray on the table. He was adjusting the bandage on his hand when the door opened and in walked Mrs. Szőllősy—a tall, slender woman whose dress swept the floor. Her waist was thin, her back was stiff, and her brown hair, interwoven with gray curls, was tied up in a knot. "Good day," came the woman's measured greeting.

"Good day," replied Gordon, standing up.

"The girl said you came from a newspaper."

"Yes," said Gordon. "From the *Evening*. We're writing an article about the coffee trade, and I would have liked to speak with your husband."

The woman seemed to calm down somewhat. She sat on the sofa and rang for the maid. "Would you like some coffee?" she asked Gordon.

"Thank you."

"Coffee, Anna."

"Yes, my lady."

"Why didn't you look for my husband in his office?" she asked, looking Gordon squarely in the eye.

"Well, I had some business in the neighborhood, and so I thought I'd try to find him at home. He heads a large corporation—perhaps he doesn't have to go in every day."

"My husband heads a large corporation precisely because he is in the office every morning at eight. And he works." With a subtle movement, the woman now adjusted her hair. Gordon saw that the skin on her hand bore the signs of aging. Notwithstanding this, she was in fine form. It was obvious that in her younger days, men had waited in droves to curry her favor. Of course, it must not have been easy for her, what with such a reedy frame, but her regal comportment and her confident expression must surely have shooed away the dowry hunters, the dandies, and the other men buzzing about her without serious intentions.

"I understand. I'd still like to ask a few questions. Just briefly."

"I am listening."

"If I'm correct, Arabia Coffee is one of the largest coffee importers alongside Meinl."

"That is correct."

"And it has stores not only in Budapest but also in Germany."

"Yes."

"In Berlin, Munich, Stuttgart, and Bremen."

"Nuremberg," the woman corrected Gordon.

"Yes, Nuremberg. Then your husband must have exceptional contacts."

"What do you mean by that?" asked the woman, jerking up her head.

"Well, Nuremberg is the hotbed of National Socialists. Hitler's rallies, the September marches, the Nuremberg laws."

"What are you actually asking me?" She slid out to the edge of the sofa.

"I am suggesting merely that it can't be easy for a Hungarian merchant to run a business in the Nazis' citadel."

"We import coffee, not fascism."

"I didn't suggest that for even a minute," replied Gordon.

"My husband worked hard to secure the German market. He made many sacrifices. He's hardly ever home; he spends so much time out there, mainly in Berlin."

After knocking softly, Anna entered the room carrying a silver tray bearing an entire Meissen china coffee service. She put it on the table and quickly left the room. The woman reached for the coffee pitcher and filled the cups while Gordon continued. "And here is my next question: What will become of your business, your empire? Will your daughter take the reins?"

He might as well have slapped the woman on the face. Her

hand stopped in midair, the pitcher trembled. She took a deep breath, set the pitcher back on the tray, and in an icy voice that only confirmed the fear and loathing in her eyes, she replied, "If you want to talk about the business, go find my husband. If it's our family you're interested in, it's best that you leave at once. Hack writers have no business looking into our private affairs. The maid will escort you out." She stood and left the room without looking back.

Gordon took a sip of the coffee. He didn't understand what all the fuss was involving Arabia and Meinl. Coffee—black and bitter, plain and simple.

The maid reappeared in the doorway. Gordon put down his cup and followed her out to the vestibule, where the girl helped him put on his jacket. Gordon sized her up. Her hair was braided on two sides; her eyes were blue and big, very big. With her bony hands, she fiddled with her apron. "What happened to Fanny?" he asked quietly.

"Good God, sir, please don't ask such a thing," replied the girl with a frightened stare.

"Why not?"

"Because no one here talks about her. I haven't been here long, but they haven't even said her name in front of me."

"How long have you been serving here?"

"Two weeks."

"And your predecessor?"

"She went back to her village."

"Which one?"

"Bükkszentkereszt—up north, hours from the city, in the Bükk mountains."

"Why?"

"I don't know."

"Did she have a falling out with your masters?"

"I don't know," said the girl, looking about with alarm, "I beg you, sir, please leave."

"What was her name?"

"Teréz Ökrös," she replied. "Goodness, she could embroider like a charm. You never saw such pieces, sir."

"That I believe," said Gordon. "So what's up with your master's daughter? What happened to her?"

The girl turned pale. "Don't talk so loudly, sir!" She got so nervous that the northern provincial accent that until now had only filtered through suddenly erupted with full force. "I said I don't know a thing about her. My masters haven't said a word about her. I was in her room only once, and it was as clean as if no one had ever lived there. They even had it painted over." She defiantly threw back her head. "Now please leave, sir, because I don't want them to fire me, too."

Gordon raised his eyebrows but didn't ask a thing. He took his hat and stepped out the door. Once outside, he turned around and looked back up at the lovely house. The curtains hung motionless and he saw no movement from within, as if no one was inside.

GORDON BOARDED A TRAM ON ITALIAN ROW AND TRANS-ferred to another on Kálmán Széll Square. He hurried home. Mór unlocked the apartment door from the inside.

"Finally, son," said the old man with a look of relief. "We were starting to get worried."

"No problem, Opa. I'm home. Krisztina?"

"She's working in the living room."

Gordon took off his jacket and went to her. Krisztina had moved everything meticulously to the side on Gordon's desk and was sitting there, drawing away. The India ink was flowing effortlessly under her hand.

"So you turned up," she said, looking up at him.

"That's right."

"And what happened?"

"I'll tell you on the way," replied Gordon.

"On the way?"

Gordon didn't answer; he was already standing by the telephone and calling a cab. He was getting so good at using his left hand that he didn't even need a pencil to dial. "Got it. We'll be down in ten minutes. Tell him we might even spend the night there, so he should come prepared." With that, he put down the phone and started rummaging about among the papers on the telephone stand. He pulled out a brochure, dialed again, and reserved a double room for two nights.

"What's this all about, Zsigmond?" asked Krisztina, standing up.

"I'll tell you in the car."

"What?"

"What I found out."

"And this is so dangerous that we have to leave?"

"It might be," said Gordon, going over to the closet. "But I'll need your help, too," he said, looking her in the eye. "I'll throw together a few things right away," he said, and he flung a couple of pieces of clothing onto the bed. "Would you get yourself ready? I'd like to leave as soon as possible."

Krisztina sighed, then angrily gathered up her drawings and packed away her pencils, pens, and notebooks. Mór meanwhile stood quietly at the kitchen door.

"Opa," said Gordon, as he turned to his grandfather. "Would you get my suitcase off the top of the closet? I can't grab it."

The old man walked over to the closet and pulled down the worn old vulcanized fiber suitcase, which had seen better days. "What have you gotten yourself into now, son?"

"Nothing I can't climb back out of," replied Gordon. "Opa, I've reached my hand into something that could go who-knows-where. I'm worried for Krisztina and for you, too. I know you don't want to come with us, because . . ."

"My jams and preserves," said Mór.

"Them. And you don't want to travel anywhere else, either. But at least keep the door locked, even when you're home. Have you bought enough fruits and vegetables?"

"I've got apples, pears, and grapes—sure, the grapes are a bit shriveled up by now—but the chestnuts will soon be ripe, too. Why?"

"I won't be so worried if for a couple of days, just a couple, you didn't go roaming away from home. You've got enough fruit now for canning. And you've also said you never have time to write down your recipes."

Sticking his index finger in his vest pocket, Mór looked at Gordon without a word.

"You're right," he finally said. "It wouldn't hurt if I wrote down the best ones."

"You see. There was the one from the other day, the apple jam."

"That," said the old man with a dismissive wave of the hand, "that was nothing special."

"It was to me. Write out the recipe. We'll be back on Wednesday. Maybe sooner."

WHEN THEY GOT DOWN IN FRONT OF THE BUILDING ON Lovag Street, the taxi was already waiting for them, and behind the wheel was Czövek, as Gordon had requested. The cabbie grinned with satisfaction. "I kiss your hand, miss. I heard we're off on an outing. Where to?"

"To Lövölde Square," replied Gordon. With a look of profound disappointment, Czövek put the car into gear and headed off. He didn't say a word; nor did Krisztina, who drew to the far side of the backseat and stared out at the traffic. Gordon quietly cursed himself for not having had Mór rebandage his hand, but he hadn't had the time. He'd ask for cold water at the hotel.

After they parked on Lövölde Square, Krisztina turned to Gordon. "Wait for me here. You don't need to come up, Zsigmond. I'll hurry." Czövek opened the door for her, and as she exited, she lit a cigarette. Gordon leaned back and shut his eyes. The trip wasn't a short one to begin with, and it would feel even longer with Krisztina in such a merry mood. But he didn't blame her.

He opened his eyes a few minutes later at the sound of the door slamming shut. Krisztina sat down next to him, and Czövek slipped back in behind the wheel. "And where are we going now?" he asked. "Back to Lovag Street?"

"To that little resort village up in the Bükk mountains. Lil-lafüred, to be precise—the Palace Hotel."

Czövek gave a quiet whistle, adjusted his driver's cap, and backed the big, bulky car out onto the street. He then drove down Andrássy Street toward Heroes' Square. From Arena Road he turned onto Kerepesi, which would take them to Route 3. Gordon looked at the speedometer. Sixty kilometers an hour. Glancing at his watch, he calculated that at best they'd arrive at 6 P.M., if not later.

The buildings gradually grew sparser along the road, and Gordon shuddered. Leaving Pest, even if that only meant venturing to the city's outskirts, invariably gave him an unpleasant feeling. He couldn't say why. It was as if he'd wound up in another world. A foreign world whose rules he could only guess at. If he'd had the choice, he wouldn't leave Pest. Gordon had not spoken of this even to Krisztina, though he suspected that she knew.

As the buildings became ever more tattered and the side roads looked muddier, Gordon felt worse. Until, that is, they had left the city altogether. Now he breathed a sigh of relief, even if he did continue to look out on the flat landscape with suspicion—small villages nestled off in the distance, dense woods, cheerful little towns. One such town was Gödöllő, where Gordon had been once before. Indeed he'd even gotten into the Grassalkovich mansion, the residence of the head of state, Miklós Horthy. The *Evening* had sent him to a reception there whose guests included several American diplomats. What with its otherworldly elegance, the mansion made a good impression on Gordon—certainly a better one than did the other people on hand. The Budapesters rode astride the high horse of their big city airs, and those from outlying regions couldn't have stripped away their stale provincialism for all the treasures in the world. This only confirmed Gordon's feeling that he was indeed in a different land.

"I said you should buy a car," said Krisztina, who was likewise looking out at the countryside.

"Furthest thing from my mind," replied Gordon.

"But there was that pretty little Graham-Paige. It cost just eight hundred pengős."

"Where would I go with a car?"

"Right now, for instance, you'd go to Lillafüred, with me."

"And I was supposed to buy a car for that? To take you to Lillafüred?"

Krisztina looked at him and shook her head, but didn't reply.

"Besides," Gordon added, "I don't have the nerves to drive in Budapest."

Krisztina turned back to the window. Only when they reached the vicinity of Gyöngyös—the town wedged between the northern edge of the plains and the foothills of the Mátra range, and whose proximity signaled that they had at last arrived in the mountainous north—did she speak again.

"Will you tell me finally what this is all about? Or do you want to keep playing the part of the cloak-and-dagger detective?"

"Of course," said Gordon, "of course."

"Then tell me. We have plenty of time yet."

"The dead girl was called Fanny Szőllősy," Gordon began. "She was the daughter of the owner of Arabia Coffee, his only child. Just how she ended up in the hands of Csuli, I don't yet know; which is to say, I know, but I don't know how things got that far. She was in love with Shlomo, the son of a rabbi, Rav Shay'ale Reitelbaum. I suspect it was the young man who got her pregnant, and then somehow word got out, whereupon the rabbi put his son on a ship to New York."

"And how did Fanny end up on the streets?"

"That I do not know."

"Did her father kick her out?"

"I don't know, Krisztina, but I believe the answer lies at our destination," he replied, filling her in on what he'd learned from the Szőllősy family's maid. And, of course, from the coffee merchant's wife.

"So the reason we're headed to this charming little resort tucked in the mountains," observed Krisztina, "is to have a chat with the former maid, Teréz Ökrös, in her nearby village of Bükkszentkereszt."

"And because you've been wanting to come here for a while," said Gordon.

"Zsigmond, there's no sense mixing up the two. We're coming because you have business here. And not for my pleasure."

"And because I didn't want you to stay in Budapest," Gordon added. "I don't think you're safe there just now."

"You're worried about me?" asked Krisztina, raising her eyebrows.

"Yes, you."

Krisztina didn't say anything. For a couple of moments she was lost in thought. "What do you figure this is all about?"

Gordon shook his head. "I don't know, Krisztina. I only have a hunch."

"What's that?"

"Something bad. I really hope what happened is not what I think."

"What do you think happened?"

"You don't want to know," Gordon replied.

"But I do want to know. It's you who doesn't want to tell me."

"I can't tell you, because I'm not sure about it yet. I'll tell you everything once I've gotten to the bottom of it."

"And when will that be?"

"I don't know. Maybe a couple of days. This week."

"This week," said Krisztina with a brooding look. "Now that you mention it, I almost forgot. I have to give Penguin an answer this week."

"I know; I haven't forgotten."

"Fine, then."

IT WAS WELL PAST SIX BY THE TIME THEY ARRIVED IN Miskolc, that bustling northern city at the edge of the Bükk range. Lillafüred was not far. Czövek drove with confidence along the windy mountain road that led to the lakeside hotel, as if he'd been here more than once.

Night had fallen. Only sometimes did they see the glimmering lights of a car approaching from the opposite direction or had to swerve to avoid a stray knapsack-equipped tourist trudging along. They stopped at the mountain railway crossing, for the charming little tourist train just happened to be chugging by, children's faces pressed against the glass of the cars as their parents sat wearily beside them. In the distance shone the lights of the Palace Hotel.

Gordon stared in silence at the building bathed in light on the shore of Lake Hámori. Ever since he'd first seen this sumptuous architectural masterpiece back in 1931, he didn't understand just what it was doing here. Even then, of course, he'd come here to work, but he couldn't fail to notice both the storybook beauty of this palace and, indeed, its utterly anachronistic nature. Such palaces were owned by ancient German families; centuries ago, their rooms played host to conversing kings, knights, and princesses. And generations lived and died in the village that stretched out below. Then the kings and princes gave way to modernity, and slowly but surely the palaces were gnawed by time. And then there was this building, which arose here hardly six years earlier, ostensibly with the aim of serving as a hotel. Built in the style of something right out of the Middle Ages, from the era of Hungary's fabled King Matthias. Gordon reflected on all this as he looked up at the imposing structure. The car now made its way alongside Szinva Creek, turning and, finally, coming to a stop in front of the hotel.

A uniformed bellboy opened the car door. Krisztina got out; then Gordon did as well. "Pull off to the side," Gordon called to Czövek, "I'll be back right away." The bellboy gathered up their bags and followed Gordon and Krisztina into the opulent lobby. Men in hunting outfits and tuxedos hurried along to the restaurants in the company of their wives, who wore expensive evening dresses and sagged from the weight of all their jewelry. Gordon headed to the reception desk.

"A reservation under the name Gordon," he announced in a measured tone, "a double room, two nights."

"Yes, sir," said the man, paging through the book before him. "Please be so kind as to follow the bellboy up to the fourth floor."

"My driver needs lodging for the night, too," said Gordon.

"Why of course. Indeed. If you prefer, I can recommend some private homes where he can sleep."

Taking the slip of paper on which the clerk had written the addresses of several local homes, Gordon turned to Krisztina. "If you want, go on upstairs. I'll let Czövek know where he can go; then I'll be right up."

"Hurry," said Krisztina, heading off after the bellboy.

Czövek was sitting on the hood of the car, having a smoke. On seeing Gordon approach, he jumped off.

"Listen, Czövek," said Gordon, "here are some addresses where you can find a bed for the night." Giving him the slip of paper and a five-pengő coin, he added, "And here's the money. This will cover your breakfast, too."

"Thank you."

"Go on ahead, and be back here tomorrow morning at nine."

THE BELLBOY HAD JUST STEPPED OUT OF THE ELEVATOR when Gordon returned to the lobby. Gordon pressed a pengő into his palm and went up to the fourth floor on his own. Upstairs, the elevator doors opened quietly and he stepped out onto the thick, spongy carpet. It was practically daylight in the hallway, so strong were the lamps. Looking at the numbers on the doors, Gordon turned right and, midway down the hall, opened the door to room 304.

A lamp burned on the little table by the balcony. From the bathroom came the sound of gurgling water. Gordon crossed over to the balcony window and pulled aside the curtain, looking out upon the silhouettes of the slender trees clinging to the steep mountainside and the light of the moon sparkling on the surface of the lake.

The bathroom door opened. Krisztina stepped out in a satin nightgown Gordon had given her as a Christmas gift a couple of years ago. Her hair fell freely about her shoulders. The light streaming out of the bathroom filtered through the delicate fabric against her skin.

Gordon flung away his trench coat, took off his blazer, and loosened his tie. Krisztina walked over to the bed and slipped under the blanket. "What are you waiting for?" she asked, looking at Gordon. "Come on over here."

Gordon didn't wait a moment longer.

Eight

It was past eight by the time they awoke. But Gordon had
started up in alarm more than once in the course of the
night: the silence was disconcerting. Every time, though,
he fell back to sleep. Finally, in the morning, he got out of bed
and went to the bathroom. At the cost of several minor cuts,
and in nearly half an hour, he'd managed to shave. He was still
in the bathroom when Krisztina appeared.

"Good morning," she said.

"Good morning."

"Are we in a hurry?"

"Czövek will be waiting for us at nine in front of the entrance," replied Gordon. "If you want to have breakfast, it
wouldn't hurt if we hurried."

By eight-thirty they were already seated in the restaurant.
Krisztina ordered scrambled eggs; Gordon, a coffee. They
watched the hotel come slowly to life with the guests going to
and fro, dressed for the day's activities. Several wore hiking

clothes as they sat at the tables, a few wore hunting outfits, and quite a few of the men were in suits, ready to enjoy the opportunities made available by the hotel, which didn't even require that they step outside. The billiard room and the card salon would quickly fill up with men, while the wives would converse among themselves in the winter garden, listening to music on the radio and gossiping.

The waiter came to their table to offer them a couple of Budapest newspapers. Gordon waved his hand dismissively. "Thanks, but this morning I'm doing fine without them." He turned to Krisztina. "Do you want any?"

"Oh, no. But I do want you to tell me what you want me to ask Teréz Ökrös."

"She should tell you everything she knows about Szőllősy's daughter," said Gordon, raising his eyebrows. He and Krisztina understood each other even without words. "I don't know how much she'll tell you, but no doubt more than she'd tell me. Just chat her up and find out everything she knows."

At a couple of minutes before nine they exited through the hotel's main entrance. Czövek was waiting for them in pretty much the same pose he'd had when Gordon had seen him off the night before: he was chowing down his breakfast while seated on a makeshift tablecloth draped over the Opel's hood. On seeing Gordon and Krisztina, he broke into a grin.

"Take a bite of this," he said, extending toward them a chunk of meat he'd presumably bought from the hog-raising family he'd stayed with. "My God, I don't know when I last had such heavenly head cheese."

"Endre," replied Krisztina with a smile, "if I'd have known, I wouldn't have had breakfast."

"No problem," said Czövek, jumping off the hood, "but the rest is in the car." He opened the door for Gordon and Krisztina, and as soon as they were inside, he got behind the wheel and started the engine. He turned left beside the lake, then began the ascent toward Bükkszentkereszt. Although the Opel handled the incline well, it couldn't go too fast, leaving them time to admire the view. Looming high above them on the left was the giant boulder called the White Stone Lookout, and they could see two figures on top. Czövek was enjoying the drive a great deal, and he handled the massive car exceptionally well. The road was lined with poplars, and they were fortunate not to encounter a single horse-drawn carriage along the way. They made it up to Bükkszentkereszt in under twenty minutes.

The well-ordered beauty of the mountaintop village surprised not only Gordon but also Krisztina. "It's as if we're in the Alps," she said, "that's how lovely it is up here." Smart-looking houses with sparkling clean yards lined the roads; indeed, this might well have been somewhere in the Alps but for the fact that the houses were distinctly Hungarian. Gordon considered the narrow, portholelike windows and low roofs of the longish houses, each of which had a verandah, some stretching right up into the hillside. As the car rolled slowly past the houses, Gordon looked in a couple of windows. His spirits plummeted on glimpsing the low ceilings with their brown-painted rafters. He could not imagine how someone could wake up here day after day, much less for an entire life. No wonder so many people in this country committed suicide, he thought. No, it wasn't "Gloomy Sunday," that popular song considered an anthem for suicides, that drove people to take their own lives, but rather the dark, oppressive homes that weighed down upon them.

"Stop right here," Gordon called to Czövek just as they drove past a woman carrying a milk can—a woman who readily pointed out the house Teréz Ökrös lived in.

They parked in front of the immaculately kept property and got out. Czövek fished a link of sausage out from under the front seat and resumed his breakfast.

Gordon and Krisztina approached the carved wooden gate. All at once, two big, shaggy black dogs—pulis—burst forth from out of nowhere, each, it seemed, barking louder than the other. On hearing the noise, an older man stepped out of the shed and headed toward the gate.

"A fine good day to you, sir!" Krisztina called out. "We're looking for Teréz."

Albeit softly, the man snarled right back at the dogs, whereupon they turned around and sat in front of the verandah.

"Do come in—they don't bite."

Gordon looked at the pulis with suspicion before opening the gate. The stout, walrus-mustached man wiped his hand on his trousers. "You're looking for Teréz?"

"That's right," Krisztina replied with a smile.

"You can look all you want, because she's not here. She went into Miskolc to arrange her servant's license."

"You're her husband?"

"I'm her big brother. And what do you want from her?"

"We want to talk with her about her former employers," Gordon replied.

"Fine by me," said the man with a shrug. "But she'll only be home in the afternoon. Not worth trying before three."

"Then we'll come back around three," said Gordon, taking Krisztina's arm and returning to the car.

"What now?" asked Krisztina.

"I don't know," replied Gordon with evident annoyance. "We'll wait till three."

"Try not to get carried away—I can see how excited you are to escape the city for a bit and see more than three trees at once."

Gordon gave a dismissive wave of his hand and got in the car. Czövek quickly packed up his breakfast and slipped back behind the wheel. "Where to?"

"Back to the hotel." All along the way Gordon stared out the window without a word.

TRAFFIC HAD PICKED UP INSIDE THE HOTEL. ONE LUXURY car after another stopped out front or headed off, taking guests to and fro. Gordon told Czövek to return at two-thirty, then asked at the front desk if a typewriter was available that he could borrow.

"Of course, sir," the clerk replied. "I'll have it sent up to your room along with paper."

"Don't tell me you want to work," said Krisztina in the elevator.

"Not necessarily," Gordon replied. "But it wouldn't hurt for me to type up what I've learned so far."

"And what good would that do?"

"So I see the whole thing on paper. Something in this story is out of place."

"What?"

"I'll tell you in the room," Gordon replied as the elevator stopped on the fourth floor.

In the room Krisztina took from her suitcase her camera, a pair of comfortable shoes, a knit hat, a pair of gloves, and a warmer jacket.

"You knew you'd have time to go for an outing?"

"No, but I figured it couldn't hurt to pack just in case. Aren't you coming with me?"

"No," said Gordon, shaking his head.

There was a knock. Gordon opened the door, took the Remington typewriter from the bellboy, and placed it on the desk by the balcony.

"Before I leave," said Krisztina, turning toward him, "tell me what it is about the story that doesn't click."

Gordon rolled a sheet of paper into the typewriter. "You've got this merchant of Jewish stock whose father converted to Christianity and whose Christian daughter falls in love with the son of a Hassidic rabbi. There's nothing so unusual about this so far, really. Then the girl is found dead at the edge of the red-light district, three months' pregnant. This is a bit unusual, but not all that much, after all. I'm beaten up by this guy with a crooked nose whose name is Pojva, and rumor has it that he's a hired thug. It's not a big leap to suppose he's probably the one who killed the girl, who, however, seems not to have existed at all, given that not even her own family wants to hear about her. I can see that, too. But not that her father had her killed."

"Haven't you heard of this sort of thing?"

"Sure, Krisztina, sure I've heard of it. But not even then does everything click. Something's not in order. I want to type it all down to see if there are any holes in the story. Did something escape my attention?"

"Well then," said Krisztina, "get to work, put your thoughts in order." With that, she hung the camera from her shoulder and shut the door behind her. At first, Gordon tried to use his right hand cautiously, but he was surprised to find that it didn't hurt nearly as much as he'd thought it would. Despite that, he was careful not to overdo it, and by the time Krisztina returned around one, he was using mainly his left hand again.

Krisztina put her camera on the bed as Gordon signaled that he'd be done shortly. On reaching the end of the paragraph, he pulled the sheet of paper from the typewriter and stood up. "Did you see lots of lovely things?" he asked Krisztina.

"Yes," she replied, "but if we don't eat right away, I'll die of hunger, and not even you could want that." Gordon folded the sheets of paper, slipped them into the inside pocket of his blazer, and they went downstairs to the restaurant.

At lunch, Krisztina's eyes sparkled with enthusiasm as she recounted her outing. She'd climbed up through the woods to the White Stone Lookout. The mountainside was so steep that the trail was at least five times as long as it would have been had it been straight, on account of all its zigzagging. "Every part of me hurts," she said with satisfaction. "My legs, my shoulders, my hands."

"At least you're happy about it," Gordon observed. "And did you take pictures?"

"Of course," said Krisztina with a smile. "Two great big deer plus two fawns, as well as some pheasants." She went on to describe the woods, the hunter's lookout towers, the brownish-yellow leaves, and the towering pines.

"So then, did you figure out where the fault is in the story?" she asked after finishing her own account.

"Maybe nowhere," Gordon replied. "Maybe I simply don't want to believe what the facts are telling me."

"You yourself said you can't argue with facts."

"That's right. But I don't have every fact in my possession yet. Let's go visit that woman, then."

THE OPEL PARKED IN FRONT OF THE HOUSE. ON SEEING them arrive, the mustachioed man, who was again out in the yard, opened the house door and gave a shout inside. A couple of moments later a plump woman came out. Determining her age was all but impossible. She could just as well have been thirty as fifty. But when she spoke, it was evident from her voice that she was somewhere between the two.

"Do come in," she said, "come in." The pulis locked their eyes on Gordon and Krisztina as they walked into the kitchen. Two children around ten years old were sitting at the table. Teréz told them to leave, then pulled two more chairs out for her guests. "Please sit down. We can't go into the sitting room: my mother is sick."

"I hope it's not serious," said Krisztina.

"Past eighty everything is serious," replied Teréz.

"We heard you make beautiful embroideries," said Krisztina, looking at the table, which was draped with a dazzling tablecloth.

"Oh, not really," said the woman, blushing.

"Show me a few," said Krisztina. Teréz went into the room as Gordon stood up restlessly and went to the door. Suspiciously he took stock of the country stove, the low ceiling, the carved chairs. A couple of minutes later Teréz reappeared with a small armful of embroidered tablecloths, runners, and pillowcases. She set them down on the table in front of Krisztina, who reached inside her purse and rummaged about for quite a while. Finally, Krisztina looked up at Gordon. "Zsigmond, I'm out of cigarettes. Would you get me a pack?"

"Sure," he replied, now turning to Teréz. "Say, where can I get cigarettes around here?"

"Oh dear, the closest place is Lillafüred. For proper cigarettes, I mean—the sort you folks smoke. Around here we only have shag tobacco."

"It'll take at least an hour there and back," said Gordon. "Can you do without cigarettes that long?"

"Go right ahead. I'll make do."

Gordon left the house, gave a nod to the man working at the far end of the yard, and went over to the Opel. "Take me back to the hotel, Czövek," he said.

In the hotel Gordon bought a pack of cigarettes. He then went to the café, gathered up the newspapers on hand, ordered a coffee, and sat down to read.

THEY COULDN'T HAVE BETTER TIMED THE TRIP BACK. Barely had the Opel parked once more in front of the house than Krisztina opened the door onto the verandah, a table-cloth and a pillowcase in her hand. She said good-bye to the woman, waved a hand to the man, and joined Gordon in the car. Czövek turned his head. "Where to?"

"Back to the hotel," said Gordon. But Krisztina put her hand on his arm. "No, let's not go there. I'm not in the mood for all those people. Go ahead and start up the car; we can stop somewhere along the way."

"May I suggest something?" asked Czövek.

"Please do," replied Gordon.

"At the house where I stayed, the widow Mrs. Károly Glum—which happens to be a name that fits her well—said there's this roadside diner up in the woods not far from the White Stone Lookout. It's more of a hunting lodge, she said, but she swore up and down that there's no better food around here. It's in the middle of the forest."

"Go ahead," said Gordon.

Czövek shifted the car into gear and headed to the far end of the village. Gordon glanced at Krisztina, who seemed lost in thought as she caressed the embroidered tablecloth. At such times, he knew, he must not say a word to her but, instead, wait for her to speak on her own. There was a time when Gordon had tried again and again to get information out of her before she was ready, but he'd gotten nowhere, and so now he let her be. Once they'd passed the last house in the village, Gordon caught a glimpse of a wooden sign whose letters had long ago been washed away by snow and rain. Since the languid October day had already turned toward dusk, Czövek turned on the headlights and pulled over to the side. Having edged his seat forward and pushed his hat farther back on his forehead, he turned around. "Widow Glum said the road is bumpy. So hold on."

Slowly he proceeded on this roadless road, which was in fact nothing more than a wide muddy trail cut by carriage wheels and pockmarked by horseshoes. Trees towered all around them toward the sky as the Opel huffed and puffed along. For a while they went on in utter silence. Czövek's every nerve was focused on the road ahead: on avoiding puddles and potholes and branches. All at once they arrived in a clearing.

"Widow Glum put one over on you," Gordon remarked. "There's no hunting lodge around here. Or else you turned up the wrong road."

"Of course not," declared Czövek.

"But we're in the middle of nowhere."

"Well, then, it's just another couple hundred meters," replied the driver as they rolled slowly on. On reaching a fork in the road, he turned right. Dusk had meanwhile turned to darkness. The trees leaned in tightly above them and forest brush scraped against the car.

Gordon turned toward Krisztina but could not see her face. Czövek simultaneously struggled with the steering wheel, the brakes, the clutch, and the gear stick. The heavy Opel slid to

and fro in the mud, and it took two tries to get up one particularly big incline. Finally, they reached the top, where a light
glimmered in the distance.

"You see," Czövek called out triumphantly, "I told you
so!" He had indeed. As they slowly approached, they saw
that the light—that of a flaming torch—in fact belonged to a
not-so-small hunting lodge, nestled in a clearing on a moder-
ately steep hillside. Smoke curled skyward from its chimney;
two sinewy, short-haired, cinnamon-hued hunting dogs—
vizslas—were loafing by the entrance; and out back stood a
huge clay oven with an open door.

As they stopped beside the barn, they could hear horses
stomping about nervously inside. The door of the hunting
lodge now opened, and out came a stout, spectacled man with
short-cropped hair. With his hands on his hips, he struck a
most welcoming pose.

"So, what do you say?" asked Czövek.

"Not bad so far," replied Krisztina.

Gordon got out and walked over to the man.

"Good evening. We heard you have good food here."

Almost imperceptibly the man's head started twitching, and
he took a deep breath. "G-g-good evening. The k-k-kitchen
won't open for another hour." He stuttered, and since he did
everything he could to avoid doing so, his speech was all the
more disjointed. It was evident that he sometimes struggled
mightily with a particular vowel, but at the same time it was
likewise clear that he couldn't care in the least. "My n-n-name
is István Bá-Bá-Bársony," he said, extending a hand and offer-
ing a genial smile. "Please c-c-come in."

The door, which he now opened wide, was a portal to the vivid scene depicted in the prewar painting hanging just inside. To the right, a fireplace poured out heat; in front of it lay another vizsla, and a cat was sleeping on the mantel. A bit farther out from the fireplace were four tables with chairs, and beside the wall was a divan flanked by a stout oak table. The walls, meanwhile, were covered by the trophies indispensable in such a venue, with candle holders placed between them. A door in the back led to the kitchen. Out popped the head of a young woman with braids. Having counted the guests, she shut the door. István Bársony now sat them down at one of the four tables close to the fireplace. "I have good grr-grr-grape-skin brandy. Would you l-l-like some?"

"We would," replied Krisztina, who then stood up and moved closer to the fireplace. She turned her back to the fire to warm up. Bársony lit the candle on their table, gave them the menus, and went to the kitchen. Czövek just sat there looking perplexed; he was not used to sitting at one table with his pas-sengers. Gordon had just taken a cigarette from his case when Bársony appeared with a tray that held four shot glasses. "Please d-d-do come," he called to Krisztina. "If you d-d-drink this, you won't be c-c-cold. You can be sure of that."

Krisztina stepped over and picked up one of the shots. Gordon and Czövek now followed her lead, and the three downed the brandy. Gordon shuddered and asked for a glass of water. Meanwhile, he handed Krisztina a menu. "What will you have?"

Krisztina quickly scanned the one-page menu, which in-cluded no soup, no dessert, no seafood, and no vegetables to speak of—wild game and not a thing more. "I'll have the roast venison with potato dumplings."

Gordon drank his glass of water, then gave Bársony their order. He was having flank of wild boar with fried salted potatoes, and Czövek, though at first reluctant to order in front of his passengers, finally settled on the relatively humble bean stew with wild boar.

"Wonderful, simply w-w-wonderful," said Bársony with a grin that stretched from ear to ear. "The most ex-exceptional choices. I couldn't have made beh-beh-better recommendations. Everything will be reh-reh-ready in an hour. If you l-l-like, I can pull the chairs over to the fire me-me-meanwhile."

"That's okay," said Krisztina with a wave of the hand. "We're going for a walk, and we'll warm up afterward."

"Just be ca-ca-careful," said Bársony. "You can see the lodge from a di-di-distance, but don't go too far." Pointing, he added, "If you go that way, you'll end up at the Wh-Wh-White Stone Lookout. It's a well-tro-tro-trodden trail, impossible to miss. If you're not b-b-back in an hour, I'll go after you with the dogs."

THE TRAIL WAS LIT UP FOR A WHILE BY THE LIGHT FROM the lodge. Krisztina took Gordon's arm, and slowly they walked ahead. They were in no hurry; there was nowhere to go and no reason to do so. Krisztina began recounting the story she'd heard from Teréz Ökrös. Incredulity lurked in her voice throughout, as if she didn't understand a single word, even though she knew it was so.

"Fanny was a polite, lovely, lively little girl. She was born in the first year of the World War, which is when her father started traveling frequently to Africa. Maybe not by chance, at least that's how Teréz sees it. He wanted a son by all means, but his wife had such a difficult delivery that the doctors said they couldn't have any more children. Szőllősy bore a grudge against both his wife and daughter. Not that he let them know exactly, but he did grow cold toward them; and while perhaps he needn't have traveled so much, there was no more simple and obvious reason to be away from his family. The girl adored not only her mother but also Teréz, who raised her— she was her wet nurse, after all. Teréz entered service with the Szőllősys after giving birth to a son at the age of eighteen. Fanny studied diligently under the tutelage of young English ladies. Never did she suffer for want of anything. She feared only her own father's cold, standoffish demeanor. She attended church regularly with her mother, and everything else was in order with her." Krisztina stopped by a fallen tree and sat down on it before resuming. "Her father decided where she would continue her studies. He sent her to the technical university in Berlin. But Fanny, who wanted to be an artist, came home and confronted her father. If he would let her go to Paris, to the Sorbonne, she would study whatever he wanted her to afterward. Business, accounting, anything at all—but what she wanted to do now was to paint. Szőllősy fell into a violent rage but eventually, under pressure from his wife, gave in.

"For three years Fanny studied painting in Paris, coming home only in the summers and for Christmas. But this spring, in the middle of the academic semester, she suddenly showed up at home, confronted her father once again, and told him she was getting married. There were no secrets Teréz didn't know about. What she didn't hear during the regular bouts of shouting between father and daughter, Fanny filled her in on."

Krisztina paused, and Gordon waited silently for more. "It turned out that while in Paris, Fanny had met the son of a Budapest Hassidic rabbi. They fell in love, but to marry him she had to convert to Judaism. Szőllősy said it was out of the question. What if his German partners found out? Word would get out that he, too, was Jewish, and then he could say goodbye to doing business in Germany. Besides, being Jewish even in Hungary wasn't exactly good luck. He'd give her hand in marriage to a Protestant before he ever would a Jew. Fanny said she didn't give a damn about the Germans and didn't give a damn about business—she wanted to marry Shlomo and marry him she would. At that, her father asked: Didn't she see what was going on here? What was going on in Nuremberg? If word got out about their ancestry, they'd be done for. And if Fanny converted to Judaism, word would surely get out. Fanny repeated that she didn't give a damn, that she would marry the boy. She'd convert. If you see him one more time, her father told her, you are no longer my daughter. Teréz didn't hear the rest—she was so scared that she went downstairs to clean the cellar."

Krisztina shook her head before continuing. "A half hour later Teréz was just coming up out of the cellar when she happened to notice Fanny with a suitcase in her hand. She looked at Teréz, who saw amid the tears in Fanny's eyes a determination she'd never seen there before. From that day on, Szőllősy's wife hadn't said a word to her husband. A couple days later, Szőllősy had Fanny's belongings and her furniture packed away; he had the room painted over and a piano put inside; and he became more gruff than ever before." Krisztina fell silent.

"What happened then?" asked Gordon.

"Not much," she replied. "Teréz figures Szőllősy's wife met with her daughter several times, but she doesn't know for sure. The woman never did speak in confidence with Teréz, who nonetheless suspects that she must have met with Fanny. On more than one occasion she suddenly got dressed and went out the door, though before, she'd always told Teréz where she was headed. Now she spoke only in general terms—she was off to the coffeehouse, to go shopping, to an exhibit. And on getting home, Szőllősy's wife would sit about for a long time in the living room, drinking wine—sometimes a whole bottle—and staring straight ahead while puffing a cigarette, even though she'd quit back in 1925."

"And why did Teréz have to leave?"

"Two weeks ago, Szőllősy summoned her, gave her two weeks' pay—this, after serving the family for more than twenty years—and sent her packing immediately. Teréz came straight home, and since that day she hasn't heard a thing about either Fanny or the Szőllősys."

"That's all she said?"

"That's it."

"I understand."

"Well, I don't understand, Zsigmond!" said Krisztina, springing up off the log. "You're always saying 'I understand, I understand.' What the hell do you understand about all this?

Because I don't understand a thing. Not a thing in the whole damn world!"

With that, Krisztina headed toward the lookout. Gordon stood up and hurried after her. Putting his arm around her, he turned her toward the hunting lodge. "It's too dark out. It'll be better back there where it's warm. You wouldn't see anything from the lookout, anyway."

Krisztina let Gordon lead her back. She slipped her arm through his, and thus they made their way back to the lights of the lodge.

Back inside, the smell of supper struck Krisztina's nose. She shuddered. "Do you have an appetite?"

"I do," replied Gordon. "You'll have one, too, you'll see. We'll sit down here by the fireplace, order a bottle of wine, have a nice quiet supper, and then we can talk back at the hotel, if you want."

Bársony peered out from the kitchen and reappeared a couple of minutes later with the tray. "A li-li-little something to f-f-fire up the a-a-appetite before supper," he said, placing another round of shot glasses on the table. Gordon took only a taste, but Krisztina gulped down the grape-skin brandy at once. "Bring a bottle of red wine, too, if you have one," she said, looking at the hunter. Bársony nodded and went back to the kitchen. Gordon helped Krisztina slip off her coat, then pulled out a chair for her. Czövek sat at the corner table, watching them in silence, a cigarette in his mouth. Gordon cast him a look that made it clear he was not to disturb them just now.

Bársony placed the venison roast and potato dumplings on the table in front of Krisztina, along with a little dish of blueberry jam. Gordon got a majolica plate containing the flank of wild boar and the fried salted potatoes. And, finally, Czövek received his bowl of bean soup with wild boar. Bársony must have sensed something, too; instead of returning to the kitchen, he sat down at an adjacent table and got to talking with them. At first, Gordon was angry at the intrusion, but then he realized that Krisztina was distinctly enjoying the hunter's vivid stories, which were laced with biting wit. As for the wine, it stirred Krisztina's appetite into action: she devoured the venison as if she were seeing food for the first time in days. Gordon was listening to Bársony with gratitude; and Krisztina was not only eating but drinking, too. By the time they'd finished, only a cupful of wine splashed about at the bottom of the bottle. Krisztina's eyes kept closing. Gordon asked for the bill and he paid. Bársony accompanied them out to the car.

"I'm g-g-glad you were here," he said with a smile. "C-c-come again."

Czövek started off, and they hadn't even turned back out onto the road in front of the hunting lodge when Krisztina's head slumped onto Gordon's shoulder.

WHEN THEY ARRIVED BACK AT THE HOTEL, KRISZTINA woke with a start. "Are we here?"

"We are," replied Gordon, helping her out of the car. He then signaled to Czövek that he shouldn't go anywhere just yet. On reaching the room, Krisztina sat on the edge of the bed and tried but failed to get undressed. Gordon helped her, then tucked her in. A couple of minutes later, Krisztina was fast asleep.

Gordon sat down at the desk, found a sheet of hotel stationery, and, after several attempts, finally found the position he needed to properly hold the pen. He leaned over the sheet of paper and began to write slowly:

Krisztina, I've returned to Budapest. I didn't want to wake you up. I hope you slept well. By the time you get back tomorrow with Czövek, I'll know a lot more. But I couldn't stay here with you now. I know you're disappointed and mad, too, but I still ask that you not be angrier than necessary. I don't want trouble to come your way. I hope I'm wrong, but I think these people are capable of anything. I have to act fast to head them off. I'll leave the car here for you. By no means should you head back before lunch. Go to Mór, not home. I'll explain everything.

He put the letter on the nightstand, then took his suitcase and went quietly out the door.

At the reception desk he asked when the last train from nearby Miskolc left for Budapest. The man glanced at his watch.

"At eight, but I doubt you'll reach it, sir."

"I'll give it a try," said Gordon. "Tally up my bill. The woman will check out tomorrow. Add breakfast and lunch, too, and throw in another ten pengős."

A couple of moments later the man slid the bill across the counter. Gordon didn't even wince on seeing the sum. He filled out a check for fifty pengős, slid it back to the man, and hurried out to Czövek.

"Giddyup, Czövek, we've got to make the eight o'clock train."

"And the little lady?"

"You'll take her to Budapest tomorrow."

Czövek jumped in the car, cracked his fingers, shifted into gear, and after careening along downhill into Miskolc at breakneck speed, he screeched the Opel to a halt in front of the station at two minutes before eight.

"Here are fifty pengős. Will that be enough for the two days?" said Gordon, extending three banknotes—two twenties and a ten—to Czövek.

"Yes, sir," said Czövek. "Plenty."

"Don't head off tomorrow before two, and take the lady to the Circle."

"Hitler Square, you mean?"

"That's what I mean," said Gordon, taking his suitcase and hurrying into the station. The conductor was already blowing his whistle when Gordon boarded the train. He sat down in an empty compartment and pulled his hat over his eyes. The conductor woke him up in Gyöngyös. Gordon paid for the ticket, stared out at the black landscape all the way into Budapest, and pondered where he would begin Wednesday and where it would all end.

In front of the East Railway Station, Gordon waved down

a cab and asked to be taken home. It was well past midnight when he opened the door of his flat on Lovag Street. He threw aside his suitcase and blazer, soaked a rag with cold water, and rebandaged his right hand. Still in his clothes, Gordon lay down on his bed.

Nine

ordon woke up early. Standing in front of the bathroom mirror, he saw that the wounds on his mouth and his forehead were healing nicely indeed. But since he looked at least ten years older on account of his stubble, he got out his razor and whipped up some cream. He tried shaving with his right hand. It worked, even if it wasn't a rousing success. He'd cut himself in several places and had torn up a few scabs, but a block of alum solved this problem, too.

He got dressed, checked that he had everything he needed, and then headed toward the Grand Boulevard. At the corner of Szondi Street, he entered the stencil shop, and after a bit of persuasion he convinced the man that, no, he didn't need a hundred copies of his couple of pages of notes but that five would be enough. They settled on a price of twenty fillérs, which was nearly five times the usual rate. Then Gordon walked to the Abbázia. The headwaiter greeted him warmly and apologized for the fact that Gordon's usual table was occupied. Gordon gave a little wave of the hand and ordered breakfast at another table. Skimming the papers, he saw he hadn't missed a thing. Citing his health, Béla Ivády had resigned as president of the National Unity Party. Meanwhile Darányi had wasted no time in submitting to Parliament the proposals accepted at the first cabinet meeting. Great, thought Gordon, taking a gulp of coffee. Ivády could resign all he wanted, but doing so was pointless; for the party wouldn't find a suitable replacement. After all, any leadership role for Béla Márton, the party's combative secretary-general, who was causing enough trouble as it was, was out of the question. Gordon read on. The usual internal struggles. Ivády, he concluded, was the least of all evils. Gordon turned the page. Miklós Kozma expressed his hope that the ban on public gatherings could soon be lifted. Gordon closed the paper, downed the remaining coffee, and headed off toward Berlin Square. Along the way, he picked up his stenciled notes. On the square he boarded Tram No. 5 and opened *8 O'Clock News*.

DR. PAZÁR HAD ARRIVED AT THE INSTITUTE OF FOREN-sic Medicine not long before. Gordon found him in his office. His secretary was still announcing Gordon's arrival as he followed her into the room. With evident annoyance, Pazár continued arranging the papers on his desk. In the ashtray was a lit cigarette.

"I'm sorry, Gordon," he said, looking up, "but I've got a million things to do. There's been restructuring in the ministry; I can't even tell my head from my toes just now."

"I don't want to hold you up," said Gordon. "The only thing I ask for is a copy of the autopsy report."

"The *only* thing?" said Pazár, jerking up his head. "It was quite enough that I showed you, and I shouldn't even have done that."

"I know, and I appreciate it. But I still need a copy of the report."

"And I need a house on Lake Balaton. I can't give it to you."

"All right, then I'll borrow it."

"You know full well we're not a lending library. Or did the sign out front say, 'Institute and Library of Forensic Medicine'? If that's what you saw, of course we'll get you a copy right away."

Gordon didn't reply.

"What do you need it for?" Pazár finally asked.

"Let's just say it's for personal use. I'm not planning to write about it, but if I do, I'd let you know."

"Personal use? You've started collecting autopsy reports? Who's kidding whom?"

"No kidding," replied Gordon, "really. But maybe I know what happened to that girl, and maybe I'd like to do something about it."

"Do?" said Pazár, looking up for a moment. "So you want to do something, do you? Well, I can't do a thing myself, but if you go downstairs right now to the autopsy room, you won't find anyone there. I'm the one who should be there, but instead I'm here, having a completely pointless argument with you, and I've even left the filing cabinet open."

"Then I won't disturb you any longer," said Gordon, opening the door.

"Mici!" shouted Pazár. "Call up the ministry at once and find someone I can speak with."

Gordon went down the stairs to the cellar, ran over to the white-painted metal filing cabinet, and after a couple of minutes of searching he found the two-page report and its copies. He took one copy, slipped it into the inside pocket of his blazer, and in minutes he was sitting on the tram. He studied the document thoroughly until reaching Crown Prince Rudolf Square.

The apartment building door was open. Gordon walked upstairs to the fourth floor and stopped in front of the familiar door. He knocked. Harder. And harder. Finally, he was pounding. He was raising his fist once more when he heard stirring from within. He stepped back. The little hinged window in the door opened first, then the door itself. Red Margo stood there, her eyes squinting and fixed on Gordon; the apartment behind her was pitch-black. Her hand shot upward to cover her face, then she spoke in a hoarse voice:

"What's it you want?"

"I want to talk about Fanny," said Gordon.

"Come back in an hour. I have to get myself together. Who's this Fanny?"

"We've got to talk now."

"The hell we do," said Margo, moving to close the door. But Gordon promptly slid his foot between the door and the doorjamb.

"Believe me, Margo, you want to let me in."

The woman stared down at Gordon's foot, then looked up at his face. Finally, she released her grip on the door and went back into the dark apartment. Gordon followed her.

"You don't even have to talk if you don't want to," he said to the woman's back.

"I know," replied Margo, "I'll just lie on my back and will hardly feel a thing. You'll take care of everything and I won't even have to move."

Red Margo reached for the curtain and pulled it open just a crack. She removed a blanket from the floor lamp she'd evidently flung on it in haste. Gordon saw that the room was just as much of a mess as it had been during his last visit. Cups and cigarette butts littered the coffee table, which had been pushed to the side, and the two armchairs were strewn with clothes. Gordon pushed aside the clothes on one chair and sat down. Margo sat down in the armchair opposite him. She looked disheveled, her eyes were baggy, and she'd hastily flung on her robe. When she leaned forward, it parted slightly. She picked up a half-smoked cigarette from the table, then reached for the box of matches. But the box was empty, and she angrily flung it back on the table. Gordon reached into his pocket, produced his lighter, and held out the flame. Margo leaned forward. She wore nothing underneath the robe. She took a drag and looked up at Gordon, who held the lighter for just a second longer than necessary. Having inhaled the smoke, Margo leaned back in the armchair and pulled the nightgown tight over her legs while not quite doing so over her breasts. She smiled from behind the smoke as she watched Gordon, who had meanwhile also lit a cigarette.

"Do you want a drink?" asked Red Margo, running a hand through her hair.

"Too early in the day for me."

"But you could use one," said Margo. "I see someone gave you a good thrashing."

"A good one."

Margo stared through narrowed eyes at Gordon, who held her gaze for a while before finally looking away. "You know," she said, "that cut really looks good on your face." Gordon leaned back in his armchair. "Going through the wringer just makes a face more attractive," she continued, sliding slowly to the edge of the armchair. The movement made her nightgown once again open up, and her left breast peeked halfway out from beneath the fabric. Gordon looked at the woman and the desire that had arisen in her eyes, and he could only sense what this was about.

"More attractive?" he asked.

"That's right," she languidly replied, coyly drawing her nightgown tight as she slowly stood up. With soft, lazy steps, she went over to Gordon and stood behind him. She put her hands on the back of his armchair, leaned forward, and now slid her hands onto his chest. "Why don't . . ." she began, slipping her left hand under his shirt. "Why don't you follow me to the bedroom?" she whispered in his ear. "You won't be sorry." With that, she straightened up and started off toward the bedroom. Gordon adjusted his shirt and turned around. Red Margo stood on the threshold of her bedroom, her back to Gordon. With a well-practiced motion, she opened her robe and drew each side up to her shoulders, and throwing back her hands, she let the robe slip right off her. Gordon stood, and looked at the woman's round ass, her thighs, her shapely shoulders. Margo turned around and leaned against the door-jamb. Her breasts slackened, in a womanly way, but her nipples stood erect. She stood there only for a couple of seconds before suddenly turning back around and vanishing into the room. Gordon heard only the creaking of the bedsprings. He went over to the little table by the window, poured gin into two glasses that looked to be in acceptable shape, and went toward the bedroom.

Margo was leaning on her side, waiting for Gordon. Her hip formed a little hill and her waist a deep vale under the sheet, whose folds only enhanced the bulging breasts underneath. Gordon stopped above her and held out the glass. The woman took the glass, sat up, and downed the gin. The sheet slipped off her. Gordon looked into his own glass and he, too, drank up. The alcohol burned his gullet and then his stomach, and finally it spread out through his veins. His nostrils were filled with the smell of the gin and the heavy stifling scent of the woman, both of which blended with the odor of cigarettes towering in the ashtrays throughout the flat. Margo slid over beside him. She reached up to his tie with one hand while her other hand brushed against his loins. "Come on," she whispered.

"We can't," replied Gordon in a hoarse voice. "Not now."

"How do you know we'll have another chance?"

"That's not up to me."

"Of course it is," said Margo, stretching out on the bed. "It's only up to you." Turning over to her left side, she took a cigarette from the nightstand. She lit it, took a drag, and blew out the smoke. "Only you," she repeated, then turned around. The cigarette hung from the left corner of her mouth, from which a thin band of smoke curled upward. Gordon gave the woman a once-over.

"I came here now so we can talk."

"Then talk," said Red Margo, removing the cigarette from her mouth.

"Come, I'll pour us another drink," replied Gordon, who then left the room. He filled the two glasses once again, and by the time he placed them on the table, Margo was already sitting in the armchair, clutching the nightgown tight just below her neck.

"Go ahead, just tell me what you want," she asked, picking up her glass off the table.

"What do I want?" asked Gordon, fixing his eyes on Red Margo. "Two things. First of all, I want to know who murdered Fanny. Second, why you didn't tell me everything you know."

"You want a lot," she said, exhaling smoke.

"I suspect it's not news to you that men want a lot."

"Oh dear!" she exclaimed, drawing in her breath as she did so and then breaking into a smile and pulling her feet under the chair. "That hurt."

"You know everything. Everything. And still you didn't tell me a thing. You stuck a letter into my hand and then let me toil away."

The woman searched Gordon's face, and gradually the playfulness vanished from her own expression. "Because you would have believed what a drunk whore tells you about an influential merchant—a Valiant Knight, a company owner held in public esteem? Fat chance."

"I would have," replied Gordon.

"Pity, pity," Red Margo chirped, shaking her head and giving a dismissive wave of the hand. "Let me ask you something."

"Go ahead."

"Now that you suspect what happened, what do you want to do about it? Leave it be?"

Gordon shook his head. "No."

"What do you want, then?"

"Let that be my secret."

"What a mysterious character you are," said Margo, pursing her lips. "You think it was so easy for me to digest what happened to Fanny? You think I didn't want to take revenge?" The last glimmer of lasciviousness now vanished from her eyes. Her expression was cold, but Gordon thought he saw in it a trace of fear.

"I don't want to take revenge," said Gordon, shaking his head.

"Sure you do. Otherwise, why would you be here? You came here because you're thirsting for revenge—either because the girl was killed or because you were beaten up. I don't know which, and I don't really care. Or are you angry only because they threatened your girlfriend? Krisztina is her name, right?"

Gordon didn't reply. He didn't ask her how she knew; he just sat there, motionless, watching the woman.

"In your shoes I'd be angry, too," Margo continued. "Infernally at that. You have every reason for revenge—whether because someone died who didn't deserve to, because they punched a hole right into your self-respect, or because you're worried for your girl."

"So the reason you didn't say anything is because you were afraid I'd fly into a rage," said Gordon.

"That's right," said Margo. "Don't go telling me your pride and your sense of justice haven't been wounded."

"Let's just drop it," said Gordon with a wave of his hand. "Tell me about them instead."

"Fanny . . ." But Margo here fell silent, incredulously shaking her head. Gordon saw with satisfaction that she had taken the bait. "What people are you talking about? What do you want to know about Fanny's family?"

"I didn't say a thing about her family," said Gordon. "I know almost everything about them. But it seems there's one thing you don't know. You see, Fanny was . . ." Now it was Gordon who fell silent.

"Pregnant!" Margo shouted. "Why didn't you tell me that before, you rotten scoundrel?" She sat up angrily in the armchair.

"Because I didn't think it necessary."

"And now you do?"

"And now I do," said Gordon, leaning forward. "Help me, Margo. Just help me a little."

"So you want to do something, after all? Catch the mur-

derer and drag him off to the police? Not even you can seriously be thinking that."

"Enough of this already!" snapped Gordon. Margo gave
him a surprised look. "The other day you tossed me a scrap of
information that allowed me to figure everything out. Practically everything. And now I'm here again. I didn't go to the
police with what I know, but to you, Margo."

"I see," replied Red Margo. "But why?"

"I came here because I'm interested in what happened to
Fanny. Because it doesn't leave me cold. Trust me, Margo. I
don't want anything more than to know what you know, too."

"There's just no satisfying you," said Red Margo.

"You're off on that point, but I don't want to prove you
wrong."

Margo stood up, went to the table, poured herself another
gin, and turned to the window. For a while she just looked down
at the street, but finally she downed the gin and adjusted her
robe, drawing it tight even at the neck, and sat back down in
the armchair. "Go ahead—ask away." Again her eyes sparkled
with fear.

"I know why Fanny's father disowned her. I also know how
she wound up with you, by way of Csuli. And that her love,
Shlomo, is now in New York. But I don't know what Fanny was
after."

"I do," replied Margo. "To put aside enough money to
follow the boy. Even her mother gave her funds."

"All I knew was that they met," said Gordon. "So she gave
her money, too?"

"You think a mother is capable of tearing her child out of

her heart just because that's what her husband says?" asked Margo with contempt.

Not wanting to ratchet up her temper, Gordon didn't say a thing.

"One time they met up by chance on Rákóczi Street. Fanny worked at night, you see, and she counted on everything—except that she'd meet up with her mother."

"When did that happen?"

"About a month ago. But Fanny didn't tell her mother what she was up to. How she was making money. If you can call it money, those couple of wretched pengős the pimp left her every night. All she told her mother is that she was working; she didn't say anything more. And right then and there her mother gave her two hundred pengős."

"Did they meet again?"

"Yes. Twice. The second time the mother gave her four hundred pengős; and then even more, almost six hundred."

"That would have been plenty for a train ticket to Hamburg," said Gordon, "and from there for a ship to New York."

"That's true, but Fanny didn't want to arrive with an empty pocket. She knew that the rabbi hadn't given his son any money, that he'd put him in the care of relatives and forbade them from giving the boy a cent. Fanny wanted her and Shlomo to start a new life without the two of them being penniless. But the third meeting with her mother turned out badly."

"What happened?"

"After their first meeting, the mother hired a private detective to figure out where Fanny was working. The man somehow got his hands on that picture Skublics took. The mother showed it to Fanny and demanded an explanation. When Fanny saw the picture, she ran away."

"When did that happen?"

"Last Sunday."

"On the fourth."

Red Margo nodded.

"And?" asked Gordon.

"And? I saw Fanny for the last time on Tuesday morning. Last Tuesday. On Wednesday I heard that a dead girl had been found on Nagy Diófa Street. When I found out what she had on, I knew right away it was her. On Saturday morning you came by, pounding at my door. And asking questions."

"I don't know what you're getting at."

"I didn't even know who you were," said Red Margo. "For all I knew, you were from the secret police or were a private eye. Look at me. Go ahead, just look at me." Gordon tried, but she averted her eyes. "Do I look that stupid? Like I'd tell everything to just any old bum who comes knocking? So the same thing would happen to me that happened to Fanny?"

"I'm neither a secret policeman nor a private eye," said Gordon.

"Now I know."

"And what happened to Fanny's money?"

"You know," she said, "I always did tell her not to keep it on her. Because that could spell trouble. You know what she replied?" Gordon shook his head. "That she might decide at any moment to buy the ticket to New York. She wanted to leave on October 28 on the *President Harding*. And she didn't trust anyone, not even me. Maybe she was right." Red Margo stared straight ahead.

"I understand," said Gordon.

"You think the mother . . ." said Margo, raising her eyes.

"No," said Gordon, shaking his head. "I hope not. I met her a couple days ago. I don't think it would have been her."

"Then what will you do now?" asked Margo.

"Sure you want to know?"

The woman didn't answer. She rose from the chair, poured herself another gin, and found a box of matches among the glasses. She lit a cigarette and replied, "You're right," turning away. "I don't need to know."

"There's one thing I don't understand," said Gordon. "Why did you open up to me at all when I first came knocking?"

Red Margo said nothing at first. She returned to the armchair, leaned back, and adjusted her hair. She crossed her legs, then looked at Gordon from under her long eyelashes. "Isn't it obvious enough?"

"Maybe," said Gordon, holding her gaze.

"What's wrong with that?" she asked, and amid a smile she pursed her lips. "You don't believe me."

"I believe you," he said, "and there's nothing wrong with that. Nothing." He cleared his throat. Gordon looked at the clothing strewn about the place: leftovers of a recent liaison. He stole a glance at the unmade bed that seemed to sprawl out in the other room, and at the thin streak of sunlight that shone upon it. Margo followed his gaze. Gordon now looked at the woman stretched out in the armchair opposite him—at her nightgown, her full round bosom, her slender ankles, her succulent lower lip. "Nothing in the whole damn world," he added, all at once catching Margo's gaze. He now saw clearly the fear in her eyes.

"Are you that scared?" he finally asked.

Margo did not reply.

"Don't tell me you realized only now what sort of people your customers are and what they're capable of."

Almost imperceptibly the woman winced.

"How long have you been doing this?"

"Too long," replied Red Margo.

Gordon rose from the armchair. "I'm off." But he only stood there, staring at Margo. "That there," he said, gesturing with his head toward the bedroom, "would have been only a reward for me doing the dirty work instead of you, huh?" The woman didn't answer. "I know you're afraid of them. And you're right to be."

"What do you think I should have done?" she asked.

"Everyone does what they know best," said Gordon.

"What are you getting smart with me for?" Looking down, she added, "You don't understand a damn thing."

"You're right," said Gordon. "I don't understand a damn thing."

"You said you're going. So go."

Gordon was already at the door when she called after him: "Wait."

He turned and looked at the woman. The sun lit her face from behind, and he couldn't see her eyes. "Nothing," Red Margo said softly before turning back to the window.

GORDON JUST CAUGHT A TRAM ON CROWN PRINCE RU-dolf Square and got to the Abbázia in fifteen minutes. This time the waiter led him to his regular table, where he took Gordon's order—a coffee and a brioche. On appearing with the tray, the man also handed him a sheet of paper.

"A note left here for you, Mr. Editor," said the waiter, and left. The message was from Jenő Strausz, who had tried telephoning Gordon at nine-thirty to say he'd be at the Ironworks Sport Club in the afternoon. Gordon put away the paper and looked up at the clock on the wall. Almost noon. He pored over the papers and drank his coffee but left the brioche untouched. He then paid and left.

DESPITE THE NIPPY AUTUMN WEATHER, MÓR'S BALCONY door was open. Gordon shook his head with irritation and went upstairs to his grandfather. He knocked. No answer. He sighed. The old man must have nodded off by the stove. Gordon knocked once more, this time with more force, at which the door began to open with a creak. On its own. His stomach was in knots. Slowly he opened the door all the way, then stepped inside. Through the dark vestibule he headed toward the kitchen. He heard no noise and smelled no smoke, but this made him all the more uneasy. Gordon was just passing the bedroom when the door suddenly opened. He spun around and there saw Mór, holding a kettle of respectable size above his head with an iron grip.

"Hey, Opa, what are you doing?" he asked with great relief.

"I must have forgotten to lock the door," said the old man, lowering the kettle. "A bunch of fresh chestnuts just arrived at the market from the hills, so I went out, bought a couple of kilos, and told myself I'd get started on the cooking right away. I went into the kitchen but forgot to lock the door on my way into the flat. Then you knocked, and . . ."

"I understand, Opa."

"No matter who it was, with that kettle I would have let them have it," said Mór.

"Without a doubt."

They went to the kitchen. "I need your help, Opa."

"No, son," said Mór, shaking his head.

"No?"

"I'm not doing a thing until you tell me what you found out. I need to know why you wound up in danger and so did Krisztina." He sat down at the table and waited.

Gordon pulled out a chair, sat down opposite his grandfather, and told him the whole story. He didn't leave anything out. Not even that he knew who had left the dead chicken in front of Krisztina's door. Nor that he'd been to Margo's. And certainly not what he'd learned about Szőllősy. Mór listened in silence, asking not a thing, even though he clearly had questions. When Gordon finished, the old man stood up and went to the window.

"I don't understand this, son," he said.

"What don't you understand?"

"What happened, I understand. But I don't understand how this sort of thing can happen."

"These things happen everywhere, Opa."

"You know, son," Mór began, "your grandmother and I really did have a privileged life back in Keszthely. We had everything—everything. Your father had a lovely childhood. They say that was an era of peace. I myself was ten years old when Buda and Pest united. We used to visit Budapest and Vienna. True, not often. Your grandmother would have gone even more, but I didn't want to. Keszthely is a small town by comparison, but there were people of all sorts of backgrounds living there, too. Germans, Jews, and even a few Poles." He sighed. "No matter. I don't understand what's going on here. I don't understand a thing about this country of ours. The war, I understood. They shot at us; we shot back. By the end, that got murky, too. And what came after, that was even more muddled up. It's been almost ten years since I moved to Budapest. I might have followed your parents to America. Not that I would have understood that country, either, but at least I would have known it was foreign. A foreign country, foreign language, foreign culture. This country here is my own, and I still don't understand it."

Gordon waited for his grandfather to turn around. "I know, Opa. I know."

"So, what can I do?"

"I want you to get on your nicest suit and your surliest expression and go to Kaiser Wilhelm Road."

"And?"

"Go up to the head office of the Arabia Coffee Company and look for András Szőllősy."

"And?" asked the old man, knitting his bushy brows.

"Tell him you were sent by an advisor to István Bárcziházi Bárczy. The undersecretary must speak with him in a confidential matter. So confidential that he couldn't say even by telephone, which is why you were sent in person."

"You can't just do that, son. Even I know who István Bárcziházi Bárczy is. He's the prime minister's right-hand man. And Horthy's trusted advisor."

"Don't you worry, Opa. There won't be any trouble. I guarantee you that Szőllősy won't ask any questions."

For a while the old man just sat there pondering the matter. "If you say so, son," he finally said.

"I say so, Opa."

"Good. So I go into his office and say that one of István Bárcziházi Bárczy's advisors sent me. And?"

"Say he wants Szőllősy to get home by five o'clock, because he's going to pay him a visit. There's been a change in the German situation that they must discuss. No one is to know."

"Do you know what you're doing, son?" asked Mór, looking Gordon squarely in the eye.

"I hope so, Opa," Gordon replied.

"That's all? And why do you need me for that?"

"Because no one would believe me if I told them I work for an advisor of the prime minister's undersecretary. And no one is capable of a sterner expression than are you. If the chestnuts can wait, I won't be going anywhere just yet; I'll go over with you."

Mór thought it over one more time, and finally he stood up and went into the bedroom. In a couple of minutes Gordon heard the bathroom door open, then close. Ten minutes later Mór stood before him in a dapper black suit, a tight-fitting vest, the thick gold watch chain hanging from a pocket, a hard felt hat on his head, and a wolf head walking stick in his hand. Unusually, even his mustache and beard looked neat and trim.

AT THE CIRCLE THEY BOARDED THE UNDERGROUND THAT ran the length of Andrássy Street, and they got off at the Oktogon. From there they went on foot, turning from Andrássy Street onto Nagymező Street, and from there to Ó Street. The Arabia Coffee office building, a stately edifice that stood practically across from Arany János Street, had the company's well-known logo on its façade: an Arabian man whose eyes alone gleamed from his face, which was otherwise covered by his raised arm. Mór took a deep breath, and after adjusting his hat and twirling his mustache, he went inside.

Gordon had a smoke while waiting. Behind him, buses and trams came and went, cars beeped their horns, and a cop kept blowing his whistle. Not even ten minutes had passed when Mór stepped out the front door of the Arabia Coffee building.

"He'll be there," he told Gordon.

"Did everything go okay?"

"Everything," replied the old man.

"Well, Opa, I thank you. Krisztina will be getting to your place around seven this evening. She'll be angry, for good reason, but not at you."

"What did you do with her?"

"Nothing special, Opa. I left her there in Lillafüred to rest a bit more."

"Then why will she be angry?"

"Because I didn't exactly talk this over with her. I'll calm her down later. The point is that you should just wait for me there. As soon as I'm done, I'll head on over to your place."

"And now?"

"I'm off to the boxing arena," replied Gordon. The old man nodded, then headed with slow, labored steps back toward Ó Street as Gordon boarded a bus.

THERE WASN'T MUCH OF A CROWD AT ALL IN THE BOXING arena at the Ironworks Sport Club, which was not surprising. The training bouts didn't draw much public interest. So when Gordon stepped inside, he saw Strausz immediately beside one of the rings. A thin cigar in his hand, he was watching the boxers go at it. Gordon realized that one of the boxers was none other than Bruno Butcher. He walked over to Strausz.

"You out to polish this diamond?" Gordon asked the coach. Strausz looked at Gordon and gave a dismissive wave of the hand.

"Who the hell knows what'll become of him. I thought I'd give it a try, that maybe I can carve a bona fide boxer out of the guy. Never mind that he's sluggish; that, you can do something about. But his head! That's where the problem is. He thinks it's enough to throw a helluva punch, and that's that, he's the winner."

"But he can throw a helluva punch, right?"

"A mother of a helluva punch, no question there. But if he finds himself up against a faster opponent, someone with technique, why then he can have all the strength in the world, he's still gonna end up on the mat." Strausz took a drag of his cigar, then stepped over to the ring. "Bruno, Bruno!" he shouted. "Don't just move that arm! Move your legs, too. I'm not asking you to dance, but don't just stand there like half a hog up against a wall." Bruno Butcher gave a nod with his thick head and took two steps to the side, whereupon his opponent went at him and Bruno leveled a punch on the other man's chin as hard as if he'd whacked a cow upside the head.

"That's more like it!" snapped the old man. "You see, this is what happens. I tell him what to do, we go over it again, he steps in the ring, and then he knocks his opponent flat in no time."

"Not bad."

"Of course it's not bad, but before long I won't be able to find him a decent sparring partner. This blockhead knocks everyone out, as if this were a slaughterhouse, and then he just stands there looking like a nincompoop." Strausz opened his arms wide. Bruno Butcher meanwhile stood about, looking befuddled, arms down, as his opponent groaned away below him on the mat.

"Come on out of there, Bruno," said Strausz. "And then go on home. I'll let you know if I find someone else for you to knock out."

Bruno Butcher climbed out of the ring and, head drooped, headed off toward the locker room.

"I got your message," said Gordon.

Strausz sat down in one of the chairs and gestured to Gordon to take a seat beside him. "You know, I really don't like this whole affair. Antal Kocsis was supposed to be here, too, but something came up for him, and so he asked me to tell you what he found out."

"What's it you don't like?"

"This whole Pojva affair," Strausz anxiously replied. "I asked around a bit. Pojva is worse than ever. He'll knock the brains out of anyone for twenty pengős." Looking at Gordon's wounded forehead and faintly swollen lip, he added, "For ten pengős, he'll do it halfway."

"Ten pengős?" asked Gordon.

"That's right."

"I would have done better giving him ten pengős to lay off me," said Gordon.

"The sort of character he is, he would have taken your ten pengős and then beat you good just because. But all that's nothing, compared to the illegal matches. Nothing interests him except money." Strausz shook his head. "For fifty pengős he'll let any opponent beat his face to a pulp. You know what the funny thing is?"

"Is there anything funny about this?"

"Just that everyone knows this about him, and lots of folks bet on him, anyway. Because I don't even have to say how much the bookies rake in on this sort of . . ." He searched for the right word. " . . . *brawl*. Because this isn't sport. This doesn't have anything to do with boxing."

"When is he fighting next?"

"Tomorrow night," Strausz replied.

"Where?"

"You want to go there?" said Strausz, raising his eyebrows.

"I do," said Gordon.

"Whatever. It's on Gubacsi Road in southern Pest, by the river and next to the Slaughterhouse Bridge, on the grounds of a factory. Supposedly it begins at six." Strausz hesitated for a moment before continuing. "You know where to find this Pojva fella?" he finally asked.

Gordon recalled his last meeting with Gellért. "Out in that slum," he said, "the Mária Valéria Colony. And who is he up against?"

"The name's Jacek," said Strausz. "A Polish kid. He's slow; he's a blockhead. Just about the same as Bruno Butcher, but if someone gets his temper up, this guy can dole out ruthless punches, I'm telling you. And he works right there in the neighborhood, at the slaughterhouse. Maybe there really is something about butchers."

"Thanks," said Gordon.

"Don't thank me. I get sick thinking about this stuff."

"So do I."

"And you haven't even seen them brawl yet."

"I'm not too happy about going, but I need to be there. And now I've got to be off; I'm due in Buda at five."

"You're writing an article about some gentlemen?"

"Something like that," Gordon replied. "Except it's not exactly an article and not about gentlemen."

GORDON CAUGHT A BUS BACK TO THE INTERSECTION OF Kaiser Wilhelm Road and Nagymező Street. He got off and looked at his watch. Just past four. If he hurried, he'd make it to Buda by five. A couple of minutes later he shut the door behind him in his flat on Lovag Street and went over to his desk. Removing the stenciled copies of his notes from his blazer pocket, he slid one beside the copy of the autopsy report while placing the rest in the drawer. He quickly changed his shirt and was on the road in no time.

IT WAS ALREADY PAST QUARTER TO FIVE WHEN HE GOT off the tram at Italian Row. At the head of Pasaréti Street, Gordon lit a cigarette, turned up his collar, and continued forward through the drizzle. Parked in front of the building was Szőllősy's car, a Maybach Zeppelin. Gordon flung away the cigarette butt and rang the bell.

In no time the maid, who had a shawl draped over her shoulders and who had clearly hurried downstairs, opened the door.

"Dear God," she spurted out on seeing Gordon, "you've come back, sir."

"Your master is already waiting," Gordon announced. "The appointment is for five o'clock."

"Yes, sir," she said. She swallowed mightily, opened the gate, and let him in.

Gordon followed her into the house. In the vestibule he handed the maid his jacket and his hat. "I'll call his lordship right away," she said, leading Gordon into the living room.

"Call his wife in, too," said Gordon, turning around. The girl shut the door behind her. Darkness reigned inside the room; a floor lamp was the only source of light. The lace curtain hanging over the window filtered out even that little light that got through the drizzle-permeated dusk. Gordon stepped over to the drinks, chose a bottle of American whiskey, and poured himself a glass. He hadn't had a respectable glass of whiskey in quite a while. He took a sip and let the alcohol linger in his mouth. He then sat down in an armchair, crossed his legs, and waited.

The door opened. In walked Mrs. Szőllősy. When she saw Gordon, her face froze and the wrinkles hardened around her lips. "You," she hissed furiously through her teeth.

"Me," said Gordon, putting down his glass.

"If you want to grill me again about my daughter, you're wasting your time. I have nothing to say to you."

"I don't know why you would have thought I'm here on account of your daughter," he said, looking her in the eye, "but you've hit the nail on the head. Except that I'm not here to grill you. I already know almost everything there is to know about your daughter. True, there are still a couple of minor details, but I can clear those up while I'm here."

The woman's face turned pale as she listened. Staggering momentarily, she leaned up against the doorjamb.

"What's that supposed to mean, that you know everything?" she asked hoarsely.

"Almost everything. But there are a few little details I have to clear up with your husband. I figured it wouldn't hurt if you're here, too."

The woman seemed not to have heard what Gordon said. Her mouth began forming silent words. Gordon waited quietly.

"What . . . what happened to Fanny?" she whispered. "Something happened to her, right? What?"

Gordon wanted to answer, but just then the door opened once again and in stepped András Szőllőshegyi Szőllősy. The man bore a striking resemblance to the great actor Artúr Somlay. He was tall, and his exquisitely tailored English suit clung almost imperceptibly to his eminent belly. He walked with great confidence. His inquisitor's gaze locked on Gordon at once. His sharp-featured face was topped off by silver, slightly curly hair combed back; and if he hadn't had a carefully trimmed mustache under his nose, Gordon might in fact have thought he was seeing Artúr Somlay. While taking stock of Gordon with cold, gray eyes, Szőllősy now shut the door behind him.

"And who are you?" he asked in a tone of profound contempt. "I'm expecting an important guest, and it's not you."

"Are you waiting for István Bárczy?" asked Gordon.

Szőllősy was taken aback. "That is none of your business."

"You can wait all you want for Bárczy. He won't be coming, so you'll have to make do with me. The undersecretary has more important matters to tend to than to waste his time on your type."

Rage filled the man's face. His eyes narrowed, and he tightened his hands into fists. "I asked who the hell you are."

"Zsigmond Gordon, journalist with the *Evening*." Gordon did not extend his hand, for he was certain Szőllősy would not accept it.

"Get the hell out of here," Szőllősy thundered. "I don't talk with hack writers."

"András, he said he wants to talk with us about our daughter," said his wife in a trembling voice.

A shadow passed over Szőllősy's expressionless face, but Gordon wouldn't have sworn to it. Before the man had a chance to speak, however, Gordon reached into his pocket, pulled out the autopsy report, and threw the first-page summary on the table.

"What the hell is this?" asked Szőllősy, not even glancing at the sheet of paper. But his wife hurried to the table, picked up the page, and began reading. The paper trembled in her hands. Szőllősy did not move. He looked at his wife and then at Gordon, who already knew he was right. He just sat in the armchair, paging through his notes, and waited.

The woman's bosom was heaving uncontrollably. The blood drained from her face as her legs buckled. Slowly she sat down on the divan. "Fanny," she groaned. "Fanny, my sweet little Fanny. My dear little girl . . ."

"What are you talking about?" asked Szőllősy, knitting his brows.

"Fanny's dead," whispered the woman almost inaudibly. Her eyes were red, though the tears were yet to flow.

"A while back I did have a daughter . . ." Szőllősy began.

"*Did* have a daughter," the woman hissed. "Well, now it really is just *did*!"

"What are you talking about, Irma?"

"Sit down! Sit down already, God damn you!" his wife shouted in a rage.

At this, Szőllősy went slowly over to the writing desk, pulled out the chair, and sank into it. His wife meanwhile composed herself, stood, and after staggering only a bit she stepped over to the desk as straight as a ramrod. She threw the first page of the autopsy report on the desk. Szőllősy did not reach for it. "At least read the part about how she died!" the woman hissed.

Having taken an eyeglass case from his jacket's inner pocket, the man now pulled out a pair of wire-frame glasses, put them on, and began to read.

"This doesn't say a thing," he said, slapping the page back down onto the table once he'd looked it over. "Besides, this is just the first page. It doesn't even have a name on it. Nothing. This is just some dead girl." Pushing the page away from himself, he added, "This doesn't prove a thing."

"No?" asked Irma, casting him a bewildered stare. "No?" she repeated, gasping for breath before she finally snapped. Her tears erupted, again her bosom heaved, and the air at times seemed stuck inside her throat. She tottered over to the divan, leaned against it with her left arm, and, hunched over, sobbed. Within a couple of minutes, though, she'd collected herself once more. She stood up straight. She took a handkerchief from under her sleeve and wiped her eyes. In vain. The tears gushed silently on. Szőllősy now raised his gray eyes to Gordon.

"You . . ." he began, gesturing with a hand toward the

door, "you can just get out of here." Gordon glanced at the woman.

"This man is not going anywhere," Mrs. Szőllősy declared hoarsely. "He is not going anywhere until we've listened to what he has to say."

"If you have a need for this, then go ahead, listen," said Szőllősy, rising to his feet. "I've got business. I'm waiting for the undersecretary."

Bowing her head, the woman stared up at her husband from beneath the lock of hair that had fallen over her eyes. She tightened a hand into a fist and stepped before him. "You have no business more important than this," she said to him softly. "You are not going anywhere."

The man hesitated for a moment only, for a fraction of a moment, but even that was enough for the suspicion to come over his wife's face. Szőllősy cast Gordon a stealthy glance. He tried disguising his anxiety by reaching for the cigar case on the writing desk. He removed a cigar, slipped off its paper band, and took out a little knife, with which he cut off the end of the cigar. He then thrust a thick match into the cigar so deep that only its tip was visible. Szőllősy stuck the cigar between his teeth and raised a lighter from the case. He lit the cigar and blew a thick cloud of smoke around himself. The woman now slowly turned toward Gordon and looked at him with anticipation.

"You can correct me if I've got it wrong anywhere," Gordon began. He spoke in a dispassionate voice, looking rarely at the notes on his knee. "Your daughter, Fanny, returned from Paris this past spring. There she'd met Shlomo,

Rav Shay'ale Reitelbaum's son, who was likewise studying in Paris. Fanny announced that she was marrying the boy. You forbade this." Gordon looked over at Szőllősy, who went on smoking. "Indeed, the same night you got in a car and went to the rabbi. What you did there I do not know, but it isn't important. I doubt you paid him off; maybe instead you threatened him somehow or, perhaps, promised something." Gordon cast Szőllősy another glance, but the man's face didn't even flinch. "The next day, the rabbi took his son to Hamburg and put him on the ship to New York. And you sat down with Fanny for a talk. It doesn't take much imagination on my part to figure out what you spoke about and in what tone of voice, for by the end you'd disowned your daughter. Your wife didn't dare confront you."

"There's no confronting you," the woman hissed.

"So then, Fanny, who thus lost virtually all her friends and acquaintances, wound up out on the streets—on Rákóczi Street, to be precise. There, a petty criminal by the name of Józsi Laboráns, who keeps prostitutes, swooped down on her. Do you want to know how he does it?"

"Go ahead and tell him," the woman replied. Gordon explained how Józsi Laboráns had terrorized their daughter. "Csuli, the gang leader, denied it, but I suspect that the man gave your daughter one helluva beating. Only then did he put her to work. You knew nothing at all about all this." Gordon held a momentary pause, then looked at Szőllősy. "All the way up until two weeks ago, that is, when you got wind that a pretty young hooker had popped up at Red Margo's." Gordon watched the man's every breath of air. He'd been certain of everything he'd said up to this point. But, here, he was just guessing. A muscle twitched on Szőllősy's face. Gordon knew he was on the right track. He continued. "Correct me if I'm wrong," he said to the man, who just sat there motionless, swathed in a cloud of smoke. "I see. Then I wasn't mistaken. You and your politician chums are regulars at Red Margo's place."

"Don't you sit there poker-faced!" Szőllősy's wife shrieked at her husband, and in one fell swoop she swept the telephone off the corner of the desk. "You think I didn't know? I even know her name, you wretch. Red Margo. What a lowlife you are."

"In short," Gordon continued, "the album—or catalog, call it what you will—wound up in your hands. I wouldn't even be surprised if you paid a visit to the Parliament building for that very reason. To have a look at this new gal for yourself. Or maybe you saw the catalog not in the Parliament building but somewhere else. It doesn't matter. You opened it up and saw your own daughter. Naked. Inviting. The way Skublics photographs the girls that come his way. I can't imagine what you must have felt when you saw your own daughter in a catalog advertising prostitutes." Gordon looked up at Szőllősy. "You won't be telling us anytime soon, I imagine, and I don't want to guess."

"So that's where the picture came from," the woman muttered. Again the blood drained from her face. She staggered over to the divan and sat down.

"That's where," said Gordon. "Of course we mustn't forget that your husband didn't tell you a thing about this, just as you didn't tell him you'd met up with Fanny. Not just once, in fact. You gave her money regularly." Szőllősy only turned his eyes toward his wife. "But you didn't know what your daughter needed the money for." The woman shook her head in silence. Gordon continued: "She was saving money for ship fare so she could join Shlomo and so they'd have something to live on until they found work."

Gordon leaned forward. "By the end of September, then, both of you knew what your daughter was involved in. Maybe even earlier. Only you didn't tell each other." Gordon looked at the woman. "You'd hired a private eye to figure out how Fanny was making money. The detective not only figured it out, but he even found a picture to prove it."

Gordon fell silent, put his notes on the desk, and continued without them. "Both of you knew precisely what had happened to her, what she'd become." He looked again at the woman. "You tried talking to her, persuading her, appealing to her better side. As for you . . ." Gordon turned back to the man. "You chose another path. You knew full well that if word got out about what your politician chums were using your daughter for, that would have been the end of you. To be more precise, you could have called it a day permanently had it come up whose daughter your buddies were romping about with. I can imagine what sorts of questions you would have been asked. Until now everyone had turned a blind eye to you. About you being a scam. A fraud. A Jew-turned-Christian doing business with the Germans. Not that there's anything unusual or contemptible about that. But folks chummed up to you, no, not because you were called Valiant Knight András

Szőllőshegyi Szőllősy, but because they knew you had to be rich, filthy rich, to get your hands on such a title. What are your merits, after all? What's made you so worthy of the title Valiant Knight?" Szőllősy listened in silence. "You never took it upon yourself to publicly have a say in politics, and while I don't know what party you fund, I suspect it's the National Unity Party. That's why folks schmoozed with you. Because you have money. You think your politician friends don't know you're a Jew? They know. Just like they know that, by now, you're Catholic. But if someone had gotten wind that your daughter was a harlot, a prostitute to politicians—a girl who, moreover, wanted to reconvert to the Jewish faith so she could marry the son of a rabbi . . ." Here Gordon paused for effect, to let his words fade away in the utter silence of the living room. "And let's not forget, either, that Mussolini meanwhile invaded Abyssinia. Which surely came in handy for you. No longer did you have to buy coffee from the Negus; you could do so straight from Mussolini. And since you're on such good terms with Nazi business circles, you might have been able to finagle an even lower price out of the Italians." Gordon looked at Szőllősy. "You think I haven't kept an eye on stock prices? You think I don't know how much you make on a hundred kilos of coffee? If you raise the price by just ten Reichsmarks, you can book yourself one huge profit even then."

Gordon stood up, stepped over to the drinks, and poured himself another whiskey. Szőllősy's face slowly began turning red. His wife listened with a broken, uncomprehending expression.

"That's when you had a word with your private secretary,"

said Gordon, sitting back down. "To take action. Your private secretary, isn't that right?" He looked at Szőllősy. "I take your silence as a yes. Your secretary somehow turned up Pojva, a defrocked boxer and a booze-brained brute, to give your daughter a scare. Not a big scare, mind you, just a small one. Just enough so she'd come home. So the whole thing would be over. Pojva found Fanny on the sixth. I don't think he was out to kill your daughter, and I have a hard time believing that you wanted that." Gordon shook his head. "The only problem is that your secretary couldn't have found a more unsuitable man than Pojva for the task. For him, giving the scare to a defenseless girl is the same as doing so to a strong guy. All you wanted was to have her beaten just a little, to have her robbed, so Fanny would come running on home. Things might even have turned out this way, though I doubt Fanny would have set foot in this house again.

"In case you're interested, I know almost exactly what happened that night, because that's how Pojva started off with me, too. Yes, ma'am"—Gordon nodded toward Mrs. Szőllősy—"your husband had Pojva sent after me, too, except that I lived through it. Your daughter didn't. But Pojva didn't set out to kill her, let's make that clear. He wanted to give her a scare. He socked her in the pit of the stomach. I got through it because I knew what to expect. But Pojva caught your daughter by surprise: he made a fist right away and hit." Gordon turned to Szőllősy. "Of course, you're a clever man. I figure you didn't tell your secretary who the girl was whom Pojva was supposed to beat up. As for Pojva, he didn't have a guilty conscience. He doesn't have a conscience to begin with, as far as I can tell, but that's another story. Your daughter died, and Pojva took the money from her purse—almost two thousand pengős. He then went on his way without even looking back. When you found out what had happened to Fanny, you acted fast. You looked up Bárczy, right?" Szőllősy was silent. "Yes, that's what I figure you did. But what did you tell him that made him call off the investigation? How the hell did he convince Vladimir Gellért not to look into the case?"

Szőllősy said not a word as he tapped the ashes off his cigar.

"Talk, you wretch!" shouted his wife, grabbing the telephone up off the floor. "Talk, goddamnit, or I'll strangle you with this phone cord!"

Szőllősy cast her a scornful stare. "I told him there was a prostitute who blackmailed me. If I didn't pay her, she'd proclaim our doings far and wide."

"And you told him you'd taken care of this girl," said Gordon, "but you weren't so sure that the cops wouldn't land on your trail in the course of the investigation. But that's not enough in and of itself. Is it big news, after all, that men of your ilk buy pleasure with cash?"

"It's not," said Szőllősy. "Bárczy knew that, too. So did everyone. But I wanted him to take me seriously. I told him that the . . . *hooker*"—he practically spit the word out—"didn't blackmail me only with this, but with something else, too."

"With what?"

"With me doing it with men," Szőllősy replied indifferently.

"That you do *what*?!" shrieked his wife.

"Of course I don't do it." Her husband looked at her with disdain. "But that would indeed have been enough to blackmail someone. I had to come up with a solid motive, one Bárczy would take seriously. Just because I had a hooker taken out wouldn't have given him reason to do anything at all."

"So you sold yourself to the undersecretary," Gordon slowly said. "You figured it would be better to have Bárczy keep you in check with him thinking you're a sodomite than for it to turn out that your daughter became a hooker serving the upper crust because she wanted to marry a Jew. You even took the risk of him setting István Cár's men on you."

"Who is that?" asked Mrs. Szőllősy.

"Cár is a detective with Unit V. Crimes against decency—that's his beat. He goes hunting for Uranians."

"I for one don't know what 'Uranians' are," said the woman.

"Slang for homosexuals," Gordon replied. "He's locked up more than one. In a word, then, you've taken on even this risk—that of being sent to a detention camp—so the truth about your daughter doesn't come out."

"You could put it that way."

"Bárczy was more than happy to have Gellért put a halt to the investigation. With this information, which, moreover, you'd freely shared with him, for all practical purposes he could hold a loaded revolver to your head. All the time."

Mrs. Szőllősy raised her eyes to her husband. "You are a . . ."

"Go ahead," said Szőllősy, "finish your sentence."

The woman did not answer. She stared straight ahead. The telephone fell from her hand.

Gordon nodded. "Bárczy got word to Kozma, and Kozma passed along the instructions to Gellért. It's clear. That's what they were talking about at Gömbös's wake."

"What?" asked the woman.

Looking at Gordon as if his wife was not there, Szőllősy explained, "And on the same occasion, Gellért told Kozma that you were snooping around."

"And that's how this information made its way back to you," said Gordon. "That's why you set Pojva on me."

"I had to somehow warn you to keep your distance from the affair," replied Szőllősy, ever more caught up in the telling of the story, as if proud of what he'd done.

"And yet you couldn't have a journalist killed, after all."

"Don't be so sure about that."

"I'm not. But I didn't let what did happen get the better of me."

"No."

"That's why you set Gellért on me, too, right? When I left the Sztambul Coffeehouse. You had him sent there."

The man nodded.

"But there you miscalculated," said Gordon, locking his eyes on Szőllősy. "Fundamentally. The chief inspector didn't scare me off, you see. Indeed, he's the one who set me on the right path. Had it not been for Gellért, I don't think I would be here today."

"You're completely right about that," said Mrs. Szőllősy out of the blue. Both men looked up with a start. The woman collected herself, adjusted her hair, and straightened her back.

The whites of her eyes were red, her face was moist from tears, and her voice was hoarse. "It's not a private detective I hired," she went on. "For I know Vladimir well. To be more precise, a long time ago we knew each other well. I've often seen his name in the papers"—she now looked at Gordon—"more than once in your articles. I didn't know who to turn to. I couldn't trust a private detective; such characters are unreliable. That's when I thought of Vladimir. At the end of September I called on him at his office. I told him in person that Fanny had disappeared. Nothing more. As for why, I didn't tell him a word." She looked at her husband. "Don't you worry, I didn't blurt out your dirty little secrets."

"Mine?" Szőllősy erupted. "As if this whole affair was my doing."

"You can discuss that later, András," said the woman, throwing back her head. Her husband moved to speak but then decided otherwise.

"What happened in his office?" asked Gordon.

"I gave him a picture of Fanny. I met with him on October 3, a Saturday, in City Park. That's when he showed me that . . ." She fell silent. " . . . that other picture. He promised me he'd save Fanny from that . . . life, if that can be called a life at all."

"You haven't heard from him since then?" asked Gordon.

"No," replied the woman. "I was in fact worried about what might have happened. That's when you showed up wanting to ask questions about our daughter. After you left, I telephoned Vladimir right away, but I couldn't reach him. I figured all the fuss involving the funeral was taking up his time. I was planning to go to his office tomorrow, but . . ."

All at once Szőllősy stood up tall and straight, stretching out haughtily as he rose.

"What do you propose to do now?" he asked, looking at Gordon.

"I don't know," said Gordon with a shrug. "Not that I have much left to do," he added, picking up his notes. "I now know all the missing pieces to the story."

"Surely you had some aim in coming here," said Szőllősy. "You want money? How much?"

"It's not so simple."

"So you want a lot. Out with it—how much?"

"It's not about money."

"You can't publish this, anyway, in case you're thinking of writing about it. I can still keep them from running it. You might even lose your job. I can still arrange for that much."

"Are you threatening me?" asked Gordon, raising his eyebrows. "Like you did with Krisztina? That chicken with the broken neck was a pretty cheap trick, after all. There was no need for that. It just speaks of bad taste."

"But it was enough to get you to take that little gal of yours by the hand," Szőllősy declared, "and run out of town with your tail between your legs."

"Of course," said Gordon. "And for a few other reasons. For example, to speak with Teréz Ökrös. I was able to type this up"—Gordon pointed to his stenciled notes—"and have them sent to our correspondents in Vienna, Berlin, Prague, and London. They also work for local papers there, you know.

You can have me kicked out of my job and you can have my article pulled. Go right ahead; don't let me stop you. But if you don't do as I say, things will start happening. The foreign papers will publish my article, which the *Evening* or *Hungary* can then feel free to run. Doing so won't spell trouble for anyone. Except you."

Szőllősy sat back down in his chair and stared at the cigar butt.

"Now you pay attention to me," Gordon continued, then reached into his pocket, pulling out a folded sheet of paper and throwing it on the desk in front of Szőllősy. "That's the address of a maternity home. Tomorrow you will wire them one hundred thousand pengős. And on November 1, another hundred thousand. The same sum on the first of every month. Until your assets are depleted. Don't tell me I'm not giving you enough time to sell the business. One hundred thousand pengős a month. As long as you still have money left."

"What the hell are you talking about?!" Szőllősy shouted, his face beet-red.

"As long as you've robbed your daughter of the chance to give birth to her child—your grandchild—then the least you can do is help others."

"What?!" exclaimed the woman, cupping a hand to her mouth.

Gordon reached into the inner pocket of his blazer, pulled out the second page of the autopsy report, and dropped it on the table. "This goes with the summary. The coroner's detailed report."

Szőllősy cast Gordon a petrified stare while his wife gasped for breath.

"Tomorrow morning I'll be calling the maternity home. Wire the money. Or have it taken over in a briefcase. I don't care." With that, he buttoned up his blazer and left them to their own devices.

In the vestibule Gordon removed his jacket from the coat-rack and pressed his hat on his head. He heard the rattling of pots and pans from the kitchen. The maid was washing dishes.

"Kid," he called over. "Be prepared to look for a new job soon."

The girl lowered a pot into the water and looked at Gordon. "I know," she said quietly. "I know."

HE BOARDED A TRAM AND LOOKED OUT AT THE GRAY, sleet-laden city. At the Oktogon he bought some roast chestnuts from a vendor, then headed toward the Circle.

Parked out front was Czövek's banged-up old Opel. The cabbie was sitting behind the wheel, smoking. On seeing Gordon approach, he sprang out of the car.

"Good evening, Mr. Editor!"

"Good evening, Czövek. Did you and Krisztina get back okay?"

"Yes, sir."

"Fine, then," said Gordon with a nod, and he headed toward the door.

"Mr. Editor!" Czövek called after him.

"Yes?"

"Your change is five pengős, sir."

"Five pengős?"

"That's right, sir. You gave me fifty, and the trip cost only forty-five."

"And how did you figure that?"

"It wasn't easy," replied the cabbie with a grin.

"Well, if I'm still due five pengős, then we'll take another ride. If you wait around a bit, then this evening you'll still have a little something to do."

Mór was sitting at the kitchen table, a bowl of chestnuts in front of him; Krisztina was nowhere to be seen.

"Don't bother looking for her, son," said the old man. "She came upstairs, said hi, then left. Convincing her to stay would have been impossible. Not that I wanted to."

"Did she tell you I left without her?" asked Gordon as he took a seat beside his grandfather.

"She did. It wasn't nice of you."

"I know, Opa. Maybe I overreacted a bit. But now I've taken care of things."

"You don't say," said Mór, raising his eyes.

"At least part of it."

The old man rummaged through the bowl of chestnuts. "What are you planning, son?"

"Nothing special, Opa."

The old man was silent for a while. Finally, he said, "You remember what your father said about revenge?"

Gordon sighed.

"He never did take revenge on anyone," Mór continued.

"He always said he just stood there holding this pipe that eventually everyone would run up through, leaving him with nothing else to do than to hold both ends shut."

"I'm not so sure I want to talk about this, at least not now and not here."

"I know that."

"Opa," snapped Gordon, "just look how far my father got with that famous pipe of his. He just stood there with that rotten pipe in his hands, waiting and waiting and waiting, and when he couldn't hold it any longer . . ."

"What could he have done? The world crisis wasn't the work of one person. He didn't know who to blame, and so he blamed himself."

"I know, Opa. I was there with him when he flung away the pipe and everything else, for that matter."

Mór looked out the window and scanned the Circle below. The light of the streetlamps traced the contours of his stout frame, his bushy beard, his sunken shoulders.

"I've got to go, Opa. I've got to go get Krisztina."

"You know where she is?"

"I suspect," replied Gordon.

"NORMAFA," SAID GORDON AS HE TOOK A SEAT IN THE Opel. Czövek started up the engine and made his way down Andrássy Street to the Oktogon, and from there along the Grand Boulevard, across the Margaret Bridge to Buda, and via King Matthias Road up toward the romantic hilltop setting that was Normafa. The traffic was sparse and the pedestrians were few as they drove along the narrow wooded road through the Buda hills. The only signs of life were the lights behind the windows of the villas they passed.

Gordon had Czövek stop by the old water tower. He got out and called back, "Wait here. I won't be long."

At the edge of the dark forest surrounding the water tower, there was a tavern, a little lamp burning above its door. The cold wind stung. Gordon turned up his collar. On reaching the tavern, he spotted Krisztina. She was sitting outside on a bench toward the other end of the little building, a porcelain mug beside her, presumably filled with hot spiced wine she'd bought inside. She gazed upon the city that stretched out far below, occasionally lifting the mug to her lips. On hearing Gordon approach, she turned around but quickly looked away.

"If I tell you not to say a word to me, you won't be able to resist, will you?" she asked, staring out at the city.

"Just in the interest of preserving the order of things," Gordon replied. "But why exactly are you still angry with me?"

Krisztina was silent.

"Because I wanted to protect you?" asked Gordon. "Because I didn't want you to maybe wind up in the same trouble I was in?"

"Sometimes I just really hate you," said Krisztina. "The problem isn't that you left me behind, Zsigmond. That's the least of it. You didn't tell me what you were planning."

"I would have told you if you hadn't fallen asleep on account of the wine and the brandy."

"I expected you to cook up a better lie than that."

"That's not a lie."

"But it's not the truth, either. And don't go telling me that you had to hurry back to Budapest because a light bulb went off in your head all of a sudden. I won't believe it."

"That *is* what happened, though."

"There's no point in this," said Krisztina, shaking her head.

"I admit I was wrong," said Gordon, sitting down beside her.

"That's awfully generous of you. You're just superb at admitting it when you're wrong."

"What do you expect me to say?"

"If you can't say the truth, then it's better you don't say a thing."

Gordon took out a cigarette, lit it, and for a while he smoked in silence. "Your wine is cold; I'll bring you another one."

"I didn't even want to drink this," said Krisztina with a dismissive wave of the hand. "But in exchange for everything you've told me, I'll now tell you something."

"Go ahead."

"This afternoon I wired London to say I've accepted the job. I'm just waiting for their reply, then I'm off."

"I understand."

"If you understood, you wouldn't have shut me out of the case."

"I didn't shut you out. It's just that I didn't want to talk about it until I knew everything. Or at least almost everything. Don't be mad."

"I'm not mad at you, Zsigmond."

"No?"

"You want me to be mad?"

Gordon shook his head. "Not necessarily."

"Then what do you want?"

"I want you to listen to me," Gordon replied. He then told Krisztina everything that had happened since he'd returned to Budapest. Krisztina listened in silence, neither asking a thing nor nodding, just sitting there staring out at the city.

"And what do you want to do next?" she asked when Gordon finished.

"I've got unfinished business with Pojva."

"What will you do with him?" asked Krisztina. "Beat him up?"

"Don't kid around," he said. "What do I care that he did that to me?"

"Zsigmond, at least admit to me that he could knock your head off with his bare hands. Even if you don't admit it to yourself, admit it to me. You want vengeance, that's what."

"Maybe you're right," said Gordon. "But it's not that simple."

"Nothing is that simple."

"Pojva thinks he's the only one who can play dirty."

"I don't want to know what you're planning."

"No?"

"I want to pack. My clothes—in a suitcase."

Gordon pushed his hat up over his forehead. "But not tonight, right?"

"No," replied Krisztina. "Not tonight. Take me home."

"All right," said Gordon, standing up. "Let's go."

Czövek was slumped over the wheel, fast asleep. Gordon

tapped the glass, at which the cabbie snapped to attention. "I'm off already," he said in a drowsy voice.

"Wait until we get in, huh?"

"Should I hurry?" asked Czövek, turning around.

Gordon looked at Krisztina, who nodded. "Hurry, Czövek, hurry."

Ten

Gordon was in the bathroom, shaving, when Krisztina appeared in the open door. "And where are you off to?" she asked.

"I'm on duty," he replied.

"Starting at 8 P.M. And now, if I'm not mistaken"—she looked at her watch—"it's just past 8 A.M."

"I've got to pay Gellért a visit this morning at police headquarters."

Gordon finished shaving; he needed hardly any alum. He put on a brown sport coat but couldn't manage his necktie.

"Will you tie this for me?" he asked, as he stepped from the bathroom.

Krisztina looked up from behind the writing desk. "Come over here."

"What are you working on?"

"Setting a few ideas on paper that have been in my head. So I have something to show Penguin."

"The publisher."

"Who else?"

"I hope they like them."

"So do I."

Krisztina leaned back over her drawings as Gordon stepped to the telephone and dialed police headquarters. Gellért was already at his desk.

"Did you accept my advice?" asked the detective on hearing Gordon's voice.

"In a certain sense, yes."

"What sense?"

"I'd rather tell you in person. And we should talk about two women as well."

"Who?"

"One is named Fanny," replied Gordon, "and the other, Irma."

"I can't talk now."

"When, then?"

"What would you say to an early lunch—at noon?"

"Fine by me. Where?"

"The Guinea Fowl, on Bástya Street. Know the place?"

"I know it," said Gordon, putting down the receiver.

Krisztina glanced at Gordon only for a moment before going back to her drawing. Gordon went to the desk and took out a little notebook packed full of addresses from a drawer. He paged through it and dialed again.

"Hullo," said a man with a strong British accent at the other end of the line.

"This is Gordon. Do you have an hour to spare this morning?"

"An hour?"

"An hour and a half."

"An hour and a half?"

"That's all."

"I'm sure I do," replied the man.

"Ten o'clock in the Abbázia?"

"I'll be there. Cheerio!"

"Bye," said Gordon, putting down the receiver.

He put on his trench coat and stopped in the doorway on his way out.

"Are you off already?" asked Krisztina.

"I've got to go," replied Gordon. "I'll call you tonight from the newsroom."

"Whatever you want," replied Krisztina, leaning over her paper once again.

GORDON GLANCED AT HIS WATCH. IT WAS JUST PAST 11:30 A.M. He waved a hand to the waiter to bring the bill. The man seated across from Gordon closed his notebook. "Lord Beaverbrook will decide if we'll start writing about Hungarian politicians and their love lives," said the correspondent from the *Daily Express*. "I can't promise a thing."

"I wouldn't expect anything else," Gordon replied.

"I can't just base this on gossip, either," said the journalist from under a shock of thick red hair.

"I know."

"You think this Margo will help me?"

"I'll have a chat with her."

"You do that." He paused momentarily. "I admit I've heard some of this already. This sort of thing isn't customary back in our country."

"That's precisely why it could be interesting."

"I'll ask around, too," said the Englishman with a nod.

Gordon paid the bill, shook hands with the correspondent, and boarded a tram in front of the coffeehouse. On Berlin Square he transferred to another to Calvin Square. He walked along Kecskeméti Street, turning onto Bástya, and was already in the Guinea Fowl a couple of minutes before noon. Gordon took a quick look around the restaurant's dimly lit interior but did not see Gellért. The tables were occupied mostly by men: a mix of students and instructors from the nearby Pázmány Péter Catholic University. Even though it was midday, the place was still not full. Not just anyone could afford to dine at the Guinea Fowl.

The waiter led Gordon to a table in the back and asked Gordon what he'd like.

"Just a coffee for now."

He had just opened a newspaper when the chief inspector appeared beside the table. A drenched jacket hung from his lanky frame, water trickling off his umbrella, his hat sopping wet.

"Lovely," he said by way of greeting, "I see that you stayed dry."

"I arrived before the rain."

"Have you ordered already?"

"Not yet."

Gellért waved for the waiter, who took away his jacket, hat, and umbrella, then brought them two menus. Gordon ordered a large bowl of consommé including not one but two eggs, and Gellért ordered beef paprikash sautéed with red wine, potatoes, and lard-fried onions.

"So what do you want to know," said Gellért, leaning back in his chair.

"You still owe me the story of what happened to Róna," Gordon replied.

The detective cast Gordon a look of surprise. "Róna? You want to talk to me about Róna?"

"Of course. I need to hand in the article."

"Well," said Gellért, lighting up a thin cigar, "I'm unable to tell you much, really. The court proceedings aren't over yet, so officially I can't even talk about the case."

"Then unofficially."

The detective raised his eyebrows. "Naturally enough," he began, "Róna was *not* bribed. It's just that in the course of another investigation, he'd gotten himself neck-deep in something he shouldn't have."

"Just what that was, you can't say."

Gellért nodded. "He'll be acquitted, but since he got the detective corps into a sticky situation, he'll be transferred. He won't lose his job, but for a while he'll have to investigate railway thefts."

"This doesn't have the makings of an article," Gordon observed.

"I told you from the start not to bother with it. Not that it did any good."

Gordon did not reply. The waiter arrived with the soup and the beef paprikash. Over lunch they stuck to neutral topics—the Spanish Civil War, Mussolini, and the Belgian king's decision to build up his army because of the growing threat from Germany.

On finishing their meal, they both lit cigarettes. Gordon waved for the waiter and then paid the bill, try as Gellért did to protest. "I owe you for the lift you gave me the other day," said Gordon.

"You're not going to ask me about the dead girl?" Gellért blurted out.

"No," Gordon replied. "I already know everything."

"Everything?"

"Everything," he said with a nod. "Well, there's one little thing I don't know."

"What would that be?"

"Did you not want to tell Szőllősy's wife that her daughter was dead, or did you not dare to?"

Gellért scrutinized Gordon's face from behind the smoke of his cigar. "Does it matter?" he finally asked.

"Not so much anymore."

"I didn't dare to and I didn't want to, either," Gellért admitted. "I'm getting old. I have two years to go before retirement. I was looking for an opportunity to tell her, but . . ."

"I can also tell you're getting older," said Gordon.

"How's that?"

"The other day you left your desk drawer open. Remember? I'd dropped by to see you at headquarters, and while waiting in your office, I noticed that you'd left one of the drawers open. You've never done that before."

"I'll ask my doctor to write me a prescription for forgetfulness," replied Gellért.

"That wouldn't hurt. The only reason I even mention it now is because what happens if an unauthorized individual goes into your office and sees an open drawer?"

"You're right," said the detective, tapping his cigar against the ashtray. "These unauthorized individuals can't be trusted." After a pause, he said, "Say, what's up in the world of boxing?"

"Harangi is still in America as a member of the European team," Gordon replied. They stood up and went toward the door. The waiter helped them get their jackets on. They stepped outside; the rain had stopped.

"I hope he wins," said Gellért.

"Me, too. From what I've heard, he's been boxing like a real champ."

"And when's the next match you're going to?"

"Tonight," said Gordon.

"Who's fighting?"

"It doesn't matter," said Gordon with a dismissive wave of the hand. "Two brutes are going to knock each other's brains out."

"Well, then . . ." said Gellért, turning to Gordon.

"Thanks," said Gordon, extending his hand.

The detective nodded, then turned to head back to the headquarters. Gordon walked back to Calvin Square and boarded a tram.

HE POUNDED ON THE DOOR IN VAIN. HE LOOKED IN THE window, too, but on peering between the narrow slit in the curtains Gordon saw no movement inside. He heard steps in the stairwell. He turned and saw the super.

"Not so loud, sir, I beg you," said the man, out of breath. "You'll rouse the whole building."

"At two in the afternoon? Who am I going to wake up at this hour?"

"Please, sir, this is a decent building." Gesturing toward the door, he added, "Even despite this. Folks here don't like an uproar. Besides, there's no point pounding at this door."

"Don't you know where the young lady is?"

The man knit his brows at the word *lady*. "She left this morning."

"Where to?"

"I really don't know—but not to the market, that's for sure. She had suitcases with her."

"You mean she moved?"

"The young lady isn't in the habit of notifying me what she does, when, and with whom," he said sarcastically.

"But you saw her when she left, didn't you?"

"Yes," said the super with a nod. "She said 'Good day,' and I replied 'Good day.' She put her bags into a taxi that was waiting out front, and they drove away. That's why I'm telling you not to pound on the door. There's no one in the flat. And now if you'll excuse me, sir, I must be going."

BEFORE BOARDING A TRAM AT APPONYI SQUARE, GORdon stopped at Liberty Square to withdraw two hundred pengős from a branch of Downtown Savings Bank. He didn't keep his savings for this kind of thing, but he didn't have a heavy heart taking out a sizable sum now. Then he got on the tram. Slowly it left behind the elegant buildings of downtown, and on Üllői Street—that busy road that crossed the Grand Boulevard and continued southeast into the dusty reaches of outer Pest—the tram clattered by ever more run-down, grayer buildings. And then came Orczy Park, from where Gordon could already make out, off in the distance, the moldering wooden barracks that comprised the Mária Valéria Colony—in a word, the slum. At Ecseri Road he got off the tram, took a deep breath, and headed along the muddy dirt road between the barracks, which would no longer have been suitable for either the soldiers or the POWs who had once been housed there. The farther in Gordon went, the more this sea of mud took on a different look. Some people had built adobe additions onto the barracks, whereas oth-ers had constructed brick outbuildings, resulting in an eerie labyrinth of sorts. After a while Gordon didn't even know if he was sliding along an actual road or, rather, an utterly unofficial passageway between two structures. His nostrils were filled with a suffocating smoke. Few people here could afford wood, so more than a few heated their homes by burn-ing old clothes and shoes. While the smell of the smoke did quell the stink of poverty, it could not hide the sorry spec-tacle that was this slum. Grimy-looking children were frol-icking about in the mud, talking and shouting in a language Gordon barely understood. They chased each other about, most of them in bare feet, howling and hooting away. Behind some windows, oil lamps flickered; behind most, darkness reigned. In a yard, two old peasants, a man and a woman, were busy dragging into their shanty a heap of brush they'd presumably lugged back from nearby People's Park. These two people, it seemed, had done everything they could to make their home look somewhat presentable. The end result was at once pathetic and touching. Water was dripping through their patchy roof; a lace embroidery served as a makeshift curtain in their window; and a cracked vase in the window held a wilted flower. Gordon stepped over to the couple and spoke.

"Good day."

The old man slowly stood up straight. "G'day."

"Can you tell me where I can find Pojva?"

"Who's that?"

"Pojva."

"Hey, Erzsike," said the old man, giving his wife a shove. "This gentleman here is looking for some character called Pojva."

"I dunno no one called that," replied the old woman from a wrinkled, kerchief-wrapped face.

As Gordon described Pojva's features, the woman made the sign of the cross and looked to the sky.

"You're looking for that . . . that broken-nosed scoundrel?"

"That's the one."

The old woman toddled out to the front of their shanty and showed Gordon which way to go. Here, street names and numbers didn't mean a thing. Gordon thanked her for the directions and headed on, trying not to sink ankle-deep into the mud as he walked. Dogs howled as they tore at their chains, and cats meowed from the roofs they'd fled to from the mud.

Soon he found the shanty he was looking for. Decaying wooden shutters hung from the windows facing the road, their tulip carvings looking rather wilted. Beside the shanty was an adobe pigpen. Two kids around ten years old were playing in the muddy yard with a bicycle wheel. They were having a wonderful time, even though the wheel wouldn't turn.

"Is Pojva home?" he asked one of them.

The child did not reply, but ran squealing into the shanty. A few moments later, out stepped Pojva, evidently in the throes of a serious hangover. His trousers had slipped somewhat under his waist, and he was naked above them. He must once have been a big and rock-hard man, but his muscles were now flabby and his skin had slackened, too. What with the combination of his crooked nose and a more or less stout frame, however, he still presented a spectacle that commanded respect and inspired fear.

"I know you from somewhere," he said to Gordon.

"I have a proposal," Gordon replied.

"You got money to back it up?"

Gordon nodded. Pojva just stood there for a while, staring at him. Gordon must indeed have looked familiar, but Pojva couldn't quite place him. "Wait here," he finally said, and went back inside. Soon there came the sound of shrieks and sobbing, and out came a fortyish woman.

"Please don't go talking to him, sir," she pleaded, "it always means trouble." At this, Pojva seized her from behind, turned her toward him, and gave her a slap. She fell to her knees. He then kicked her in the back, which sent her flying into the mud.

"What business is it of yours who I talk to," he sputtered, then waved a hand to Gordon. "Come right in."

The shanty stank to high heaven. Something was bubbling away in a pot on the stove, and curled up in the corner was a sopping-wet dog. Water dripped from the ceiling into a cracked metal vat on the kitchen table, and an oil lamp flickered beside it. Pojva plopped down on one of the chairs, stuck a cigarette into his mouth, and kicked the other chair out from under the table toward Gordon. "How much?" he asked.

"You don't even know what this is about," replied Gordon.

"You didn't come here because you need a gardener," said Pojva, scanning Gordon's face in the hope of recognizing him, but in the end he just gave a dismissive wave of the hand.

"Twenty," said Gordon, putting two ten-pengő banknotes on the table.

Pojva reached over greedily, snatched up the bills, and cried out: "Woman!" His frightened wife stuck her head in the door. "Here's some motherfucking money, goddamnit. Now get going. Go buy some oil and some real grub." Giving the stove a sound kick, he added, "Not even the dog is gonna eat this shit." The thick, suspect fluid in the pot splattered on the woman's leg. Wincing, Pojva's wife stepped just close enough to take the ten-pengő bill held out by her husband, then got going fast.

"Now let's have it," Pojva spat out, "whadayawant?"

"Tonight you're having . . . a bout."

"Not me."

"Sure you are."

"How am I supposed to know you're not a cop?"

"Would a cop have given you twenty pengős?"

Pojva pondered the matter. "And let's say I did have a bout?"

"Then you'd be up against that Polish kid, Jacek, at the factory grounds on Gubacsi Road."

"If I did have a bout," said Pojva with a nod, "that's where it would be."

"And who would win?"

"In an honest match you never can say," pokerfaced Pojva replied.

"Not even for fifty pengős?"

Pojva's eyes glittered with greed. "No way for fifty, but maybe for a hundred."

"I understand," said Gordon. "If it's possible to say for a hundred who's going to win tonight, why then, the winner might even be Jacek. Let's say in the second round he could knock you out."

"For a hundred pengős," said Pojva, licking his lips, "he might even win."

"Say, Pojva," asked Gordon. "Did anyone else come by asking if you'd have a bout tonight? And if you did, who would win?"

"No," Pojva replied. "The bookie is always asking, but no one else."

Gordon now reached inside his wallet and pulled out five twenty-pengő banknotes. Pojva snatched out for them, but Gordon was faster. He pulled away his hand. "On one condition."

"What's that?"

"I give the money to your wife," said Gordon.

"Not a chance!" cried Pojva.

"Sure there is. Would you rather go to a detention camp?"

Pojva knit his brows. He thought long and hard. Finally, he licked his lips and slowly nodded.

"If tonight's fight ends the way we suspect it will," said Gordon, "we might even do business together regularly."

"No problem," said Pojva, and Gordon could see in his eyes that he would beat the money out of his wife.

"Let's be sure of that," said Gordon, rising from the table.

"There won't be," said Pojva, who then picked a bottle of denatured alcohol off the floor and took a swig. He gave Gordon the once-over. "Get going already—I've got to get ready for my match."

"Box like you mean it," said Gordon. "Mr. Szőllősy doesn't like to be let down."

"Who?"

For a moment Gordon thought he'd made a mistake. "The gentleman who sent his secretary to see you."

"Oh, him?" said Pojva, looking up at Gordon. "He also said his boss likes a job done just right. Well, I sure didn't let him down."

"You sure taught that girl a lesson. Did he tell you to knock her dead?"

"No," said Pojva, shaking his head. "Just to give her a scare. How was I supposed to know that dame was such a lightweight?" he asked, talking to the bottle before him. "I barely waved my hand at her, and she up and died. No matter, she was just some slut, anyway."

"That's right," said Gordon with a nod. "Just some slut. And what did you do with the money?"

"What money?"

"Calm down, Pojva, the gentleman doesn't care about the money. It's just me who wants to know what happened to it. How much did she have with her? Almost two thousand pengős?"

"Only about a thousand five hundred."

"And what did you spend it on?" asked Gordon, looking around. "Medicine?"

"What do you care?" snarled Pojva, taking another swig. "Debts. Sharks."

"Did the gentleman's secretary say you should take the money?"

"Of course. He said whatever she's got on her is all mine."

"How did you do it?" asked Gordon. Something was not right with Pojva's muddled stare.

"What do you care?"

"We like to know how our employees operate."

Pojva only shook his head, but then answered all the same. "First I gave her a slap; then I took her purse. She was lying there on the ground, and I took it from her hands."

"And that's when you saw how much money was inside?"

"Yep."

"And that's when you socked her in the stomach."

"Yep."

"After seeing how much money she had with her."

Pojva nodded.

"And what else did she have in her purse?"

"Just the money, plus a bunch of junk. I gave that stuff to my little woman and the kids."

"But you left a book inside," said Gordon.

"Some sort of book," said Pojva. "I figured as long as she's dead, they might as well bury her with that. Besides, we don't read."

"And you don't pray."

"Who am I supposed to pray to?" asked Pojva, staring at an odd-shaped heap of straw in the corner of the room that had once been a piece of furniture but whose cover had long since shredded away.

Gordon followed his eyes, then slowly nodded. He turned to leave, but then called back. "Do a good job tonight, huh?"

"I will. It's my specialty, after all," he said, drinking down what remained in the bottle.

Outside, it was starting to rain. Gordon looked inside the pigpen. There he saw not pigs but Pojva's wife and the two kids. They were cowering in the mud; there was no straw inside, and the cold wind was blowing in through gaps in the walls and the roof. The kids were so used to it that they weren't even shivering. Gordon leaned inside the pigpen and reached out the money toward the woman. But she only shook her head, her eyes filled with terror.

"Take it already, goddamnit!" bellowed Pojva from the door of the shanty. "And buy some food, too, you hear?!"

The woman took the money. Gordon looked at the two children. "Are your parents still alive?"

"They're down on the plains," the woman half whispered with a nod. "If I ever get free of this"—she shook her head toward Pojva—"I'd go back there right away with the kids."

"Take good care of the money," said Gordon. "It might yet help get you a train ticket."

Gordon walked back out to the muddy road, turned up his collar, and headed in the direction of Üllői Street. While waiting for the tram, he looked at his watch. It was just past four. He would get to Gubacsi Road sooner than he'd planned. When the tram reached the corner of Könyves Kálmán Boulevard, he got off and entered a tobacconist's shop.

"May I use the phone?" he asked, putting a twenty-fillér coin on the counter.

Opening up his notebook, Gordon looked up the number of the maternity home, then dialed. The central switchboard transferred him to the director's line. His secretary answered.

"The director has already left for the day."

"My name is Zsigmond Gordon. I'm a journalist for the *Evening*, and I'm writing an article about the state of affairs at maternity homes. Has the public been in a giving mood lately?"

"Giving?" came the woman's confused reply.

"Are you getting donations?"

"Once in a blue moon."

"You haven't gotten a sizable sum lately?"

"If we had, we'd be heating the bathrooms, too, not just the wards and the operating room."

"So you haven't received any big donation."

"Unless you yourself are planning to help us out," said the woman in a joking tone of voice.

"I'm planning on it," Gordon replied. "I am."

After stepping out of the tobacconist's shop, Gordon boarded the tram for a short ride along Könyves Kálmán Boulevard. He got off at Mester Street and walked a block toward the Danube to Gubacsi Road. The last workers were straggling home from the oil refinery. The massive iron gate of the factory building beside it was closed, but Gordon noticed that men in groups of two or three began arriving regularly at its side entrance. He drew into the doorway of the building opposite and for a while looked quietly on. Before long, five middle-aged men arrived in the company of a much younger man who looked more like a kid. He proceeded with slow, plodding steps, but his jacket almost burst on his back. One of the shorter men in the group hurried over to the side entrance and went inside. Less than a minute later he gestured for the others to follow him in.

When another group arrived, Gordon hastened over to the other side of the street and stepped up behind them. The man leading the way opened the side gate and waved a hand at the caretaker's booth. Now inside the grounds, Gordon separated from the group for a look around. But he saw nothing special; nor could he determine exactly what sort of factory this was. Most probably it housed several smaller operations—judging from the smells, a cabinetmaking facility and a furrier, at the very least. Gordon hurried to catch up with the group. They had turned left into an alleyway of sorts, stopping to open a heavy iron door. Gordon waited for the door to slowly close behind him. The group was now well ahead of him, having walked down what seemed to be a pitch-black, narrow hallway. Since Gordon couldn't see a thing, he edged his way forward, following sounds. Another door opened, then slammed shut. He moved in its direction. Finally, Gordon found the door, on the right side of the hallway, and opened it. He now stood outside or, rather, in the building's inner courtyard. In fact, he'd gotten there just in time to catch a glimpse of one of the men vanishing from the courtyard into a doorway that, from what he could make out, led down to the cellar. Gordon's footsteps echoed off the cobblestone courtyard. The barred windows of the five-story building loomed darkly above on all sides.

Gordon opened the cellar door. The smell of sweat struck his nose at once and he heard laughter. Unbuttoning his jacket, Gordon headed down the stairs. At the bottom stood a weasel-faced old codger with a shifty gaze. Gordon took a pengő from his pocket and pressed it into the man's palm. The man stood aside.

Gordon was surprised by the cellar's colossal size. Never would he have imagined that such a large space existed under this building. In the middle was a boxing ring surrounded by a throng of men with their coats flung over their shoulders. In one corner a young boy was tapping beer from a keg. Spotting the bookies in the crowd wasn't hard. With slips of paper in one hand and thick clumps of banknotes in the other, each of them kept stridently announcing the ever-changing odds by the minute. Just how they went about calculating was a mystery to Gordon. Pushing his hat up over his forehead, he stepped into a corner, lit a cigarette, and stood there watching. An iron door occupied each corner of the cellar. It took Gordon only a couple of minutes to understand that at least three of these doors were locked. But the fourth soon opened, and out came a boy of around fourteen carrying a bucket of water. The door closed behind the boy, but Gordon walked over and opened it again. He found himself in a hallway occupied by several small groups of men. A scruffy man with thick eyebrows stepped up to Gordon.

"Where to? Let's have it."

"Antal Kocsis said this is where I could find Jacek," Gordon replied.

"You know Kocsis?"

"Didn't I just say so?"

"And what do you want with Jacek?"

"What business is it of yours?"

"Everything here is my business," said the man, crossing his arms over his chest.

"I'm here to offer him work."

"What kind of work? And, anyway, who the hell are you?"

"A little work on the side," said Gordon, pushing the man out of the way.

"I don't buy that," said the man, seizing Gordon's right

arm. The others had meanwhile gone back into the main part of the cellar, leaving Gordon and the man alone in the hallway.

"Let go of my arm."

"You haven't told me yet who you are," hissed the man. "But you don't have to. I'll drag it out of you." Only when Gordon turned toward him did he loosen his grip on Gordon's arm. Gordon now came so close to the man that their faces were almost touching. "You'll drag it out of me, will you?" he asked.

"I will," replied the man. At once Gordon tore himself free of the man's grip and swung his right fist into the other's cheekbone. The man staggered and then slumped against the wall but did not fall down. He just stood there, head drooping. Gordon was about to step past him when the man looked up. Gordon did not wait to be attacked. This time he delivered a deep uppercut to the chin. The man's head hit the wall with a thud, his eyes went blank, and he began sliding toward the floor. His eyes moist and fist sore, Gordon again moved to walk past the man now lying on the floor. With a sudden start, the man grabbed his ankle. Gordon spun to look down at the man. Blood trickled from the corner of his mouth to the floor and his eyes were foggy, but his hold did not slacken. Gordon tried to yank away his foot, but the man somehow gripped even tighter. He then leaned up on his left hand and the life returned to his eyes—eyes that looked with such loathing upon his foe that Gordon didn't hesitate another moment before planting yet another punch on the other's cheekbone, this time with his left hand and every ounce of strength he had. The man fell flat at once, his head knocking against the floor. The blood trickling from his mouth began to form a little puddle.

Gordon slumped against the wall and slid slowly to his knees. He moved the fingers of his right hand. They worked, but hurt terribly. He could hear the man's hushed gurgling breaths. Gordon took a deep breath and stood up slowly, shaking and massaging his right hand. He opened the door his attacker had been guarding. Inside the room, a burly man was shadowboxing; his movements were slow but strong. Gordon stepped inside and shut the door behind him. Without saying a thing, Jacek watched Gordon from the corner of his eye. Gordon just stood there by the door, looking on until the boxer finally lowered his arms and, with a slight Polish accent to his otherwise clean, crisp Hungarian, spoke.

"What do you want?"

Gordon pulled out a chair from under a table and straddled it. "I have a business proposal."

"What sort of business?"

"I heard that the result of this evening's match has been decided in advance."

Jacek slammed a fist down on the table. "But we agreed with Pojva that we'd play clean for once."

"I think you don't understand. Pojva is bragging that tonight he's not going to sweat it out, because someone has paid you off."

"Me?" Jacek flared up. "Me? I never sold a single match in my whole life. Understand?"

"I understand. I'm sure you're right. But I thought I should let you know."

"This will be my twelfth match, and I've never taken a dive. How dare Pojva say that?" thundered Jacek, veins bulging on his neck.

"That much I don't know," said Gordon, rising from the chair. "That's all I wanted to say," he said, heading toward the door.

Jacek just stood there stewing helplessly in his rage, but then he called after Gordon: "You mentioned some sort of business."

"Why of course," said Gordon, slapping his forehead. He reached in his pocket, took out fifty pengős, and set them down on the table.

"What's this?" asked Jacek.

"Just a little contribution to Hungarian-Polish relations."

"To what?" he asked, looking at Gordon with incomprehension.

"To that, son, to that. Besides, you yourself said you never lost a match. So don't you lose now."

With that, Gordon stepped out the door. The man was still lying in the hallway. Amid his halting breaths the bleeding had stopped and the puddle was gradually congealing. Gordon stepped over him and went back to the main part of the cellar and the ring.

The match was to begin in a couple of minutes. The room

was filled with a terrible cacophony of voices. The bookies were doing their utmost to outshout each other, and the referees were standing in the ring with their sleeves rolled up. The smell of smoke, sweat, and beer permeated the cellar. Gordon passed his eyes over the crowd. Everyone was on hand: factory workers, carriage drivers, office workers, and, of course, more than a few dubious characters. A bit farther from the ring were gentlemen dressed in meticulously tailored, top-quality suits, and Gordon was not surprised to see them there.

The iron door opened at one minute before six. Pojva was the first to come out, with a surprisingly calm expression, and he was followed by Jacek, whose resounding steps were replete with both resolve and rage. His face spoke only of determination.

"Kill him, Pojva!" someone yelled. This voice was now joined by a chorus: "Kill him! No mercy!" At this, the other fighter's fans broke in: "Show him no mercy, Jacek! Go for the head!"

The two boxers reached the ring. One of the referees lifted the rope, and the fighters stepped in. Jacek was stretching his neck and relaxing his shoulders, while Pojva looked on with a grin. They wore neither gloves nor even handwraps. There was no weighing in, though Pojva and Jacek looked to be about the same weight. The head referee herded them into opposite corners, whereupon an older man in a tux and a top hat stepped into the ring and, shrieking in falsetto, introduced the two fighters.

"In the blue corner we have the famously brutal Pojva,

who knows no fear—Pojva, owner of the most dangerous fists around!" The crowd flew into a passion. Now the old fellow moved toward Jacek. "And in the red corner is the butcher and slaughterman from Łódź, the man whose fists the Poles are so afraid of that he had to come all the way to Budapest—none other than Jacek himself!" More cheers. Men lined up in front of the bookies to place last-minute bets: eyes glittering, they jostled to push their way to the front, waving banknotes. Then the old man in the top hat climbed from the ring, and the head referee called on the boxers to shake hands. Both stepped to the middle of the ring. Pojva reached out his hand while gloating at the crowd. Jacek seized his hand and squeezed it tight. All at once Pojva's face contorted, and the referee had to push Jacek out of the way. The bell rang, the referee gave the signal, and the boxers moved toward each other again. Pojva began with a few faltering jabs that Jacek effortlessly avoided before going on the attack. With his long arms, he aimed for Pojva's chin, but missed. Pojva now moved forward, and to the extent that he could, given his age, he took to dancing about to avoid the other's punches. But with a well-directed swing, Jacek caught him on the chest, which sent Pojva staggering. He did not fall, but the grin froze right off his face.

Even from a distance, Gordon could see clearly when the two boxers began wrestling, as it were. It seemed as if Pojva had said something to Jacek, who responded by pushing him away and swearing at him. This sent Pojva on the attack. Jacek's right hand swung, but all at once Pojva caught it under his arm and wouldn't let go, hitting the Pole with his left elbow. This was too much even for the referee, who separated them. The bell rang again: the round was over.

The two boxers flopped down onto stools in their respective corners. Their assistants washed their faces with ice water and fanned them with towels. Pojva leaned back, eyes shut, gasping for breath. But Jacek shook off the water and sprang to his feet. Pojva stood only at the sound of the bell. The referee gave the signal, and they fell upon each other. Pojva tried every dirty trick in the book. While putting his left arm around Jacek's waist, he leveled a blow at his opponent's kidneys. The referee stepped between them. At this, Pojva now let his left fist fly with surprising agility, tearing up Jacek's eyebrow in an instant. The referee stopped them. He examined the wound but saw that it wasn't bleeding too much. Jacek shook himself off and moved forward. Pojva gave a desperate knee kick toward the other man's groin. Again, the referee stepped between them. The crowd was in a rage. Screwed-up faces egged on the boxers, who heard nothing of it. Pojva defended his head with both hands. Jacek had found the right moment. He sent a punch flying at his opponent's belly, at which Pojva lowered his left hand. At that instant Jacek's right fist delivered an uppercut onto Pojva's chin.

Time stopped. Even from afar, Gordon could hear the cracking of bones. Pojva's head snapped back, his eyes rolled upward, and his arms flopped down lifelessly to his sides. He collapsed like an empty sack of potatoes. For a moment the crowd fell silent and then, all at once, began to roar. Jacek was still standing in the middle of the ring. The referee pushed him into the corner, stepped over to the body lying on the floor, and, kneeling down, put his hand around Pojva's wrist.

By now a good number of onlookers had hurried toward the steps leading out of the cellar. The referee held Pojva's wrist in his hand for a while, and then he shook his head. He stood, went over to Jacek, and raised his hand in the air. But the crowd was already surging up into the courtyard. The referee whispered something to Jacek, who nodded, quickly lifted the rope, and headed toward the iron door.

Gordon did not leave. His right hand hung limp by his side; his left raised a cigarette to his mouth. The iron door opened again, and two men emerged, one of them pushing a wheelbarrow. The cellar had emptied out with surprising speed, and by now even the referees had fled. Gordon watched from the shadows as one of the men jumped up into the ring and kicked Pojva's body to the ground. His partner grabbed the corpse under the arms and pulled the upper body onto the wheelbarrow. The other man now took the legs, flung them up as well, and then they hurried off toward the door.

Gordon went up the stairs to the courtyard. The more daring bookies and their clients were still there hastily arranging their affairs. Gordon followed the dark hallway back out to the factory grounds. A horse-drawn carriage stood at one of the delivery ramps, half filled with firewood. The door leading to the ramp now opened, and out walked the two men he'd seen in the cellar. They were pulling a sack, which they now picked up and flung on the back of the carriage. One of the men jumped in after the sack and in no time covered it with firewood. The other got in the driver's seat and cracked the whip, whereupon the caretaker, who had already left his booth, opened the gate. Gordon stepped out the side entrance onto Gubacsi Road and watched the carriage fade into the night.

Eleven

Gordon walked over to Soroksári Road and stood at the tram stop. When the tram arrived, he flung away his cigarette butt and got on. The city turned increasingly colorful and bright the closer they got to downtown. Fewer and fewer people on the streets were making their way home from work, and ever more were looking for evening entertainment. Illuminated boats swayed out on the Danube, and on this crisp autumn night every single window of the fortress up on Castle Hill was clear as day. Calvin Square was teeming with cars, and the traffic was heavy in front of the hotels. Restaurant windows revealed packed tables and, occasionally, the glint of a Gypsy band leader playing his violin. The National Museum sprawled out in all its stateliness from behind the tall trees on its grounds. Neon lights flashed on Apponyi Square, marked by the quiet chaos of buses, trams, and horse-drawn carriages.

An enormous clock in the display of a jewelry shop showed the exact time: seven-twenty. Gordon headed toward the newsroom.

Only a couple of people were still in the office. Gordon greeted Valéria, hung his jacket on the coatrack, and headed to his desk. But Valéria now looked up from her novel and called after him in a raspy voice.

"There was a telephone message for you."

"You're kidding," said Gordon, turning around.

"It was Krisztina. She wants you to call her, something about her asking whether . . ." Valéria leaned closer to the sheet of paper, for she couldn't even read her own handwriting. ". . . to reserve a table."

"I understand."

"Or if the preserve is edible . . ." she added, then went back to reading.

Gordon pulled out his chair, switched on his green glass banker's lamp, and sat down. For a while he just stared at the typewriter, but then he pulled his notebook from his pocket and turned the pages. He rolled a sheet of paper into the typewriter, drew the machine in front of him, and slowly began to type. Not that he'd learned anything new from Gellért about Róna, but Gyula Turcsányi was already eagerly awaiting the article. Gordon got down to writing what little he knew until an apprentice reporter walked up to him: a thin, pimply boy barely twenty years old and wearing a blazer one size too big.

"What do you want, son?" said Gordon, raising his eyes.

"If you don't mind, sir," the boy anxiously replied, extending a typed page toward Gordon, "could you look over this article? The deadline is tomorrow."

"What is this?"

"An article. I . . . I wrote it," he stammered. "No one else was in to write it. Mr. Turcsányi said you were out sick."

"And?"

"He also said you'd be in tomorrow and that I should show you then."

"Fine, then. Show me tomorrow."

"I'd really appreciate it if you'd look at it now," said the boy, his face flushed. "I've never written an article like this."

"And what is it about?"

"A suicide."

"How many suicides does that make for the week?"

"I don't know, Mr. Editor," replied the boy.

"Let's see it."

Gordon put the sheet of paper in front of him and reached for his red pencil. The pain had by now subsided sufficiently in his hand. Gordon read, underlined, crossed out, and corrected.

"Please, sir, don't cross out the word *suspicious*," said the boy.

"Why not? A suicide can't be suspicious."

"Sure it can," the boy protested. "I called police headquarters a little while ago, and one of the detectives said the man died under suspicious circumstances."

"Who did you talk to?"

"Chief Inspector Szrubián."

"Well then, you just go on over to the telephone and call

Chief Inspector Vladimir Gellért, who is also a section head. Tell him I told you to call. Maybe he's still in."

The boy nodded. Gordon took out his cigarette case and lit a smoke. A couple of minutes later the boy returned.

"Chief Inspector Gellért said it's not suspicious."

"You see," said Gordon with a nod. "So then, the title of this article should really be: 'Wealthy Merchant's Unexpected Suicide.' It would be suspicious if the detectives suspected that someone had killed him." He looked down at the article, then back up. "A stranger. Or his wife. But that's not what happened, is it?"

"No," replied the boy with a frightened look. "Chief Inspector Gellért said everything about this case is perfectly clear, and that it was a suicide."

"The rest is fine," said Gordon, taking a drag on his cigarette. "Just be careful with what comes first in the lead. That's very important. You wrote, 'This afternoon in his home on Pasaréti Street, using a revolver, the owner of the Arabia Coffee Company took his own life.' The important thing is neither when nor where. But who. Thus: 'The owner of the Arabia Coffee Company took his own life with a revolver this afternoon in his home on Pasaréti Street.' And who he left his estate to, that doesn't belong in the lead, either. It's enough if you mention the maternity home only farther down. So then, go on back now and retype the article."

The boy took the sheet of paper and headed back to his desk.

"Son," Gordon called after him.

"Yes, sir?"

"There's one thing you shouldn't forget. Your job is to write what happened. Leave out the speculation. It's not your job to go guessing about the *why*."

The boy sat down at his desk and began rewriting the article. Gordon typed the final keystroke of his own article and pulled the sheet of paper from the machine. Pulling on his jacket, he placed the article on Turcsányi's desk. Then he went to Valéria's desk, picked up the telephone, and, with a less than certain grip, started to dial with his right hand.